HELL ON WHEELS

I LEFT HERE A MAN BUT CAME BACK A BEAST

PENNY DEE

Hell on Wheels
Kings of Mayhem MC Series Book 4

Penny Dee

This book is a work of fiction. Any references to real events, real people, and real places are used fictitiously. Other names, characters, places and incidents are products of the Author's imagination and any resemblance to persons, living or dead, actual events, organisations or places is entirely coincidental.

All rights are reserved. This book is intended for the purchaser of this book ONLY. No part of this book may be reproduced or transmitted in any form or by any means, graphic, electronic, or mechanical, including photocopying, recording, taping, or by any information storage retrieval system, without the express written permission of the Author. All songs, song titles and lyrics contained in this book are the property of the respective songwriters and copyright holders.

Disclaimer: The material in this book contains graphic language and sexual content and is intended for mature audiences, ages 18 and older.

ISBN: 978-1089215769

Book design by Swish Design & Editing
Cover design by Marisa at Cover Me Darling
Cover image Copyright 2019

First Edition
Copyright © 2019 Penny Dee
All Rights Reserved

DEDICATION

To Carol,
Thank you for being so wonderfully you.
I miss you.

And to Bindi,
Who also passed away during the writing of this book.
My best buddy. My writing companion.
The best dog in the world.

PATH OF FAMILY

The Calley Family
Hutch Calley (deceased) married Sybil Stone
Griffin Calley
Garrett Calley (deceased)

Griffin Calley married Peggy Russell
Isaac Calley (deceased)
Abby Calley

Garrett Calley married Veronica Western
Chance Calley
Cade Calley
Caleb Calley
Chastity Calley

The Parrish Family
Jude Parrish married Connie Walker
Jackson Parrish (deceased)
Samuel Parrish (deceased)

Jackie Parrish married Lady Winter
Bolt Parrish (deceased)
Indigo Parrish

The Western Family
Michael 'Bull' Western
Veronica 'Ronnie' Western

KINGS OF MAYHEM MC

Bull (President)
Cade (VP)
Chance (SAA)
Caleb
Ruger
Davey
Vader
Joker
Cool Hand
Griffin
Matlock
Maverick
Animal
Yale
Tully
Nitro
Hawke
Ari
Picasso
Caveman

Reuben (honorary member)
Prospect 1
Prospect 2

Employees of the Kings
Red (Chef, clubhouse housekeeper)
Mrs Stephens (Bookkeeper, administration)

HELL ON WHEELS

I LEFT HERE A MAN BUT CAME BACK A BEAST

PENNY DEE

PROLOGUE

Before

I woke up to a blanket of dark hair moving slowly across my chest. Her breasts, ample and full, were pressed up against my pecs, her long legs entangled in mine as she stirred against me. A hand slid down from my shoulder, over my chest and across the dips and grooves of my stomach, moving lower and lower. My body responded in all the usual ways it did when a beautiful woman curls her fingers around your morning wood.

Lips parted, my breathing picked up speed. My eyes fluttered and slowly opened as she gently began to rub me, her palm gliding up the length of me, her fingers paying special attention to the wide, smooth head of my cock. I breathed out a moan, feeling the pleasure stir in my balls. As my brain started to function, I reached for her slowly, my body already minutes ahead and wanting more. I pulled her down to me and kissed her hard, enjoying her whimpered moan of pleasure in my mouth.

She rose, her warm body hovering over me, nipples hardening against my chest as she positioned herself onto me.

Her kisses were sweet and hot, her tongue filling my mouth as her body came alive against mine.

As she sank down on my cock, I was lost to her while she rode me slowly, her slim hips rocking against me, her firm thighs straddling me, her pussy milking me. But it was more than that. These physical feelings, the ones that had been so hard to deny at first, now took a back seat to what was growing between us. What had *already* grown between us. I could love this woman. Give her my all. Take her back to my home in the US. To my life before here. To my family.

"Oh, Chance," she whimpered my name as she started to come. Her head fell back, her long, dark hair swirling over her smooth, sun-kissed shoulders as she lost herself to the orgasm.

I followed quickly, exploding inside her. Pulsing. Filling her. And when the pleasure receded and the euphoric haze descended upon us, she collapsed against me, her gloriously smooth body blanketing me.

I closed my eyes, my heart slowing, my breathing evening out as my post orgasm bliss settled into me.

"It's almost dawn," she finally said, her sexy voice hoarse and sleepy. "I need to go before someone sees me."

I hated that she had to leave before anyone realized she was here. Hated that we had to move around in the shadows because of who she was and who I was. Two people divided by war. She was born here. I was a soldier on a classified mission. We'd tried to deny our feelings. Tried to ignore the attraction pulling us closer and closer every time I walked past her family's little restaurant on the far side of the village. We met in the darkness of the alley. Stolen moments of whispered conversations and longing-filled kisses.

"Wait." I didn't know what I wanted to say, only that I wasn't ready for her to leave. When she turned back and smiled down at me, I reached up and cupped her beautiful, sweet face. I could fall for this girl. See a future with her. Make her mine. Every goodbye was getting harder. "Will I see you tonight?"

Her dark eyes gleamed with the mystery I'd come to love about her. "I will try."

It was her standard response, something I'd come to expect every morning when we said our goodbyes in the cool pre-dawn light. Sometimes she would show up and we would spend the night in each other's arms, drinking wine and making love with wild abandonment. I'd spend other nights alone in my small, one-bedroom dwelling just off the dusty main street of the little village, missing home, missing my family, missing the familiar sights and sounds of a life half a world away.

I ran the back of my fingers down her arm. Her skin was smooth, golden, and perfect. She glanced back at me again.

"I want to meet your friends," she said.

"You've met my friends ... when we come for dinner."

Her father owned the small restaurant my unit frequented. He loved Americans and would fuss over us with enthusiastic delight whenever we visited his establishment for a meal and a night where we could forget we were in the throes of war.

"But I want to meet them as your girl." She raised her chin slightly. "I don't want to sneak around anymore."

"I don't like it either, but we need to wait until my unit is reassigned somewhere else. And then we'll tell your father." I sat up and pulled her hand into mine. "Then we can be together."

Until then I couldn't afford for anyone to know about us.

It was too dangerous. While this village was considered safe, there were eyes and ears everywhere. Some people who didn't want us here and she could easily become a target. I couldn't risk her getting hurt. This was war.

She frowned, her mood darkening. "It's always wait, wait, wait. Wait until I get reassigned. Wait until its safe."

I moved behind her and pressed a kiss to her shoulder. This wasn't the first time she'd cried about having to hide our relationship. She wanted to be a part of my life. Wholly and openly. She wanted to walk through the streets holding hands. She wanted to kiss me and touch me and not worry if anyone saw us. She wanted to come with me when my unit dined or had drinks at the nearby bar we frequented.

"We will. I promise. My unit will move on soon, and I will be able to stay for a while as a civilian." I tangled my fingers in hers. "Then I'll walk the streets holding your hand. Kissing you. Hell, I'll even take you in my arms, dip you, and kiss you senseless for the whole world to see!"

Her eyes shone brightly, but she jutted out her chin. My lighthearted promise was lost on her. "It has to be now."

She rose to her feet and moved away from the bed, the sheet slipping away from her body. Naked, she was perfect. And confident. She moved across the room and stood at the window. Outside, the pale streaks of dawn lightened the sky, and I admired her silhouetted curves in the dim light.

"Tomorrow night, you and your unit are celebrating something. What is it?" she asked, not turning around.

The mood had changed. My promises didn't appease her anymore. And maybe if I'd been paying more attention, I would've realized that I never once mentioned anything about celebrating Sergeant Healy's birthday the following night. I never told her anything about my unit or the men in it.

Instead, I sighed and rubbed my eyes with the heel of my palm. "It's someone's birthday."

"And you're going to a bar?"

"I'm not sure."

She turned back to me. "Take me with you. Or we're done."

I was a little caught off guard. There had never been an ultimatum before.

Hell on Wheels

But before I could reply, she quickly crossed the room and climbed onto the bed, pushing me back onto the pillows with a sudden frenzied energy, and straddled me. She kissed me hard, *pleadingly*, her pussy rubbing against me as she tried to convince me to take her with me the following night. Her hand reached between us, grabbing my cock and rubbing it through the damp folds of her pussy. She nudged the head inside, surrounding my crown with creaminess and sending a flare of pleasure through me.

But this craziness had to stop.

I pushed her hands off me and rolled away from her.

"What are you doing?" I breathed.

"I want to be a part of your life now. No more waiting." Her eyes were dark fire, her hair a wild mess as it tumbled over her shoulders. "It starts now. Or it stops now."

"You know I can't—"

"Then we are done!" She climbed off the bed and snatched up her clothes.

"Don't do this," I said.

But she said nothing. She tossed on her clothes and stormed to the door where she paused and turned around. "You should have let me come."

She disappeared out the door, letting it slam behind her.

I hadn't seen her in over a week. I'd visited her father's restaurant, but it seemed her frostiness extended to him as well. He said it was a good idea if we didn't go there anymore. I couldn't lie. That hurt. And it confused me. How she could cut me off like that and disappear? And where was she? She wasn't in town. She wasn't in my bed. She wasn't anywhere.

My job kept me busy. Kept her from my mind. Our final mission had come through; we were due to leave in less than a week.

We'd been slowly annihilating the same cell across several villages along the countryside, and intelligence indicated it had arrived at the village where we were stationed. Weeks of waiting for this to happen was now paying off. Our SEAL mission was to take out the cell leaders: a woman known as *The Dark One* and two men who were thought to be her brothers.

I leaned down and pressed my eye to my scope, and then she appeared. My target. The person responsible for the catastrophic attacks on several marines, resulting in high casualties. I pulled back, my brows knitting together. No. It couldn't be. Blood whirred in my ears as my pulse quickened. I peered into the scope again and watched my target moving through the street, walking with the two men known for orchestrating attacks on American and allied soldiers. There was a fleeting moment where I wondered if she was somehow being held against her will, that perhaps she was not involved in any of this. But her body language wasn't that of someone who feared for her life. She walked with purpose. Confidence. The beautiful body I'd spent hours making love to was relaxed. Those long legs, the ones she'd wrapped around me as she rose to meet the thrust of my cock, strode confidently alongside her companions. The mouth she had kissed me with a thousand times spoke fast and with purpose. And those eyes ... the ones that had looked at me with so much lust and affection, and at times with what I was sure was love ... were now hard, sharp, and *deadly*.

My finger twitched on the trigger. My jaw tightened. In my ear, my commander instructed me to take the shot. I had a clear line of vision; my weapon was accurate. *Take the shot.* If I squeezed the trigger, a .338 caliber bullet would rip through several hundred yards of air and thrust into her, devastating every tissue fiber in its wake as it carved a deadly path through her body.

Slowly, everything came into focus and started to make sense.

How she had pursued me.

Encouraged me.

Used my loneliness against me.

How she had come to my room at night and warmed my body with hers.

Take the shot.

All this time she had been lying.

Working against me.

Using me.

Take the shot.

The reason she wanted to meet my friends?

She wanted to kill them.

And me.

Take the shot.

Bitterness tore through me.

My finger grazed the trigger.

Take the shot.

As I squeezed, an almighty eruption lifted me up from the ground and cartwheeled me across the room of the abandoned building. I heard the startled shouts of my unit as the explosion ripped apart our surroundings, turning our world inside out and upside down. I hit the floor, my face smashing against something hard and rough. Heat and fire flashed across the room, searing the uniform on my body and sending a sharp burning pain deep into my skin.

Confusion smothered my brain, suffocating me, disorientating me.

Who was I? Where was I?

And then it slowly came back to me.

I was a sniper in a land far, far away.

And I had taken the shot.

CHAPTER 1

CHANCE
Eighteen months later

I stood beneath the shower stream and let the warm needles of water pound into my flesh. My temples throbbed with pain, but that was nothing new. I'd seen the bottom of more than my share of bourbon bottles, and last night had been no different.

Squeezing my eyes shut, I groaned as the heat of the shower engulfed me, relaxing my muscles and relieving the tension in my brain.

When I'd come home from several months in a military hospital, my family and the club had closed ranks around me. They were worried about the broken soldier with violent scars. To get me out of my shell and back to the old Chance, they'd put me right in the middle of MC life: the clubhouse, parties, drinking. *Women.*

But I felt none of it.

Wanted none of it.

Ok, maybe the drinking.

But not the parties.

And definitely not the women.

Even if it was just for one night.

I lived at my mom's when I first got home, but Mom's relationship with Ari had become serious while I was overseas; he lived with her now. They were really into one another, and even though it was my home and I felt welcomed, it was hard not to feel like a third wheel—especially when you came down the stairs to find your mother and her boyfriend in a passionate embrace. Or worse... when their muffled moans drifted through the thin walls when you were trying to sleep after another nightmare.

I just didn't need that shit.

So, last night I packed up my duffel bag and moved back into the clubhouse.

I knew it was a mistake the moment I walked in and saw the party in full swing.

They got me hammered.

So hammered I could barely see straight.

So hammered I wasn't even aware of the girl in my bed until I felt her fingers slide across my naked chest and her arms wrap around me. In my drunken haze, my heart ached with longing because I hadn't felt the touch of a woman in a long, long time. Not since *her*. And every physical part of me longed for the comfort and peace and the softness of a woman's caress.

But my mind was in a state of decay. It fought my heart. Ferociously. It didn't want her. Didn't want the warmth of her arms around me. I didn't deserve it. Not after what I'd done.

So I had untangled her from my body, rolled over and drifted into a disturbed, restless sleep.

She was still in my bed when I woke up this morning with a raging hard-on and a desperate need to jerk off.

Not in the mood for small talk, I escaped quietly to the bathroom and now found peace beneath the stream of hot water, my eyes closed, my cock still hard. I moaned and closed my eyes, feeling my muscles relax and the tension leave my body.

I was about to take care of the throbbing erection between my legs when the shower door opened and last night's girl stepped in, butt naked and beautiful. Before I could stop her, she rose to her tiptoes and kissed me. It was tender and soft, and somewhere inside me a tiny heartbeat of longing began to beat. She was offering her body to me, offering her kiss and the kindness of her arms around me.

But I didn't know how to accept her comfort, only the uncomplicated offer of her lips as she dropped to her knees and took me in her mouth, in the shower.

My mind warred with the pleasure while my body wanted the sweet suckle of her mouth. My brain told me I didn't deserve the pleasure. Wasn't worthy of her tongue licking at my cock. Wasn't worthy of her lips and mouth making my balls swell with the intensity of an approaching orgasm.

She moaned, her mouth full of me, and the rising tension inside of me snapped. Anger collided with desire, and I braced myself against the tiled wall, feeling the approaching release of my orgasm. I closed my eyes. My breath was quick, my lips wet with water. I was close and if she kept fucking me with her luscious mouth, I was going to come despite the agony taking place inside my head. But she didn't. Instead she released me from between her lips and rose to her feet, pressing her velvety body up against mine.

I felt her kiss me. Felt my surrender burst through the surface. The last woman I had touched was *her*, and the sting of *her* kiss still lingered on my lips. Now I was jamming them against another woman's mouth, savagely kissing this woman as if I could somehow kiss the memory of *her* from my mind.

Growling, I pushed her up against the wall and hooked her leg over my arm. My first thrust was hard and deep, and she gasped, taken by surprise by the ferocity. Then she moaned and bit down on her lip, raising her arms above her head as my second and third thrusts plowed into her just as deep.

It was fucking. It wasn't love. It wasn't intimate or gentle or the beginnings of anything. There was no promise, no hope, *no lies*. Just a primal instinct and one man running from his truth. I kissed her fiercely, my hands winding tightly around her neck as light and darkness raged inside of me. Lust roared through me, wild and fierce, and my hands began to squeeze.

At first she whimpered, but then she let out a strangled, almost mocking laugh.

Her eyes darkened and my mind followed as my orgasm possessed me. I squeezed my eyes shut, overpowered by the battle of pleasure and pain as I came violently, rocked by the power of my release as it pumped out of me in perfect time with the blood pounding in my head.

As I started to come down, I became aware of her punching at the hard muscle of my shoulders.

My eyes opened to find hers wide and bulging as she frantically kicked and punched for me to let her go.

Suddenly realizing what I was doing, I loosened my hands around her neck and she dropped to her feet, slumping against the wet tiles, gasping for air.

Alarm tore through me, quickly followed by shame and guilt because I had almost choked her unconscious.

What the fuck.

That wasn't me.

I was a King and we didn't lay a finger on women.

We honored and served them. *Protected them.*

We didn't tolerate violence against them. And I would be the first to step up to any man that dared try it in front of me.

Fuck.

I was losing it.

I looked at the girl, and she watched me with terrified eyes.

"I'm sorry," I said hoarsely.

"Are you fucking crazy!" she cried, grabbing her throat.

Scrambling to her feet, she almost fell out of the shower cubicle trying to get away from me.

"You should go," was all I managed to say as I wrapped a towel around my hips.

She snatched her clothes off the floor. "They told me it was an easy gig. No weird shit. If I'd known you were into that, I would've charged them more."

I stared at her, confused, but then anger lit me up like an atom bomb. She'd been paid to fuck me.

I had no idea by who. But I would find out.

"If you like that shit, it'll cost you more—" She stopped and her eyes widened again. It took me a nanosecond to figure out why. My scar. I didn't have a shirt on and there it was as plain as day for her to see. *To judge.* She gasped, her face twisting into an ugly expression of disgust and pity. "What the fuck?"

"Get out of here," I said, my calmness a direct contradiction to the agony pouring out of me.

But she didn't move. She just stood there, her wide, glassy eyes darting from my face to the scar tissue on my back. "What did they do to you?" She gasped.

Her pity might as well have been a fucking bullet coming straight at me. Because I hated pity and I'd seen enough of it in the last year to last me a fucking lifetime.

"If you don't get out, I will throw you out," I warned her in a calm voice.

But she just stared at me like she couldn't believe her fucking eyes. "It's horrible."

In that moment my mind snapped. I knew it was fucking horrible. I wasn't blind.

"I said get the fuck out!" I yelled.

Terrified, she took off out of the room, barely covered by the clothes cradled against her naked body.

I slammed the bathroom door behind her and stood there, letting the shock waves ripple over me. I felt rocked, and in pain, the heated sense of shame knotting tightly in my chest.

Walking to the sink, I leaned against the porcelain counter and stared at my reflection in the mirror, hating what I saw.

A beast.

From this angle, there was only a slight hint of my scars curling around from the back of my neck. But when I turned, the mass of scar tissue stretched from the top of my neck, across my shoulder blades, claiming my back all the way down to my hipbone. Layers of melted skin. Shiny and silvery pink. Scars of war. *Scars of hate.*

I turned to face the mirror, and my eyes moved to the deep wound on my face. It carved through my eyebrow and up the side of my forehead. It was deep. Pink. *Ugly.* A constant reminder of what I had become that day.

A beast who took the shot.

But the scars on my body were nothing compared to the brokenness inside. In time, the burns and shrapnel scars would heal, but the invisible ones inside never would. They were open wounds of pain and hatred.

And today that pain and hate had broken free, forcing my hands around the neck of the girl I was fucking and squeezing until I'd almost choked the breath out of her.

I was losing it.

Not holding it together like I kept telling everyone I was.

I ran my palm across the back of my neck and shut my eyes tightly.

Hell on Wheels

It wasn't just my scars that made me a monster.
It was the darkness inside.
And I knew it was growing stronger every day.
Because the military had made me a soldier.
But war had made me a beast.

CHAPTER 2

CHANCE

Later that afternoon, I rode with my brothers, Cade and Caleb, to Stockade Square. The town was getting ready for Founding Fathers' Day celebrations, and there was a real buzz in the air for the approaching holiday. Posters about the parade and fireworks plastered every street corner, and storefronts were filled with holiday displays. Decorations in red, white, and blue decorated the town square.

Today, it was busy with people.

We pulled up in front of Iron & Salt, a bar off the main street, and sat in the outdoor terrace with beers.

I loved my brothers.

But I wasn't like them.

Not anymore.

Once upon a time, we were three peas in a pod. The Calley boys. The cocky kids of the MC, sharing the same dark hair and blue eyes, and the same easy-going charm we threw around like fucking fairy dust to get ourselves out of the trouble we always seemed to get in to.

Hell on Wheels

That was before life kicked me in the balls.

Now we were vastly different, and our paths couldn't be further apart.

They had their wives who adored them. Stunning queens who loved them fiercely and who gave them beautiful children who climbed all over them. Cade's son, River, was the spitting image of his father, and at almost two years old, he was as adorable as he was mischievous. And Caleb's daughter, Ruby, my sweet little niece, was the apple in her father's eye, and I had to admit, in her uncle's as well. Somehow, *and God only knows why*, she absolutely loved me. Whenever I was around, she would reach out her little arms and whine until she was held snugly in my arms. And that smile. Man, it just melted the scar tissue in my heart until all I could feel was a pure, avuncular love coursing through my veins.

I loved spending time with my niece and nephew. It was really the only time I was happy because they held the darkness at bay.

My brothers were lucky sons of bitches.

But that life wasn't for me. And whenever I found myself longing for what they had, I quickly replaced the ache with anger and hate. I would never have what they had, and it was for the best. A wife deserved love, and my heart was too much of a desolate wasteland for love to grow.

Besides, I didn't have time for anything but the club. When I returned as a full-time member of the Kings of Mayhem, I was voted in as Sergeant at Arms because Grunt had to move back to Indiana when his youngest sister was injured in a car wreck. At the time, Bull had been considering a few candidates for the position. He needed someone he could trust. Someone who wasn't afraid to step up when he needed them to. Someone who always had his back and put the club first. A good Sergeant at Arms possessed a certain amount of crazy, and I had a fuck-ton of crazy to bring to the table—not to mention the pent up rage. It was a useful resource when the club needed you to keep them safe.

Club business aside, when I wasn't busy having my president's back, I had a small side project to keep me busy. It was my grandmother's idea. *The infamous Sybil Calley.* The original biker queen. Fierce and wild. A fiery redhead with a penchant for blinged-out caftans and red lipstick. To help with my recovery, she had given me an old fisherman's cottage to renovate. It was a dilapidated shack that sat across the river from the family cabin. It was unloved, unlivable, and in such a state of disrepair I could work on it for one hundred days and it still wouldn't be close to finished.

Which was exactly why my grandmother had given it to me. She wasn't a fool. She knew I needed help settling back into life outside of the military. She knew I'd find a lot of myself again while I worked on that beat-up old house. I hadn't yet, but I hoped that one of these days I would find some kind of peace.

Until then, I would bury myself with club business and forget the other part of me that wished things had worked out differently.

I thought about this morning's encounter and another punch of shame twisted my gut.

"I swear to fucking Christ, you have the attention of a two-year-old," Cade said, annoyed. "Did you just hear anything I said?"

Nope.

"Where the fuck are you, Brother?"

In my bathroom, with my hands around a club girl's throat, choking the life out of her while I come.

I felt a flush creep up the back of my neck and shifted uncomfortably in my seat.

"Are those headaches back?" Caleb asked, raising his beer to his lips.

"I have good days and bad days," I said.

Apparently today was a bad day.

"You still seeing the doctors over in Humphrey?" Cade asked.

I was fucking sick of doctors.

And something told me I was seeing the wrong kind of doctors.

That *something* being my hands squeezing a girl's throat as I came.

No, that wasn't me.

I shifted uneasily. If it was, then I didn't need a doctor. The only thing that was going to save me was a bullet.

The approaching rumble of a familiar Harley told me that Bull, our president, *our uncle*, would be joining us.

Watching him pull up to the curb, I felt the shoe drop for the second time that day. My brothers had lured me away from the clubhouse. But this wasn't a friendly ride into town for a couple of beers. This was a fucking intervention.

I glanced at my brothers, who both pretended like nothing was amiss.

"Assholes," I muttered, sitting back in my chair and lighting a smoke. "If you wanted to know if I was alright, you should've just asked. Not arrange a fucking intervention like I'm some kind of strung-out tweaker."

"And what would you have said if we did?" Cade asked, knowing there was no point denying it. "You would've told us everything was alright. But it's not, Brother. You don't sleep. You don't talk."

"Something is going on with you, man," Caleb added. "Talk to us."

Out of my two brothers, I was closest to Caleb. Growing up, Cade was always busy with Indy, which meant Caleb and I spent a lot more time together.

When I was lying in a hospital bed like the living dead, his phone calls and visits saved my sanity. Sometimes he'd just call and talk shit to me. He knew I couldn't reply, but he understood how important it was for me to know there was life outside of that hospital room. A life worth fighting for. I needed to know there was a place for the lifeless to live again. Because I'm not going to lie. I spent more time wishing I would die than I did wishing I would live.

"Was it you two who paid that girl to fuck me?" I asked.

The look of confusion on their faces told me it wasn't them. It didn't surprise me. This reeked more of Joker and Vader than my younger brothers.

"What girl?" Caleb asked.

I took a drag of my smoke and told them about the girl. Everything except the choking.

"It was probably Joker and Vader," Cade said, echoing my own suspicions.

"They're worried about you, man," Caleb added. "It would be their way of trying to help you out."

"I don't need that kind of help."

"Then what do you need?" came Bull's voice from behind as he approached our table. He sat down and lifted his dark sunglasses. He had the weirdest fucking eyes I'd ever seen on a human. Almost demonic. It was caused by his acute color-blindness, which made him sensitive to light. As a result, you very rarely saw him without his dark sunglasses.

"I saw Tammi-Lynn leaving your room this morning," he said. "She was shaken up. Not to mention *naked*. Seemed she couldn't get out of there quick enough. Want to tell me about it?"

"There's nothing to tell."

We both watched Caleb get up from the table to take a phone call.

"Seemed to me she was a little upset."

My jaw twitched as I took another drag on my smoke. I didn't need this right now. "It was a misunderstanding."

"I see shit like that and I get concerned."

"There is nothing to be concerned about. Like I said, it was a misunderstanding. It won't happen again." My headache was drilling into my temple like a fucking jackhammer. "Look, I appreciate your concern. But it's misplaced, okay? I'm fine."

Bull didn't move. He just fixed those otherworldly eyes on me as his mind worked in silence. To most people it was unnerving, but it didn't work on me. I wasn't about to admit anything to my president. *My uncle.* There was no point. I couldn't be helped.

"Fuck me," Caleb growled, walking back from taking his call. "That was Remy from Gunslinger. They can't make it tonight."

Gunslinger was the band we used for our celebrations at the clubhouse. They played raw rock and blues. Tonight's party was to welcome Ruger into the chapter.

Ruger was Bull's brother-in-law and was patching over from the Kings of Mayhem's Louisiana chapter.

Bull had been married to his sister Wendy years ago. Crazy in love, their union had been cut short by a drunk driver after only three months of marriage. Back then, my father was president and Bull was vice-president. Almost losing his mind with grief, Bull had skipped town for Canada and spent the next few years riding across the provinces.

In Bull's absence, Ruger joined the Louisiana chapter of the Kings of Mayhem and rose through the ranks to vice-president. Now he was patching over to the original Kings of Mayhem because he was ready for a change of scenery.

Ruger was a handsome son of a bitch. The club girls fell all over themselves when he arrived. Caleb's wife, Honey, called him a silver fox. Whatever the fuck that meant. Ruger took things in his stride. He was a big man. Powerful. But he was a thinker. He listened. Strategized. And then slayed with lethal force. He was a good addition to the club.

Caleb threw his phone on the table.

"Bet this shit never happens to Mrs. Stephens," he moaned.

Caleb had somehow become the clubs unofficial event coordinator while the club's housekeeper, Mrs. Stephens, was on a three-week vacation in the Bahamas.

"What about Talk Show?" Cade suggested. They were another band we sometimes used.

"I'll see, but it's going to be hard to find someone with such short notice," Caleb replied, picking up his phone again.

I glanced at Bull. His face was still cast in my direction, his jaw tight, probably trying to work out what to do with me.

But there was nothing he could do.

There was nothing anyone could do.

It was as simple as that.

Later in life, I would remember this moment as the *before*.

The moment right *before* I heard her.

Because that's how it happened. I heard her before I saw her. Her voice reached out across the town square to where we were sitting outside the bar and hit me in the chest like a fucking bolt of lightning.

I looked up and there she was, perched on a wall near the statue of Colonel James Dylan, one of our town's founding fathers, strumming her guitar and singing a song about feeling

Hell on Wheels

like a misfit, about being dark and twisted inside, and not fitting in.

I knew the song. It was vaguely familiar. A pop song. Probably something I'd heard on the radio when I was half-dead, lying in a hospital bed, burned to a crisp with a massive head injury.

She sang about feeling like a misfit.

Lady, you don't know the half of it.

About being dark and twisted.

These words from a woman who looked like she'd fallen from Heaven.

About not fitting into the format.

Darlin', I'm so far out of format not even Google could find me.

I took a drag off my smoke, trying to distract myself, but she was impossible not to notice. I studied her from behind my dark glasses. She was pure California, with a voice like sunshine and skin the color of whiskey. Her blonde hair was long and thick and tumbled over smooth brown shoulders in golden waves. Even from this distance, I could see that her eyes were as bright as sapphires. And as she strummed her guitar, the silver rings on her fingers glinted in the sunlight.

She was fucking mesmerizing.

My uncle and brothers thought so too because the conversation had stopped.

"Her voice is amazing," Cade finally said. He looked at Caleb. "There's your answer to finding someone to play at Ruger's patchover tonight."

Caleb raised an eyebrow at him. "Are you kidding? There is no way she is playing at the clubhouse. Imagine trying to keep Vader and Joker's hands off her. Not to mention Yale. I don't know him well enough yet, but something tells me he's a deviant motherfucker."

Yale was new to the club. A seven-foot Scandinavian who didn't say a hell of a lot.

"She looks like a fucking angel. You bring her into the clubhouse and it'd be like dangling a carrot in front of their eyes," Caleb added.

My brother wasn't wrong. She did look like an angel.

An angel that was awakening something inside of me.

I looked away from her, my eyes shifting to the scruffy looking kid in dirty jeans and a hoodie acting shady as he leaned up against a brick wall, watching her.

It was second nature for me to observe what others missed. It was my job in the Navy; our marine patrols relied on my experience to spot things out of the ordinary. And this kid, he was definitely out of the ordinary. I watched him push off the wall and slowly walk past her.

She finished her song, and the small crowd in the coffee shop and bars surrounding the town square clapped politely. People walked past and dropped money in the top hat she had sitting on the ground in front of her. She smiled broadly and started singing a song about California. Which was fitting, considering she looked like she'd stepped right off the bus from the golden state.

My eyes shifted back to the kid in the hoodie. He was smoking and eyeing the top hat. He was up to no good, and if I was right, he was going to make a grab for it. I waited, watching him take a final drag from his cigarette and flicking the butt to the ground. Then just as I anticipated, he suddenly lurched forward, grabbed the top hat, and took off running through the town square, almost knocking an old lady over in the process.

I was out of my chair and chasing him down before Bull, Cade, or Caleb had a chance to react. I leaped over a small fence and sprinted after the kid, my mind focused on one thing and one thing only. *Get the target.* As he disappeared down an alleyway, determination roared through me, and I ran faster, ignoring the burning in my lungs as they screamed for oxygen. The kid was a fast runner, I'd give him that, but I was faster. Months of rehab and grueling post-hospital gym sessions helped. When he jumped onto the chain wire fence to escape the alley, I grabbed him and threw him down on the concrete.

Hauling him to his feet, I hurled his scrawny body against the wall.

The stench of poor hygiene hit me in the face. This close I could see the grey skin, the mouth full of decay, and the meth-dead eyes. This kid was a tweaker.

"Don't hurt me, man," he cried.

Every inch of me wanted to do *exactly* that. *Hurt him*. To jam his rotted teeth down his throat. Because thieves were scum and junkie thieves were the worst of the bunch. But then I realized it wasn't about him at all. I just wanted to hurt something, and that sudden knowledge stopped me. I let him go and he took off.

But it was too late.

The blonde-haired beauty was running down the alley toward us. And she'd see me. Seen the monster. I could see the alarm on her face.

She ran up to me and suddenly I was engulfed in the sweet scent of her. Up close, I could see she was the kind of girl you lost your heart to and never reclaimed it. The flawless skin. The luscious, full lips. Eyes the color of the sky. Blonde curls swirling around a perfect face.

I tried not to notice any of it. But then she smiled up at me, and every cell in my body reacted like they were detonated by a fucking atomic bomb.

She was innocence and beauty.

Light and goodness.

And the last thing I fucking needed.

CHAPTER 3

CASSIDY

Twelve dollars and fifteen cents. The would-be thief got an ass kicking from the hot guy who chased him down for a measly twelve dollars and fifteen cents.

I bent down to pick up the money scattered on the concrete then straightened to look at him.

There was no denying he was attractive. Dark hair. Eyes the color of a tropical ocean. A slight cleft in his chin with the right amount of scruff along his jaw. He had a deep scar running from his forehead, through his eyebrow and down his cheek. His scar looked like the wound would've been severe. Painful. Life changing even. Yet somehow it added to his beauty. It made him different. Stronger. *Beautiful*.

But I saw the look in his eye when he thrust that kid up against the wall. Sure, he had restrained himself from beating that kid to a pulp, but I'd seen what that gleam turned men into when they could no longer hold back.

Yeah. I had a few scars of my own thanks to that fucking *gleam*.

"Thanks," I breathed out.

"You're welcome. The kid was a tweaker."

"I don't think he would've gotten far with twelve dollars," I joked lamely.

He looked at me through a furrowed brow.

"You okay?" he asked.

I smiled awkwardly because damn this guy was hot as fuck. He was tall with massive shoulders and a face I couldn't stop looking at. He wore a hoodie, dark pants, and a pair of kick-ass motorcycle boots.

I nodded. "Yeah, thanks."

A strange pause lingered between us before he spoke again.

"You're a good singer," he said. "I really liked the one you opened with."

"Oh, that wasn't one of mine." I noticed how bright his eyes were as we talked. "That belongs to Ava Max."

Like fucking bright blue.

He smiled and I felt my knees slightly weaken. This guy already had a sexy intensity about him but when he smiled it was simply breathtaking.

"Do you play paid gigs?" he asked.

"Well, yeah, sometimes," I replied, surprised. "Why, you know someone who needs a girl with a guitar?"

"Yeah." He smiled again and *damn*. "As a matter of fact I do."

"I'm listening."

"I need someone to play at a party we're throwing tonight. How does two hundred dollars for six songs sound?"

Like a lifeline.

"It sounds pretty amazing—"

I was seconds away from accepting his offer when I noticed the leather vest under his hoodie.

He was a biker.

No. Not just a biker. According to the patch on the front, he was the Seargent at Arms of the Kings of Mayhem motorcycle club.

My heart sank.

I'd heard about the Kings of Mayhem. You didn't live in Destiny and not know who they were. They were like rock stars in this county and held the real power in this town.

Which meant they were to be avoided at all costs.

Well, for me anyway.

I didn't care how hot they were, or how powerful and lusted after they were, those vests were a giant red flag.

It was my experience that with status came power. And with power came the misguided ignorance that you were better than other people. Some saw this as a license to abuse. Or worse. *Destroy.*

Disappointment rushed through me. This guy was something else—from those vivid blue eyes and the muscles for days, right down to that scar running through his eyebrow.

My disappointment sank deeper in my gut.

Two hundred dollars for six songs.

The offer was good, but the vest was a deal breaker.

He raised an eyebrow at me. "It sounds pretty amazing, but ...?"

"You're a biker," I blurted out.

He frowned. "And?" My sudden change in demeanor was as obvious as a snowstorm. I didn't want anything to do with bikers, and I was doing a bad job at hiding it.

"Listen, it's a really decent offer, but I'm going to have to decline."

His expression didn't change. Except his eyes darkened a little. He didn't bother asking why. He could tell I was put off by his vest because I was looking at it like it was a piece of satanic literature and I was a nun.

Hell on Wheels

I held up the money I'd earned for the day. "Thanks again."

His expression remained unchanged as his eyes locked with mine. "No problem. If you change your mind..."

I wasn't going to change my mind.

I was good at calculating the risk in most situations—I had to be—and this man and that damn vest, was too high of a risk. Hauling my ass across town to a biker clubhouse to play in front of drunk, sweaty bikers wasn't in my immediate future. That would be asking for trouble.

And I was already running from a fuck-ton of it.

CHAPTER 4

CHANCE

I couldn't shake her from my mind as I left the bar. It had been hard to miss the frown on that pretty face of hers and the way her nose screwed up when she noticed my cut. That was new. The cut usually earned me a wink or a suggestive bite on the bottom lip—and quite often an invitation of some sort. But disgust? Not until ten minutes ago.

It annoyed me more than it should have.

I should be happy she pushed me away.

So why couldn't I get that angelic face and those big blue eyes out of my head.

And why the fuck did just the thought of those luscious lips and flawless, honey-colored skin make me want to kiss her?

This morning I had sworn off women.

Now I was getting hard over one.

I broke away from my brothers and took my bike for a ride on the highway where I could really open her up and let her fly. It was good therapy. The sun on my face. The wind whipping against my skin. The freedom I felt as I pushed my bike to her limits. Sometimes it was the smallest things that took the biggest steps toward healing.

After half an hour of roaring through the empty highway, I turned back toward town and headed for the clubhouse.

Needing a pack of smokes, I pulled up outside a convenience store and parked my bike at the curb. It was a small store jam-packed with overpriced groceries and souvenirs for the tourists that flocked to Destiny for fishing and watersports on the river. The bell dinged when I walked in, and Kimmy, the young cashier with the tight blue smock and big dangly earrings, looked up from her magazine and gave me an appreciative smile.

"Hi, Chance," she said, her eyes sparkling and roving up and down the length of me as I approached the counter.

"Hey there, Kimmy, how you been?"

"Good. Got you in those Hot Tamales candies you like," she said proudly.

"You did?"

I got hooked on the cinnamon candy overseas. Another sniper named Pennsylvania Pete used to eat them like they were a staple to his diet. His mom used to send him over boxes of them, and pretty soon she was sending them to me too. I hadn't had any since returning stateside and must've mentioned it to Kimmy at some point.

"I convinced Merle to get them in special."

"Well, I appreciate that. Thanks, sweetheart." I gave her a wink and a pink flush crept up her neck and across her cheeks. "Give me a pack of Marlboros and two of the Hot Tamales. Thanks, darlin'."

Thrilled because I was buying the Hot Tamales she run up the sale and took my money. But she only charged me for the smokes.

"They're on the house today," she said, batting her long lashes.

I was about to insist on paying for them when I heard raised voices behind me. I glanced over my shoulder and saw Merle, the store manager, arguing with someone hidden by a stand of Doritos.

Shoving the smokes and Hot Tamales into my cut, I stepped closer and to my surprise saw the blonde angel from earlier arguing right back at him.

He was accusing her of shoplifting.

"Everything alright?" I asked.

Both of them looked at me. Merle's face was bright with anger while she rolled her eyes.

"I caught her trying to steal from me," Merle said.

"And I told you I wasn't!" she exclaimed.

"Then explain the cans of soup I saw you put in your guitar case," he demanded.

He went to yank her guitar case from her, but she jerked it away from him. "Get your hands of it."

"Listen, I think I know what happened here," I said stepping in.

"You know this girl, Chance?" Merle asked.

She looked at me. My eyes never left hers as I replied, "I do. She's playing at the clubhouse tonight, Merle."

"Is that true, little lady?"

She could barely hide her annoyance, and I didn't even try to hide my smugness.

Eyes still on me, she replied through gritted teeth, "Yes."

I couldn't help but grin because her mouth said yes but the look on her face said no. And her eyes spelled *murder* as she glared across at me.

I smiled and looked at Merle. "Listen, what we've got here is a misunderstanding. She's simply put those cans in there and then forgot about them. I'm pretty sure this is just a big mistake." I pulled out my wallet and handed a fifty-dollar bill to the grumpy store owner. "Here's some money for the cans. Keep the change."

"That's fifty-dollars," Merle exclaimed, distracted by the gross overpayment.

I winked. Crisis averted. Even if it did cost me fifty fucking dollars.

"Consider it a tip for the inconvenience," I said, taking the girl by the elbow and heading for the door. "Have a good day."

Outside, she yanked her arm away.

"You didn't need to do that!" she snapped, stepping away from me. "I had it under control."

"Yeah, you really had it under control. Merle was two heartbeats away from calling the sheriff on your ass."

"So you decided to play the hero?"

"No. I'm just a normal guy who stepped in to help someone who clearly needed it."

Her eyes narrowed. "And now I suppose I owe you something."

I thought for a moment. We still needed someone to play at the clubhouse tonight. And if the stolen cans of soup were anything to go by, this girl obviously could use the cash.

"That's usually how these things go," I replied.

Those fucking amazing blue eyes of hers traveled over my cut. "And I suppose that means I have to put out or something equally as gross."

I admit I was taken back by her comment. Just because I wore a biker's cut I was suddenly an asshole who took advantage of young girls who were busted shoplifting, and then expected a sexual favor in return.

But no one fucked me out of obligation.

And no one would.

Ever.

"Whoa there, California," I said, taking a step back and raising my hands in surrender. "That's not what I'm talking about."

"Cassidy," she said, irritated by the nickname. "My name is Cassidy."

"Ok then, *Cassidy*, its nothing like what you're suggesting."

She still looked suspicious. "What, then?"

"The offer still stands. I want you to play at the clubhouse. It's a genuine offer. Six songs. Two hundred dollars."

Her eyes widened, only for a split second, but long enough to let me know the offer was too good to refuse.

"Just six songs." She looked at me dubiously. "For two hundred dollars?"

"That's what I'm saying."

Her suspicions weren't easily appeased. "And nothing else?"

Jesus, this girl really had the wrong impression of me.

"Nothing. Else."

Finally, she held out her hand. "Six songs. Two hundred dollars, and you have yourself a deal."

I shook her hand, and the moment my skin touched hers I felt a jolt run through me. I shook it off, just like I did when I kidded myself that I was helping her out because she looked like she needed a break. That was a lie. I didn't know why I was doing this. Only that I wanted to.

I wrote down the address of the clubhouse on an old receipt she had in her bag. "I'll make sure the guards on the gate know to expect you."

"Guards? You don't look like the type of guys who need guards," she said, folding her arms across her chest.

"Who says they're for us?" I climbed on my bike and put on my sunglasses. "See you at seven."

She smiled. "Only because you asked so nicely."

I couldn't help but smile back. "And California—try not to get yourself arrested between now and then."

CHAPTER 5

CASSIDY

Six songs. For two hundred dollars. It was a life-changing offer. Maybe not for some, but for me it meant Missy and I could get out of this shithole and catch a bus out of town.

Hope was as warm as the sunshine on my shoulders while I made my way through the sleepy streets. When the rundown dump I called home came into view, my stomach dipped and twisted, but not even the sight of the little house I hated so much could dampen my spirits. Things were looking up, thanks to a rather gorgeous biker named Chance.

I told him my name was Cassidy. It was almost the truth. I didn't become Cassidy until I met my best friend, Missy, on a bus trip from Sacramento to Las Vegas two years earlier. She'd asked me my name over a shared bag of potato chips, and I'd been Cassidy ever since.

I wouldn't tell her my real name.
I wouldn't tell anyone.
Because that girl was dead.
She was dead the moment she ran away.

Penny Dee

The little wooden gate creaked and whined as I pushed it open and made my way up the overgrown path to the front porch. For the first time in months I felt a ray of hope. I couldn't wait to tell Missy what had happened. We could make plans and be somewhere else this time tomorrow.

Six songs. Two hundred dollars.

Inside, I dumped my guitar at the front door and headed for the bedroom I shared with Missy but stopped cold when I saw the door was slightly ajar. I had closed it. I always closed it. And I knew Missy was at work.

Cautiously, I pushed it open and stepped back in horror when my brain processed what the hell I was seeing.

Missy's sleazy brother, Craig, was sitting on my bed, jerking off with a pair of my lace panties in his hand. Despite being startled, when he saw me, he gasped and his eyes went wide. In that god-awful moment he came all over his hand and my lace panties in pulsating white waves.

"What the hell are you doing!" I screamed, mortified and furious, fighting back the sudden rise of bile in my throat. Blood buzzed in my ears as rage and disgust collided inside of me. "Get out! Get out!"

Craig didn't even bother pulling up his pants in his haste to get away. He leaped off my bed, his semi-flaccid cock dangling between his legs and my cum-soaked panties still in his hand as he fled the room.

I slammed the door behind him and leaned against it, my body suddenly racked with tears of rage and shock. I shouldn't be surprised. He'd been acting weird around me ever since Missy and I moved in two months ago, always staring at me and making suggestive comments. After he'd walked in on me in the shower, I always kept the doors to the bathroom and my bedroom locked. Always.

I slid to the floor as the tears streamed down my cheeks. I felt sick. Disgusted.

Hope gone.

It was time to hit the road.

Again.

I cried until my inner strong girl rose to her feet and told me to pull myself together. This was nothing compared to what I'd already endured.

The sudden pounding on the door made me jump.

"Cassidy?"

It was Craig.

"Go away!" I yelled.

Knowing he was so close made the hair stand up on the back of my neck.

Fucking pervert.

"I'm sorry, Cassi. Really, I am. I don't know what came over me. I promise I won't do it again."

Just the sound of his voice made me want to puke. And how the hell was I ever going to get the image of him jerking off with my panties out of my head?

It was hard not to gag.

"Cassi?"

I hated anyone calling me Cassi.

"What, Craig?"

There was a pause before he asked, "Are you going to tell Missy?"

I suddenly felt exhausted. Traveling from town to town was finally catching up with me. I was ready to leave Destiny, but a tiny part of me longed to put down some roots somewhere and just relax for once in my life.

"Well, are you, Cassi?" Craig pressed.

I exhaled heavily. Telling Missy could work against me. She was protective of her brother. If I mentioned this to her, there was a good chance she would turn it all around and make it my fault. As much as I loved her, sometimes she could be moody and unpredictable. Since coming to Destiny, a gap had started to form in our friendship, and I didn't know why. She'd been acting strange lately, even becoming secretive. And in the last few weeks she'd spent less and less time at home.

While things were a little strained, I wasn't going to mention this.

"Do you promise to never do that or anything like that again?" I asked.

His voice sounded meek through the door. "I promise."

"Then I won't tell her. But if it happens again—"

"It won't. You have my word."

At least he sounded apologetic.

I closed my eyes at the thought of living in the house with Craig, knowing what a fucking creep he was. But after tonight I wouldn't have to worry about it. I would play at the clubhouse, get the two hundred dollars, and then Missy and I would be on a bus out of town.

"Ok, then. We'll keep it between us."

"Thanks." There was a pause. "Cassi?"

"Yeah, Craig?"

"Do you want your panties back?"

Another urge to gag hit me.

I didn't want to see those panties ever again.

But I didn't want him keeping them either. He'd fuck them until they were threadbare.

"Just leave them by the door."

I would burn them. I would douse them in gasoline and burn them in the fire pit out in the backyard until they were nothing but ash.

"Ok, I will," he said.

I heard him crouch down and then straighten again.

"And, Craig ..."

"Yeah?"

"If you ever touch anything of mine again, I'll cut your fucking balls off. Do you understand?"

His voice was barely audible through the door. "Ok."

I heard the floorboards creak as he walked away, and I let out a deep breath despite the knot of pain tightening in my chest. I bit back the tears.

Then for some strange reason, I thought of Chance and a peaceful warmth spread through me, instantly filling me with endorphins and calming my wildly thumping heart.

I was able to catch a breath, and I relaxed.

Drawing in a deep breath, I climbed off the floor.

Everything was going to be okay.

It had to be.

CHAPTER 6

CASSIDY

I called a cab to take me to the gig. When I told the cab driver the address, he looked me up and down and raised his brows but said nothing. I didn't know what that meant, but whatever it was it didn't feel positive. So, I reminded myself why I was doing this for the billionth time that afternoon. Two hundred dollars for six songs.

And nothing to do with an overly confident biker called Chance.

Twenty minutes later, we pulled up out the front of the Kings of Mayhem clubhouse. It was a large single-story building on a massive compound protected by six-foot gates. Paying for my fare, I climbed out and cautiously approached a man in a Kings of Mayhem cut who was on guard duty.

Through the gate, he called for a guy named Vader, who appeared a few minutes later and escorted me to the clubhouse.

So far so good.

I was still alive.

Nervously, I glanced around me. At the rear of the property, shops backed onto a shared parking lot, and to the left of the

Hell on Wheels

clubhouse was a small playground. By day I imagined it looked like an innocent industrial area but by night it was party central. String lights and fully-lit gallon drums threw off enough light to see across the compound to the far end of the property.

I followed Vader inside the clubhouse, where the smell of beer and tobacco smoke collided with the scent of sweat and perfume. Immediately to my left, a young woman was making out with a skinny biker, and further along, two girls in bikinis were sitting on the lap of an older biker, kissing.

Gnawing the inside of my cheek, I started to realize I had made a mistake accepting the gig. My music wasn't going to cut it here. Especially considering Stone Temple Pilots' "Unglued" was blasting through the speakers.

Six songs and I was out of there.

Six songs that they would probably ignore.

As we walked deeper into the club, I looked around. To my right was a bar with a wall of gleaming liquor bottles behind it. To my left was a row of shiny booths where men in biker vests smoked and drank and flirted with their female companions.

Between the two were three large pool tables, but only one of them was occupied.

Across the room, a huge blond man was arm wrestling another giant who had long, sun-bleached hair, their massive biceps bulging and their faces turning red as they battled it out. They were growling and grunting with the strain, and around them girls in very tight clothing and a lot of exposed flesh cheered them on.

Vader led me over to a small stage set up at the back of the clubhouse. It was the perfect size for a five or six-person band, but tonight there was just a lone stool in the center of it with a mic stand and amp. My guitar was a regular acoustic guitar, so he set me up with one I could plug into an amp.

"Believe me, you'll need it with this lot," he said, nodding toward the crowd who were paying no attention whatsoever to me.

"Thanks," I replied, suddenly overcome with nerves.

It was a risk accepting a job like this. Paid gigs usually meant cameras. And cameras meant danger. I couldn't afford for someone to post my picture on social media. But I would be leaving here soon, so if *he* found out I was in Destiny, I would already be long gone before he got here.

Besides, these guys didn't look like they spent a lot of time on Facebook.

"Hey, relax. From what Chance told me, you're going to knock them dead," Vader said, giving me a wink. I couldn't help but smile at his friendliness.

Signaling across the room for someone behind the bar to turn off the music, he turned to the mic, switched it on and said, "Alright, you motherfuckers. Give it up for Cassidy."

There were a few blank stares and curious glances but no one really paid any attention. Then I opened my mouth and everything changed. That was when everyone, including the hot looking biker with a deep scar running through his eyebrow, turned to watch me sing.

If there was one thing I was confident about, it was my voice. One day, when I was about twelve years old, I opened my mouth and this powerful, perfectly pitched voice with a broad range came powering out of it, and I hadn't stopped singing since.

During the dark days, it was the only thing that got me through the torment.

Which was ironic. Because I found my singing voice when my other voice was silenced.

Singing had been my savior in other ways too. I had moved from town to town with the money I earned from singing on the streets, and the occasional gig I got at some dive bar somewhere.

Hell on Wheels

I was once offered a really good gig at an exclusive yacht club in Seabrook, Texas, but I had to turn it down because I couldn't perform where the rich and fortunate congregated. I couldn't risk *him* finding me. But if I stayed in the shadows and played in the seedy bars and places like this, I was safe.

And I could afford to eat.

I focused on the words I was singing. Chance had mentioned he liked the Ava Max song he heard me sing, so I made sure I included it in my set—along with the Bahari song "California" that had inspired his nickname for me.

I also did an acoustic version of Jewel's "Only One Too."

I was a little nervous about my song choices. Considering the crowd I was singing to, I thought I would lose them. After all, these guys were all about rock 'n' roll and I was more acoustic pop.

But I was wrong.

Just like I was wrong about those damn vests.

I couldn't have had a better audience if I tried.

Especially when I threw in Dolly Parton's "Jolene." That got me some serious audience love.

But nothing could compare to my version of Heart's "Barracuda." That seemed to set them off like a nuclear bomb.

Six songs turned into eight.

Then ten.

People were dancing and having a good time. Big bikers and their women. They were encouraging with their clapping and their singing and their friendly interaction with me.

By the end of it, I was accepting requests. And at one point, a guy who looked like he'd stepped straight out of a Metallica concert, with his long strawberry blond hair and handlebar mustache, joined me on stage to sing Dolly Parton's "Nine To Five."

The crowd ate it up.

This was from people I thought would eat me alive.

In the end, I had to stop singing because my voice was growing hoarse, and I needed a drink. My cheeks were also hurting from laughing and smiling so much.

I glanced over at Chance, who stood watching from the bar, his big arms crossed over his broad chest, and a wave of appreciation washed over me. Tonight had been fun, not to mention life- changing because tomorrow I was on a bus out of here.

Perhaps I had been too quick to judge him because of the vest he wore.

Maybe there was reason to everyone's madness when they dropped their panties for these guys.

Maybe they weren't the power-hungry bullies I thought they were.

I glanced over at Chance, who was still watching me, and felt a thrill travel up my spine.

I started to lower my guard.

I mean, where was the harm in one night?

Especially if I was leaving town tomorrow.

CHAPTER 7

CHANCE

I was late to Ruger's patchover party because I had to visit the sexual health clinic over in Humphrey. Fucking anyone without protection wasn't what I was about, and this morning's event in the shower was further proof I wasn't myself. I knew Tammi-Lynn was one of the actresses who worked for the Kings of Mayhem adult film production company, Head Quarters. I knew they had strict health checks so they could fuck on film without condoms. I knew she would be clean and knew I would be okay.

But I visited the clinic anyway.

As a result, I got to the clubhouse just in time to see Cassidy get up on stage and start singing.

And goddamnit, my insides lit up like fucking fireworks when I saw her up on the stage, her bright blonde hair gleaming under the lights and those beautiful glossy lips singing into the microphone. But it was that voice, that rich, smoky voice that reached across the clubhouse to where I was standing at the bar and punched me square in the chest.

She was fascinating, and as the minutes turned into an hour, I grew more and more drawn to her. Even though I knew it was pointless, it was hard not to when she was up there singing like a goddess and making a room full of bikers and their old ladies eat out of her hand.

When she finished her set, the room erupted with raucous appreciation. I watched, intrigued, as she thanked the crowd then stepped off the stage and made her way to where I stood at the bar.

"Not bad, California," I said, trying not to notice how her skin glowed with a golden sheen of sweat. Or how long her lashes were.

Or the fullness of her juicy, pink lips.

"Here," I handed her an iced tea. "I ordered you a drink."

I watched those luscious lips slide over the rim of the glass and felt the flare of attraction burst in my gut.

"Oh God, it tastes so good." She beamed up at me. "Thank you."

"You looked like you were having fun up there," I said, resisting the urge to wipe the small beads of sweat from above her mouth.

"Maybe." She grinned. "It wasn't as bad as I thought it would be."

"Not the seventh realm of Hell?"

She laughed. "No. I had fun. I'm sorry I reacted so badly about you being a biker when we first met. I'm just cautious, you know?"

"Don't mention it. You helped us out. They really loved you."

"It was fun." She fanned herself. "But I think I need some air. It's hot under those lights."

"Come on. Let's go sit outside." I took her by the hand and led her out to the barbecue tables in the playground, where we stared up at a starry sky, talking. She told me about traveling with her friend, Missy, and how they had spent the last two years roaming across the country, picking each new town by putting names in a hat and pulling them out. She liked to be free, she said. To explore. She was spirited. Inquisitive.

I was jealous of her freedom. Not just the freedom to roam but also the freedom from the darkness. Because she was wild and carefree. Untouched by the blackness. I was like the night, while she was pure fucking sunshine.

The hours seemed to pass like minutes.

"I suppose I should go," she finally said, pulling out her phone.

"Let me give you a ride."

She shook her head. "No, it's okay. I'll call a cab."

I watched her order her cab, not wanting her to leave even though I knew I should let her go.

When she hung up, I suddenly remembered I hadn't paid her.

"Here ... before I forget." I handed her the wad of cash.

"There's three hundred here. It's too much."

"You sang more than the agreed six songs. You earned it."

"I couldn't let my adoring fans down when they kept asking for more," she joked.

"I think Joker became your number one fan."

"Is that the guy with the epic mustache, who looks like a young James Hetfield from Metallica?"

"The one and only."

"He had some killer chords."

I chuckled. "I think he fell in love with you."

When she smiled, something crackled between us. Our eyes remained locked together. And before my brain could fathom it, she leaned forward and grazed her lips across mine.

Fuck.

My breath left me with a desperate moan as her lips glided over mine. They tasted just as sweet as I thought they would, and I felt my entire body react. From the acceleration of my pulse to the thickening behind the zipper of my jeans. Because Jesus Christ, this woman had me to so turned on I couldn't think.

But I couldn't kiss her back. I wanted to. *Badly*. But I had to stop it, because if I didn't I would do something stupid like take her beautiful face in my hands and kiss her a thousand ways to Sunday. And I wouldn't stop there. After losing myself in her lips and the torture of her succulent mouth, I would take her to my room and peel every inch of clothing from her luscious body and spend the rest of the night making love to that amazing body of hers until neither of us could take any more.

I throbbed in my jeans just thinking about it and shifted awkwardly, resisting the urge to adjust myself.

I abruptly pulled away, and she looked up at me, startled.

"I'm sorry, did I misread the moment?" she asked, her cheeks slightly flushed.

"No, you didn't," I said, hating myself. My eyes dropped to her luscious lips, and my entire being begged me to kiss them again.

To just say *fuck it* and dive right in.

But I wouldn't.

Because this girl deserved more than what she was asking for.

"You're a beautiful woman, Cassidy," I said, tucking a lock of hair behind her ear. "But you're kissing a goddamn frog. You should stick with the princes."

She looked down and her brow wrinkled with a frown as she considered what I'd said.

When she looked up, the brightness was gone from her eyes. Either I had hit some kind of nerve or she felt rejected.

In a way, I kind of needed her to feel that way. Because if she came at me with that kiss again, I couldn't be held responsible for what happened next—which would be a whole lot of kissing and a fuck-ton of me exploring every inch of that beautiful body

Hell on Wheels

of hers with every part of my body that was capable of getting hard.

I was so lost thinking about the things I wanted to do to her, I didn't realize her cab had arrived.

"I suppose I should get going then," she said, climbing off the table and pulling on her denim jacket. I watched her pick up her guitar. "Thanks for tonight. I had a good time."

I climbed off the table and followed her over to where the cab was waiting. Something hung in the air between us. Something unsaid. A broken kiss. A missed opportunity. An instant attraction. She bit down on her bottom lip, and I fought back a groan, wanting desperately to taste her again.

But the moment passed quickly, and she turned away to open the car door.

"Will I see you again?" I asked before I could stop myself.

She turned back to look at me, those fucking amazing blue eyes sparkling like sapphires in the dim light.

"I don't think so. I'm leaving town tomorrow." She held up the cash I'd just given her. "Now that I can afford that bus ticket out of here, who knows where I'll end up." She smiled and damn if that smile didn't crush my heart.

With nothing left to say, she climbed in, closed the door, and the cab pulled away. I watched it leave the parking lot, and as the taillights disappeared into the darkness, I couldn't help but wonder what I had just let slip through my fingers.

CHAPTER 8

CASSIDY

I was pleased I was leaving town so I never, *ever* had to see him again.

I was embarrassed. The kind of embarrassed where you wished the floor would open up and swallow you down to Middle Earth.

Thinking he was interested in me, I'd practically shoved my tongue down his throat, when in reality he was just being nice. I groaned and felt my cheeks flush with heat. I looked at the six fifty-dollar bills in my hand and felt relieved. They were my ticket out of this damn town.

The lights were on in the house when the cab pulled up at the curb, and I couldn't get inside quick enough to show Missy the money. I hadn't seen her to tell her about the gig at the clubhouse, but I knew when she saw the money, she'd be just as excited as I was.

She was in the bedroom we shared, sitting on her bed scrolling through her phone.

Hell on Wheels

"Get packing, honey. We're out of here," I said excitedly, grabbing my already packed bag out from under the bed. I swung around, my heart blooming with excitement and an urgency to leave. "Where do you think we should go? New Orleans? Atlanta? New York? God, I've always wanted to go there." I grabbed my gold *Hope* necklace off the shabby old dresser by the window and put it on. "They say Central Park is mind-blowing when it's covered in snow." I turned around. Missy hadn't moved and was as still as a mouse. "We can go anywhere we want—"

"I'm pregnant," she said quickly. And all of a sudden the air vanished from the room.

I straightened. "To who?"

I didn't know she was having sex.

Missy's face came alive. "Johnny," she said.

My mind worked quickly to put all the pieces together.

"You mean, Johnny Miller—your boss at the bar?"

She nodded and crossed the room to sit on my bed, tucking one leg under her.

"Oh, Cassidy, he's treatin' me real nice," she gushed. "Always kissing me and stuff. Callin' me beautiful, telling me he can't stop thinking about me. He calls me his doll face. And he has this real nice way about him."

"But he's married!"

She raised her chin slightly. "He loves me."

All I could do was gape at her.

"But... he's married!" I reminded her again.

A storm cloud passed over her lovely face. "He's going to leave his wife for me."

"Did he say that?"

"Yes. Last night. When we were making love."

I sat down on the edge of the bed.

Missy took my hand. "Please be excited for me, Cassidy. I'm so happy. Please say you'll stay and help me with the baby. I know you don't like it here. I know Craig makes you feel uncomfortable. But Johnny and I will get a house and you can come live with us. You can help me with the baby." She shook my hands because I was non-responsive. "Please say you'll stay and help me."

Slowly, I turned my head to look at her. I felt like the wind had been kicked out of me. I hadn't seen this coming.

I owed Missy a lot. She taught me how to survive on nothing as we traveled from one adventure to another. She also saved my life. Last year when we were traveling from Scottsdale to Phoenix, the car we were riding in crashed and flipped on an almost empty desert highway. I was trapped in the front seat, hanging upside down and unconscious. A fire started in the engine and smoke began to fill the car. Missy was able to crawl out her window. When I came to, she was undoing my seatbelt and pulling me from the wreckage while the driver was on the phone to the police. A minute later the car erupted into a ball of fire.

I owed her my life. I couldn't leave her now when she needed me.

"Of course I'll stay and help," I said, forcing a smile.

Suddenly, getting out of Destiny was an impossibility, and I had to fight back the nausea when the realization hit me.

I was stuck here.

CHAPTER 9

CASSIDY

Two days later, I started work at a diner in town.

It was only three hours a day, four days a week. The money was bad, but despite being on the wrong side of the river where the homes were trailers and there were more bars than stores, most of the customers were good tippers.

Plus, Molly Jenkins, the owner, was kind of cool. Somewhere in her sixties, she flustered easily and was angry, prone to eye-rolling and head-shaking, but she hadn't lost her sense of humor, even after life had given her *two dud husbands and three no-hope kids*. She was kind. Funny. She also knew a desperate case when she saw one. Because even though I had absolutely no waitressing experience whatsoever, she threw me a lifeline and gave me a job.

She also threw in breakfast. Because according to her, I was too skinny and looked like I would disappear if I turned sideways. So before my shift started, she all but force-fed a bowl of grits and gravy into me. Which was good because when I'd gone to make toast before work, I discovered Craig and Missy had eaten all the bread.

There was one other waitress besides me, Molly's grand-niece Daisy, a chatty drama queen who liked her uniform as tight as it was short and her heels as high as they were shiny. She wore a lot of makeup and chewed gum like it was exercise. She was fun, confident, and flirty. Straight away, she had my back. When I spilled milk on the lap of a rather pissed-off trucker, she swooped in to take care of matters, and after a lot of flirting and eyelash batting, she had him convinced it was completely his fault and not mine. She was good at her job. Great at PR. And had the opposite sex eating out of her hand.

She made my first day fun.

Not to mention saved my ass more than a couple of times.

Because, hell, waitressing was a lot harder than it looked.

After the lunch crowd cleared and the afternoon diners came and went, Daisy and I heard the approaching rumble of Harleys. We stood at the window, and Daisy pulled down the curtain for us to watch five bikers rumble past, all of them looking like formidable gods with their dark glasses and cuts as they controlled big metallic beasts between their legs. We watched as they disappeared down the street to where they pulled up to a cigar bar, reversing their bikes to park in front of the curb.

Daisy looked like a lovesick teenager.

"They're so dreamy," she sighed.

"They're bikers," I said. "Outlaws."

"They're not just any bikers, Cassidy. They're *Kings*."

Right.

My mistake.

She pushed the curtain down further to get a better view of them.

"See the one that looks like Jason Momoa ...? That's Maverick. He's so hot he could melt iron," she gushed. "Oh, look, there's

Hell on Wheels

Cade. He's their VP and is married to Indy, who is a doctor. Next to him is his brother Caleb—oh my God he is so delicious I could eat him with a spoon. His wife owns a cupcake shop on the other side of town and is expecting twins."

She seemed to know an awful lot about them. And I couldn't help but smile at her enthusiasm.

"The one climbing off his bike ... that's their president, Bull."

I thought about Bull and his piercing, ethereal eyes. I had only met him briefly the other night.

"And there's Chance..." She sighed dreamily, resting her head against the glass window. "That boy is pure sex on a stick."

A small thrill ran up my spine at the mention of his name. I looked out the window, and my eyes lingered on him as he climbed off his bike and secured his helmet to his handlebars.

"You know a lot about them," I said, ignoring the lust pooling between my thighs.

I didn't tell her that I had played at the Kings of Mayhem clubhouse two days earlier. Or about Chance chasing down the would-be thief to get my money back. Or how damn sexy he looked as we sat out under the stars and talked for hours.

And I certainly didn't mention how I had practically assaulted him with my mouth as we waited for my cab to arrive.

Because when you spend your life running from your past, it becomes second nature to keep things to yourself.

The flush of embarrassment licked at my cheeks again when I thought about the kiss. And how for just a second those lips had felt so incredibly amazing against my own.

Without thinking, I reached up and touched my mouth, as if the brush of his lips still lingered there.

"Around here, they're a big deal," Daisy explained. "A lot of local girls try to get their hands on a King. Even for just a night, you know?"

I did know.

Two nights ago I was one of those girls, entertaining the idea of a night with my King.

My King?

Oh *hell* no.

What the fuck was wrong with me?

I had no King.

He had made that as plain as the sky was blue.

I sighed and shook my head, refocusing on Daisy.

"How old are you?" I asked.

"Old enough," she said, looking at me with a wicked gleam in her lust-filled eyes. She turned back to the window and sighed. "Boy, what I'd give for one night with *any* of them."

"Even the married ones?" I raised an eyebrow at her.

"*Any* of them. But of course Cade and Caleb are all about their wives and would never cheat on them. And Maverick ... well, apparently he's so smitten by his girlfriend he's asked her to marry him like *a thousand times* even though she keeps saying no every time. And Bull... well, everyone knows he lost his heart years ago when his wife died in a car wreck. The rumor is he swore he'd never fall in love again. But a girl can fantasize." She pressed her hand to the glass. "I guess that leaves Chance."

Again, my heart started to dance at the mere mention of his name.

Because, clearly, I was losing my mind.

I shook my head to get the craziness out of it as I walked away, leaving Daisy to her King stalking. It would be stupid for me to get caught up in it. As soon as I worked out a new plan, I would be moving on from this town.

Carrying a tray of dishes, I pushed through the swing doors leading into the kitchen and headed toward the sink. Lost in ridiculous thoughts about how good Chance looked climbing off his bike, I didn't see Molly walking in the back door from the alleyway before it was too late. She opened the door and it sent

Hell on Wheels

the tray of dishes in my hand flying. Coffee sloshed down the front of my uniform as cups and plates smashed to the floor.

"Oh my God, Molly, I'm so sorry!" I cried.

I dropped to my knees and began picking up pieces of shattered porcelain.

"It's okay, pet. Don't fret."

She crouched down and began helping me clean up the mess.

"I'm not usually so clumsy," I said, feeling like a klutz. First the spilled milk on the truckers lap then a dropped piece of cherry pie on the floor. Now this. My first day could end up being my last day.

"No point in crying over spilled milk," Molly said.

"Or in this case coffee," Daisy added lamely from the doorway.

I looked at her with a sarcastic *thank you* then turned back to Molly.

"I really am sorry. Please let me pay for the dishes."

But Molly brushed it off. "Don't worry your pretty head over it. Best you go home and get yourself cleaned up. No point hanging around here any longer looking like you mopped the floor with your blouse."

"Are you sure?"

"Of course. And make sure you take that there box of leftovers I've fixed you." She pointed to a white cardboard box sitting on the counter.

"Well that's just great! She breaks dishes and gets an early mark," Daisy huffed, dramatically throwing her hands up in the air. "*And* she gets dinner!"

She pushed the swinging doors leading out into the café and resumed her spot at the window, dreamily gazing down the street.

"I really am sorry," I said to Molly again. "You're not going to call me later and tell me to not come in on Friday, are you?"

She smiled warmly as she patted my cheek. "I'll see you back here at ten o'clock."

I was so relieved I could've hugged her. Now that I was staying in this town, I needed this job.

"Thank you. I promise, no more broken dishes."

As I passed Daisy, she smiled at me. "Good work today."

"Really? You think I can make it as a waitress?"

"No. But I like having you around." She gave me a wink. "See you Friday."

I left the café with a smile on my face and walked home in the late afternoon sunlight, armed with a box of leftovers that included sandwiches, potato salad, and a slice of pecan pie.

Thirty minutes later, I walked down my street but came to a halt as soon as I saw the car in the driveway. It was a Pontiac. An *unfamiliar* Pontiac.

Fear began a slow crawl up my spine. In six weeks, Craig and Missy had never had a visitor. Craig was basically a loner, and Missy did most of her socializing at the bar where she worked.

I approached the porch cautiously and paused at the front door, listening for voices, but all I could hear was someone playing a Metallica song on an electric guitar. I frowned and pushed the screen door open, stepping inside where I found Craig sitting in the living room, murdering "Wherever I May Roam."

What the hell?

Since when did Craig own an electric guitar?

My eyes went to the Xbox packaging beside him on the couch.

Or an Xbox for that matter?

I looked around at the discarded boxes of *things* littering the floor.

Craig had been on a spending spree. Electronics. A sound system.

A Pontiac in the driveway.

Hell on Wheels

Craig didn't have a job. Didn't have an income. So what bullshit scam was he involved in that he could afford all of this stuff? I thought about asking him. But in all honesty I didn't want to know. I didn't want him dragging me into whatever redneck bullshit he was a part of.

Instead, I walked upstairs and found Missy in her room.

"Hey," I said, flopping down on the bed. "Am I seeing things or has Craig been on a crazy spending spree?"

When she didn't answer, I became aware of the tension in the room. She was folding laundry from the basket and putting it away, doing everything she could not to look at me.

I sat up. "Is everything okay?"

"Why do you give him a hard time? You know he's a bit slow. You don't need to be such a bitch to him."

Whoa.

"Okay..." I said, confused. "I'm sorry, I didn't mean anything by it. But you must admit, it's a bit suspicious that he's got all this new stuff. How did he pay for it? He doesn't even have a job."

"Oh, so now that you've got a job you're suddenly better than him. Is that it?"

I was taken back. "No, that's not what I was—"

"Why don't you cut him some slack, Cassidy. What has he ever done to you?"

I thought about him jerking off with my underwear.

But I didn't mention it.

"You must admit, it's a bit curious..." I let the sentence trail off because Missy seemed really agitated and I didn't want to add to it. "Hey—I'm sorry if I offended you."

"It's fine," she replied stiffly, pulling out a T-shirt from the laundry basket. She started folding it, and either it had pissed her off and she was taking out her anger on it or she was pissed at me about something.

I climbed off the bed. "Are you sure you're okay because I'm picking up some pretty negative vibes. Has something upset you? Have I?"

She threw the half-folded T-shirt back into the basket and rounded on me with mean eyes. "Admit it, you can't stand that I've found someone. That a man wants to be with me."

Her accusation came so far out from left field it gave me whiplash as she hurled it at me.

"What are you talking about?" I asked, confused.

"You hate that I'm having a baby with Johnny."

"I don't hate—"

"You don't think I should be with him."

"Because he's married!"

"See! You look down your nose at me like you're better than me."

"That's not true." I didn't want to fight with her, so I tried to defuse the situation. "Listen, Missy, I don't know why you're so angry at me—"

"You need to go."

I looked at her, dumbfounded, unsure if I'd heard her correctly. "What?"

She picked up the T-shirt again and began to fold it hastily. "I don't think you should live here anymore."

I stared at her in disbelief. "Why?"

"I'm settled here. I don't want to leave."

"I thought you wanted me to help you with the baby—"

"I don't need your help. Johnny is going to take care of me and the baby."

It suddenly occurred to me that she hadn't looked me in the eye since I'd asked her why she was throwing me out. And now that I realized it, it became obvious. She was having trouble looking at me because she was lying.

I climbed off the bed. "Fine, I'll leave but not before you tell me why."

"I just told you."

"I mean the truth."

"I don't need to do anything." Still no eye contact. "Because this is my house and I'm telling you to leave."

I couldn't believe what she was saying. Tears welled in my eyes and the hurt pounded through me with such force that I felt breathless. I didn't understand what was happening or why she was doing this. We'd been through a lot together, hard times, poor times, rough times, and now she was throwing me out? I struggled to swallow my hurt.

"Fine, I'll move out tomorrow."

Finally, she made eye contact. "I want you gone tonight."

"Where will I go?"

She turned back to folding her washing. "That's the thing, Cassidy, I don't care."

CHAPTER 10

CHANCE

We were just leaving the cigar shop on Main when I saw her. She was walking down the street.

No, not walking.

Stomping.

She was *stomping* down the street carrying what looked like all of her worldly possessions. One canvas bag, a guitar case, and a world of trouble on her shoulders.

And just like that, a new war took up inside of me.

Leave her to deal with whatever it was that lead her onto the street at dusk with all of her belongings.

Or help her.

Hate told me to walk away.

Just kick the Harley into gear and hammer down in the other direction.

I'd already let her go the other night. And even though I'd thought about her constantly in the time since then, she was out of my life.

But I couldn't shake the feeling that something wasn't right.

Hell on Wheels

Fuck. Fuck. Fuck.

I looked at Caleb and the others. "You go. I'll catch up with you at the clubhouse later."

They glanced over at Cassidy then nodded and roared off down the street. The noise caught her attention, and she looked up. The moment our eyes met, I knew I was going to help her. Call it a sixth sense, but I just knew I wasn't done with this girl yet.

I kicked the Harley into gear and rode over to where she was standing on the curb.

"I thought you would've left town by now," I said.

"I'm on my way," she said, clutching her bag of clothes in her hands. But instead of looking happy about it, she looked sad.

Pissed.

Yep. Something wasn't right.

"Where's your friend? The one you're traveling with?"

If she looked sad before, now she looked completely devastated. But it was only a flicker before it was gone and quickly hidden behind a bright, phony smile.

"I'm flying solo this time. She's staying here."

The way she said it, I knew there was more to the story.

"Is everything okay?" I asked.

She huffed out a breath and looked away, tears glimmering in her lovely eyes. She bit down on her bottom lip to calm her quivering chin, and I couldn't hold back the lascivious thoughts that flickered across my sex-starved brain.

"Cassidy?"

"She threw me out," she snapped suddenly, the emotion fierce on her delicate features.

"Your friend?"

"My supposed *best friend*," she said angrily.

She gave me a very brief explanation about her roommate suffering from baby brain and how she threw her out because

Cassidy disapproved of the affair she was having with her married boss.

Her friend sounded like a real piece of work.

"So you're leaving town tonight?" I asked.

She shook her head and held up a crumpled bus timetable. "The last bus left at four-forty-five. I'm going to sleep at the bus station tonight and get on the next bus out of town in the morning."

Yeah, that wasn't going to happen.

The bus station wasn't a safe place for sleeping. It was unpatrolled with a lot of people coming and going. Once it closed down for the evening, it wasn't the place for a young woman to spend the night alone.

"Come on, I can't leave you out here," I said, revving the Harley. It came to life with a bark and a rumble, the sound echoing down the street. "You can't stay at the bus station."

"I've stayed in worse places."

I gave her a pointed look. "It's not safe. In the daylight it might seem harmless, but at night the desperate and the tweakers spill out of the shadows. Come on, I'll find you a safe place to sleep tonight."

"I'm not staying with you," she said, taking a step away from me.

I raised an eyebrow. "Good, because I wasn't asking you. I'll take you where no one will bother you. Now will you climb on the back and let me help you."

Reluctantly, she slid behind me, her bag of clothes resting between us and her guitar strapped to her back. With a pull on the throttle, the Harley roared to life, and we took off into the dying light.

Ten minutes later, we arrived at the Black Cherry Inn, a little motel just outside of town. Cassidy slid off the back and looked across the parking lot at the small motel with the bright neon cherry flashing on the roof.

"I can't afford this," she said, alarmed.

"Again, good. Because you're not paying."

"You're paying for me to sleep here tonight?" Her surprise turned to suspicion. "Just because I kissed you the other night doesn't mean I want to sleep with you."

I raised an eyebrow at the suggestion.

"Do you always make it this hard for people to help you?"

"Only when they want me to fuck them in return for their help."

I climbed off the bike and walked over to her. Leaning in close, I whispered, "I *don't* want you to fuck me."

I walked off and made my way across the gravel parking lot toward the manager's office while she stayed put, watching me, probably weighing her options and whether or not she could trust me. Finally, she sighed, and I heard the sound of her boots on the gravel as she chased after me. Before I got to the door she grabbed my arm.

"You really don't expect anything in return?"

Jesus, what was this chick's deal?

"Not a damn thing." I turned away and opened the glass door leading into the office.

I paid with cash and put the room under my name. Cassidy said nothing, but I could feel her eyes on me as she watched me sign for the key. I couldn't figure her out. One minute she was trying to kiss me and the next she was acting as if I was some kind of skeeze. Talk about mixed messages. All I wanted was to do the right fucking thing here, and that was making sure she wasn't left to sleep on the goddamn street.

When we stepped outside, she looked at me suspiciously.

"If you don't expect me to sleep with you, then what *do you* want?" she asked, when I handed her the key.

Jesus Christ ... this again.

I lit a cigarette and let it hang off my lip.

"That's the thing, sweetheart. I don't want anything." I shoved my wallet into my pocket and walked back to my bike, climbing on. "Room's paid up 'til eleven. See you around, California."

I was walking away. I didn't need this shit.

If she didn't want my help, I wasn't going to fucking force it on her.

I'd done what I'd set out to do. She had a roof over her head for the night. What she did after that was up to her.

I got as far as putting on my helmet when she called out to me.

"At least let me buy you breakfast in the morning. You know, to say thank you."

I raised an eyebrow at her. "You can't afford to buy me breakfast."

She smiled. And fuck me if I didn't feel that smile right along the length of my cock.

"Three hundred dollars says I can." She smiled and held up her cash.

I scowled at her. Telling the whole world you had cash was a good invitation for getting mugged. Sometimes I wondered how this angel survived traveling across the country without getting rolled.

"I'll pick you up at 10:45." I flicked my wrist and my Harley roared to life. "And, California—"

She looked up from putting the key in the door. "Yeah?"

"Lock the fucking door behind you."

And with that, I rode off into the late afternoon.

CHAPTER 11

CASSIDY

The door clicked and my eyes flicked open. At this hour, I knew that sound meant trouble. The house was still and quiet, but my heartbeat roared in my ears. He was coming for me.

He said nothing when he reached me. Even when I began to struggle against him, he said nothing.

I shook my head from side to side, but he clamped his hand down over my mouth. Experience told me to lie still. Because he got off on the struggle. But it was my instinct to fight—and fight him I did, even when he overpowered me, even when he ripped my panties and took me, I continued to struggle.

By the time he was finished with me, I was face down on the bed and naked below the waist.

My body ached but it was nothing like the pain in my soul.

I woke up with a start, my skin cold but my hair damp with sweat.

My eyes darted around the dark, unfamiliar room as I struggled to catch my breath, the fog of sleep slowly lifting.

As my dream receded, my breathing evened out and my heart began to slow.

I was safe.

He didn't know where I was.

There was no way for him to know.

I had been careful.

One day it wouldn't have to be this way.

One day I would be truly free of him forever.

I didn't know how.

I could only have hope.

It was the only thing that kept me going.

The alarm woke me five hours later. Reluctantly, I climbed out of bed and took a long shower. Standing under the spray of warm water, my muscles softened, and I began to feel relieved about leaving Missy's mom's house. Here in this little motel room I was free from Craig's leering and the possibility of him walking in on me at any given point.

I was also free from Missy's craziness.

Her selfishness.

Her impulsiveness.

But I felt sad. She was my only friend. And despite her unpredictable, and often self-centered behavior, I couldn't understand why she turned on me like she did. She told me it was because I wasn't supportive of her involvement with Johnny, but I couldn't help but feel like there was more to the story.

Now I was alone.

Truly alone.

Hell on Wheels

Except for the kindness of one lone biker.

My cheeks heated when I thought of the kiss and how he'd pulled away.

I had only asked him to breakfast to say thank you for his kindness. The guy had done me a solid by giving me a roof over my head for the night. Not to mention a paid gig at his clubhouse. It was the least I could do. Even if the memory of our *non-kiss* made my spine tingle with embarrassment.

I dressed quickly in my favorite boho dress and boots, shoving my arms into a denim jacket. I threw my bag on the bed and started repacking it but paused when I realized my entire life was in front of me. Everything I owned in the whole world, apart from my guitar, fit into a canvas backpack. It was kind of pathetic, really, but it was the way it had to be. For now, anyway. I couldn't afford for anything to slow me down.

My eyes shifted to the silver gun sitting next to my pair of Converse high tops. I picked it up and stared at it in my hand. When we were in Texas I took a firearm course and spent hours honing my skills at the firing range. Now I was good at three things. Singing. Running. And shooting a fucking gun.

When you were running from what I was running from, you needed some kind of protection in case you got caught.

Could I use it if I had to?

Abso*fucking*lutely I could.

I shoved it into my handbag and continued repacking my backpack.

When I heard the rumble of an approaching Harley I went to the window and watched through the parted curtain as Chance pulled up front.

A knot tightened in my stomach.

Sliding off his bike, he looked like all kinds of sin as he approached the porch. Dark glasses. Broad shoulders. Just the right amount of scruff on a sexy as fuck jawline. I quickly let the curtain fall back into place and ignored the pulsating between my thighs as I answered his knock on the door.

"Didn't get mugged for your three hundred dollars?" he asked with a smile that totally disarmed me.

"Someone very wise told me to lock my door." I raised my hands up in wonder. "Whataya know? It worked. I'm still rich."

He gave me a big smile, and again I wasn't prepared for the impact it had on me.

"Ready to go?" he asked.

I nodded.

"Have you picked out a place for breakfast?" I asked, closing the door behind me.

"Yep. And it's super expensive. So it's good you've got money, honey."

I slid on the back of his bike and wrapped my arms around him.

He was big. The kind of big that made you feel safe. And for a moment I let myself enjoy the warmth of his body and the hardness of the muscle I felt beneath my arms as we rode into town in the morning sunshine. My heart felt light, and despite the craziness of the last couple of days, I could feel that comforting flicker of hope warming my heart. I rested my cheek against his leather vest, and for the first time in a long time allowed myself to feel content.

To breathe.

But that all came crashing down when we rode past a shiny pickup truck, and I saw Missy at the wheel.

Missy didn't own a pickup truck. And she certainly didn't have the money to buy one either.

Something wasn't right.

I tried to reason with myself. Maybe it was Johnny's. Maybe he'd loaned it to her.

But something nagged at me.

Hell on Wheels

Yesterday, Craig had bought a car.

Now Missy was driving a new pickup.

Things weren't adding up.

Had Craig gotten her involved in something illegal?

Again, I tried to reason with myself. It wasn't my problem anymore. Missy had shoved me out of her life with a big fuck you. I would probably never know why, and maybe it was better that way.

But at the end of the day she had been my friend, and I didn't want her getting into any trouble because of her loser brother.

And this reeked of Craig.

Chance pulled up outside a diner called *Perky's*, a coffee shop with shiny red booths and black-and-white checkered linoleum on the floor. We sat by the window overlooking the street and accepted menus from a waitress called Viola, who devoured Chance with her eyes. I was getting used to it. The Kings were a big deal in this town. Rock stars of the county. I got it.

But I couldn't get Missy out of my mind. Or shake the thought that she'd gotten herself into something bad. Was it drugs? Had Craig stolen credit cards or gotten her mixed up in something equally as illegal?

It ate at me. So when I saw her pull up across the street from the diner, I couldn't help myself; I had to know what was going on. I had to know she wasn't involved in something that could send her to jail.

Without a word to Chance, I got up and burst out onto the sunny street and confronted her.

Missy looked surprised.

No. She looked *busted*.

"Cassidy, w-what are you d-doing h-here?" she stammered, glancing around us nervously. "I thought you left town."

She had on a full face of makeup and the dress she wore was new. This close, I could smell the expensive perfume.

"Well, you thought wrong." I looked over her shoulder at the shiny red pickup. "Nice pickup. Is it Johnny's?"

"No." She looked uncomfortable. "Why haven't you left town? You were supposed to go yesterday."

"Stop trying to change the subject. Who does the truck belong to?" I narrowed my eyes. She was up to something. She and Craig. "Oh my Lord, Missy, did you steal it? Did Craig make you do this?"

"No!" She raised her chin. "For your information, it's mine."

"Yours?" Two days ago, she didn't have two pennies to rub together. Now she had a new car? "Where did you get the money to buy a pickup?"

When she looked away, the tingle of an alarm started at the base of my spine.

"Answer me." I grabbed her wrist. "Missy, where did you get the money to pay for it?"

She yanked her wrist free. "Why didn't you tell me you came from a rich family?"

Her words floored me. I mean, she couldn't have surprised me more with a sledgehammer to the face.

I took a step back. "What do you mean?"

"All this time we've been struggling on the street, going without food, working our fingers to the bone, when all along you're a rich girl."

Panic rushed from my toes to my head, making me see stars and stealing the air from my lungs.

"I'm not rich," I managed over the lump in my throat.

"Yes you are. Craig found out all about you online. Saw your missing person poster. Your real name is Chelsea. Your father is Kerry *fucking* Silvermane!"

My hand went to my stomach. I felt winded.

"My *foster* father," I rasped.

"Whatever. He is worth billions. And he has been looking for you."

"You contacted him?" I asked breathlessly.

Blood whirred in my ears.

"Not him, *exactly*. If you must know, we spoke to your brother."

Oh God.

My knees went week.

"You don't know what have you done," I breathed out, dazed by the sudden knowledge that my life was in extreme danger.

If Missy noticed my panic, then she didn't show it. In fact, she rounded on me like I had done something terrible to her by not letting her know where I came from.

"We went for days without anything to eat. Slept under bridges and in bus stops because we were so broke. We hitched rides with men we didn't know. We went without so much, but all this time you were fucking rich!"

The footpath felt like liquid beneath me. I stumbled backward, fighting the bile rising in my throat.

"You told Barrett where I was."

It wasn't a question.

"For the right price," she replied.

"He paid you?"

"There was a reward out for information on your whereabouts."

I was going to be sick. My nightmare was coming to life.

"You just killed me," I whispered, dizzy with fear.

But Missy simply scoffed, because not only didn't she understand what she'd done, she didn't care.

I needed to get out of there.

I was losing time as it was.

Without another word, I staggered away from her and began sprinting down the street as the realization that Barrett would already be on his way hit me.

Or worse.

He was already here.

In the diner, Chance must've seen me take off down the street because I heard him call out my name. But I didn't stop. I had to get back to the motel. I had to grab my things and get out of town.

Missy didn't know it, she was too naïve to realize, but she and Craig had signed my death warrant the moment they spoke to my brother.

I heard the Harley roar up the street, heard it come closer, and as I raced across the road, Chance cut me off.

"Please," I cried, about to have a meltdown in the middle of the street. "I need to get back to the motel."

He didn't waste time with questions. Instead, he guided me onto the back of his bike, handed me a helmet, and we took off for the motel.

My heart was in my throat as we rode.

Was Barrett here?

Could he see me now?

The terror was like ice in my veins. And if it wasn't for the warmth of Chance's body against mine as I held onto him, I would be trembling from the fear.

When we arrived at the motel, there were no other cars in the parking lot—but an empty parking lot didn't mean he wasn't waiting for me inside the room. A bomb of fear exploded in my chest.

The Harley was barely parked when I climbed off and raced toward my room. My legs shook, and my breathing was labored as I paused at the door. I was mentally bracing myself. If he was inside, I would run. I would run so fast from this place my lungs would burn and my muscles would melt from overheating. And even then I would keep running. I'd keep running until I died.

Breathing heavily, I opened the door and the relief was instant when I saw the room was empty.

Pausing in the doorway, my eyes darted around the room.

It was exactly how I left it.

Like a rocket went off under me, I raced inside and started grabbing at my belongings, shoving them into my bag and making sure there was no trace of Cassidy Lewis left behind in the room.

I was barely aware of Chance walking in. He said my name, his voice gentle at first. When I continued to hastily pack up my stuff like a crazed person, he said it with more force.

"Stop!" He stalked over to me and put his hands on my shoulders, forcing me to look at him. "You need to take a breath."

"You don't understand. He'll be here soon."

"Who will be here soon? Who are you running from?"

My chin quivered. My heart pounded. Fear had me in its claws, and I couldn't shake free. "The fucking Devil."

CHAPTER 12

CHANCE

She was scared to the point where she was talking crazy. She called him the Devil, and I could see how frightened she was. I barely knew her, but her reaction was genuine. I studied her beautiful eyes. They were overflowing with fear and torment, and her hands were shaking. She wasn't just afraid. She was *terrified*.

"What are you talking about?" I asked, taking her by the hands.

"Please, we have to get out of here before he arrives."

"Who?" I gripped her hands tighter.

"My *brother*. Missy told him where I am, and it's the worst thing she could've done. He'll be here soon."

She tried to pull her hands away, but I held onto her tightly. In order to help her, I needed to know what was happening. "Listen, I can help you. But I need to know what is going on."

"We're wasting time. He's probably already in town."

"Why are you running from him?"

"We have to get out of here."

Hell on Wheels

"You need to tell me what's happening."

"Are you deaf?"

"Why are you running—"

"Because he raped me!" she yelled.

It was like a sonic boom went off in the room and the shockwave settled over us. Time stopped as the R-word rippled in the air. I released my hold on her, and she took a step back, wrapping her arms around her waist.

"Your brother?" I finally asked.

"My *foster* brother."

I wanted to know what we were dealing with, but right now I needed to get her somewhere safe where we could work out what to do next. I needed to get her calm.

If her brother didn't already know where she was staying, he would soon. He would search the most likely places for her, like motels, diners, taverns, and then he'd enquire at gas stations, the post office, and other stores in town.

But I knew one place he wouldn't look.

"I'll get you out of here," I said, pulling out my phone to call Caleb. He answered almost immediately. "I need a favor. Can you meet me at the Black Cherry?"

"Sure, is everything okay?" he asked.

"No, but it will be. Can you bring the black van, the one Red uses to run errands?"

Caleb must've checked to see if the van was in the parking lot of the clubhouse because he paused before replying, "Sure, I'll bring it."

"Great, I'll see you soon. And Caleb—?"

"Yeah?"

"Drive fast."

When I hung up I went to the window and checked the parking lot. It was clear. There were no cars or guests, and the street was empty. Crossing the room, I picked up Cassidy's bag, stopping to put a reassuring hand on her shoulder. She was trembling.

"Caleb's coming with the van. It'll be safer transporting you to the clubhouse in it than riding on the back of my bike, okay?"

"The clubhouse?"

"I'm taking you back with me. We'll work out where to go from there."

"You don't need to do this. Getting involved is dangerous."

Her voice was calmer, but I could see the violent pounding of her pulse in her neck.

"Danger is my middle name, sweetheart." I gave her a wink, and a weak smile tugged at her lips. "Let's get you out to the clubhouse. Then we'll work out what comes next."

The drive from the clubhouse to the Black Cherry Inn was twenty minutes. Caleb got there in twelve. He didn't ask any questions, but judging by the look he gave me I had a lot of explaining to do once we were alone.

"You take her in the van with you, and I'll follow behind on my bike," I said to my younger brother.

When Cassidy was in the safety of the van, I quickly visited the motel office and slipped the manager fifty bucks for his silence.

"If anyone asks you who was in that room—"

"I'll tell them it was an out of town businessman here with a lady friend."

"And his name?"

"George Brown. Probably an alias. Arrived by cab. Paid cash. Checked out early."

I nodded. "Thank you."

"No," he said. "Thank *you*, soldier."

His words stopped me.

"I know who you are," he explained. "My son was a marine. I know the SEALs provided our marines with the critical cover

Hell on Wheels

they needed while over there. I know what you did, what you saw, the decisions you had to make with only seconds to decide. My son would write home about it. He was good writer. Used to tell me what went on over there before he ..."

He didn't finish his sentence. He didn't have to. I knew the look on his face, knew what it meant. His son never made it back.

"I'm sorry," I said. "This country has lost a lot of good men."

He nodded regretfully, the pain still ripe on his face. "You have my unwavering respect, sir. Thank you for serving our country."

His appreciation was unexpected and evoked an uncharacteristic surge of emotion in me. But my face remained rigid. My eyes hard. My teeth clamped together. I gave him a sharp, albeit appreciative nod before I turned and disappeared out the door.

I felt humbled by his appreciation. *Grateful*. But I put it behind me the moment I stepped onto the pavement. Because he was right. I *was* a SEAL. A trained observer who noticed what other people didn't. And I couldn't afford for any emotion to distract me or cloud my instinct.

Because a devil was coming to town, and I knew they only responded to fight and force. You had to face them head-on and take them out with lethal precision.

Yeah, I knew a thing or two about devils.

Because I was the son of one.

CHAPTER 13

CASSIDY

They took me back to the Kings of Mayhem clubhouse. Caleb parked the van next to a row of gleaming Harley Davidsons. Before I knew it, the passenger door swung open and Chance appeared.

"You okay?" he asked.

"Dude, you really think my driving is that bad?" Caleb joked as he climbed out and closed the door behind him. "She's fine."

"Thanks for your help," Chance said to him.

Caleb nodded. "Anytime." He looked at me and his face filled with gentle empathy. "Whatever is going on with you, darlin', you're safe with him."

I bit back tears. He was being kind and it was the straw that broke the camel's back on this overly emotional Wednesday morning. He threw the keys to Chance and then winked at me before sauntering away.

"I'm going to pack up a few belongings and get us some supplies from the kitchen," Chance said as we approached the entrance to the clubhouse.

"We're not staying here?"

"The clubhouse is not a long-term solution. Guests are usually only permitted to stay one night." He guided me out of the sunshine and inside the building, and it took a moment for my eyes to adjust. "My grandmother has a cabin on the river just out of town. We can stay there until we work out what you want to do. Okay?"

I didn't need to work out what I *wanted* to do, I already knew what I *needed* to do. *Run.*

Dazed by the morning's events, I followed him through the spacious bar, past a couple of pool tables and over to a set of booths on the other side of the room. Black Stone Cherry's "Burnin" was playing on the surround sound, and in the bar a one-armed man was carrying around a clipboard and taking some kind of stock of liquor bottles.

"Wait for me here. I could be a while." He gave me a reassuring but closed-lipped smile. "You want anything to drink or eat while you wait?"

If I put anything in my stomach, I was going to bring it right back up again. My life was spinning out of control, and I had no idea where I was going to land.

I shook my head and tried my best at a smile.

"No, thank you. I'm fine."

"I'm going to talk to Bull, and then we have chapel. Afterward, you and I will talk and work out a plan." He paused, his beautiful eyes trailing over my face. "Try to keep calm. He's not going to find you here."

I huffed out a breath and forced a smile. He really didn't know who he was dealing with.

As Chance walked away, I watched his broad back with the Kings of Mayhem patch blazed across it and felt a stab of longing, wishing this wasn't unfolding this way. He was the kind of man you could fall in love with if your life wasn't as frenzied as a shark attack.

I watched him disappear around a corner before I pulled out my phone and brought up Facebook. I had an alias account, Hope Lee, with a profile picture of an Asian girl that I'd stolen from the Internet and a few fake posts with more images that didn't belong to me. Every month I added a new post about something that never happened, with people who didn't exist, in a town I wasn't in. It was my only means of keeping an eye on my foster brother, Barrett. It was my only link to him. And at times, my only peace of mind, because knowing where he was meant I could stay ahead of him.

It made me sick to befriend him. And when he accepted my friend request, that connection alone was enough to make me violently ill. But it was necessary because I needed to keep my eye on him.

And he made it easy because Barrett Mather Silvermane was an arrogant rich boy who liked to show off, and Facebook was the perfect playground for him to boast. To shout to the world about how awesome he was. Not to mention handsome. Rich. Charming.

Criminally insane.

Something he conveniently left out of the façade he created on social media.

Instead, he showed the world the made-up Barrett Silvermane. A successful realtor who knew how to work hard during the week and then party harder on the weekend with his lascivious buddies and a string of beautiful women. The handsome man with a charismatic smile that hid a twisted mind. Pictures of a pretend life. Playful images with a dog I knew would mean nothing to him because he didn't have feelings. Only a primal instinct to inflict pain and fear.

Hell on Wheels

Instagram was the same. Just like I did with Facebook, I created an Instagram account, but I didn't follow him. I simply searched for him whenever I needed to know what he was up to. Social media gave me an advantage; it meant I could see him without him seeing me.

At first, I used to check it every day. But seeing his posts left me feeling sick and anxious, so I only let myself check once a week, and usually before I went to do something I knew would keep my mind preoccupied afterwards.

Now as I brought up his page, I felt the bile at the back of my throat. My hands began to shake and my stomach churned, but I needed to see when he last posted something and where he was.

Relief flooded me when I saw Barrett had posted this morning. It was a picture of him in front of a property he'd just sold in Huntington Beach. He posed with a married couple and was shaking hands with the man. Smiles all around. The caption read: *So happy to see this beautiful property to go such a beautiful couple. Congratulations Mr. & Mrs. Sanders.* With the hashtag #soldtoday

The syrupy sweetness was hard to swallow.

I quickly hopped out of Facebook and into Instagram. There were two new posts. The first was a picture taken outside a very exclusive restaurant in Newport with the caption: *Heading to this dive to celebrate another generous sale.* #SoCalEats #slummingit

The second was a split picture of two different watches, a gold Rolex and a diamond-rimmed Cartier, with the pretentious caption: *Couldn't decide. Rolex or Cartier. So I bought them both.* #iwearcartier #rolex #richboy

I looked at the images on the screen with disgust then quickly closed out of social media. Just as I closed my phone, Caleb reappeared with two women. One was a very attractive blonde with a killer figure and eyes so brown they were almost black.

The other was a striking brunette who was very, *very* pregnant. He led them over to where I was sitting in the booth.

"Ladies, this is Cassidy. Chance's friend."

The two women looked surprised. Then all three of them shared a weird look as if my presence here meant something.

Caleb laid those baby blues on me. "This is Honey, my wife." He gestured to the gorgeous brunette.

"Hey," the very pregnant woman said as she awkwardly slid into the booth across from me.

"And this is Indy. You met her husband the other day in the town square. He's my less charming brother, Cade."

Indy raised an eyebrow at him and gave him an unimpressed look before turning those big brown eyes in my direction.

"Hey." She sat down in the booth next to Honey, who could barely get her huge belly between her and the table.

"I'm heading to chapel. Do you ladies need anything before I go?" Caleb asked.

"I suppose getting these babies out my stomach is asking too much," Honey said.

"Out of my hands, baby girl."

"Then no, I'm fine. You go to chapel and I will just sit here and incubate your babies in my gargantuan stomach."

"That's my girl," Caleb said with a cheeky grin. "You know, I'd kiss you goodbye but—" He gestured to the table between them.

"Don't worry about it. You'd probably just get me pregnant again anyway."

He threw her a wink before walking away.

"Thankfully, it doesn't work that way," Indy added.

"I'm not kidding. That man's sperm is powerful shit," Honey said, rubbing her hand over her big belly. "Sometimes I think he only needs to rub up against me and I fall pregnant."

"When are you due?" I asked.

Hell on Wheels

"Not for a few weeks. But the way my husband drags me everywhere he goes, you'd think I was about to go into labor at any minute. He won't leave my side, and it's driving me crazy."

Caleb sounded like a doting husband.

"He's just protective of you and his babies," Indy offered.

"Babies?" I asked.

"Twin boys," she said, rubbing her belly. "And I have a nineteen-month-old daughter, but she's out with her aunty Autumn today, being spoiled rotten I imagine."

"Do you have any names picked out?"

Honey rolled her eyes, slightly exasperated. There had obviously been a heated debate about it.

"Caleb wants to call them Robert and James."

"Those are good names," I said, slightly surprised by the traditional choice.

"He only wants those names because of Robert Plant and Jimmy Page." She sighed. "My husband with all the Led Zeppelin tattoos on that deliciously sinful body of his wants to name our first sons after members in a rock band."

A rush of energy entered the clubhouse as a gorgeous young woman with thick hair the color of chocolate swept across the room and slid into the booth next to me.

"Please tell my brothers that I am not having my birthday party at the clubhouse," she wailed dramatically. Up close she was gorgeous. She had the same dimples and bright blue eyes as Chance, Cade and Caleb, so I assumed they were the *brothers* she was talking about. "Indy, you *have* to have a word with them. They'll make it this big MC princess thing, and it's going to be *so* over the top!"

"I think it's too late," Indy said, playing with the crown pendant around her neck. I noticed that Honey had one around her neck too.

"Please don't say that! I just want something quiet."

"Yeah, I don't think quiet is quite what they had in mind," Honey added, rubbing her belly again.

The beautiful brunette grimaced. "*Great*. It's going to be completely over the top, isn't it?"

"Yep," Indy and Honey said in unison.

The brunette dropped her head back and let out a dramatic sigh. "Why was I born into an MC? No… Why was I born into the Kings of Mayhem MC? Ugh." Then, as if seeing me sitting there for the first time, she straightened and looked at me with wide eyes. "Oh, hey there. I'm Chastity."

She offered me her hand.

"Cassidy," I said, shaking it.

"Cassidy is a friend of Chance's," Indy said with an odd inflection to her voice.

Then the three of them shared a look that again told me my presence here as *a friend of Chance's* meant something.

"Okay, that's the second time in half an hour you guys have done that," I said. "So spill. Why is it such a thing for Chance to bring me here?"

Honey looked at Indy who looked at Chastity who looked at Honey.

"It's just my brother doesn't usually bring girls to the clubhouse," Chastity said.

"He doesn't?"

I didn't know why that made me a bit warm inside.

"I haven't seen him with anyone since he's been back from his deployment," Indy offered.

Oh. Okay. They thought Chance and I were involved.

"We're not together," I said. "He's just helping me out."

Chastity looked disappointed. But Indy and Honey both looked like they didn't believe me.

"I wasn't with Caleb either," Honey said. "We were just *friends*. Now he can't stop knocking me up."

Hell on Wheels

"And I married my best friend, so ..." Indy shrugged.

I liked these women. They were funny and kind and being around them distracted me from the turmoil churning my insides.

"We really are just friends," I insisted. Even though they didn't believe me.

"How did you meet him?" Chastity asked, then suddenly snapping her fingers, added, "Now I remember! You played at Ruger's welcome home party the other night."

Inwardly, I grimaced, remembering my *non-kiss* with Chance. The non-kiss I instigated and the one *he* ended.

"Played?" Honey asked.

"She's a singer and a guitar player," Chastity explained. "Had all the boys eating out of her palm the moment she stepped on that stage. She's really good."

Chastity was sweet.

"I wish I had been there," Indy said. "But I pulled a late shift."

"Indy is an ER doctor," Chastity clarified.

"And I was having an *I'm pregnant and feel as big as a whale moment*, so I stayed home with a tub of ice cream and Netflix. Oh, and a husband who refused to leave me for five minutes in case I spontaneously give birth to his sons on the living room floor."

"Can you really blame him though?" Indy asked. "You *did* give birth to his daughter in the backseat of my car."

Honey laughed. "Good point."

I was about to ask her what happened when a group of men in Kings of Mayhem cuts poured into the room and headed straight for the bar. There were about twenty of them, but Chance wasn't with them. I looked at the clock on the wall and was surprised to see over an hour had passed.

Just as Chastity started talking to Indy about the party again, my phone buzzed with a message from a number I didn't recognize.

I opened it and saw it was a link to a video on YouTube. I hit play and immediately my heart went to my throat as I watched a man on the screen begging for his runaway daughter to return. He was a handsome man with sandy blond hair, sparkling green eyes, and a California tan. He spoke with confidence and charm into the camera like a man in politics who was used to speaking to the media and making public appearances. He pleaded for his daughter to make contact and offered a reward for information on her whereabouts.

This is what Craig had found.

The man on the screen was famous. He was well-loved. Looked up to. And I had no doubt his political campaign would be reaping the rewards of his devastated father routine.

Anger flared in me, but it was nothing compared to the fear. Because this video meant someone knew who I was, and they knew my phone number.

Was it Craig and Missy fucking with me?

Or worse ... *Barrett?*

I quickly turned off my phone.

Looking up I saw Chance approached the table and my stomach knotted.

"You doing okay?" he asked.

I nodded, thinking about the message and who the fuck had sent it. They were toying with me.

It had to be Barrett. This shit stank like his psychopathy.

I nodded. "Yeah, just feeling a bit freaked out about everything."

"Bull thinks we should stay here for the night and then head out to the cabin first thing," he said. "He's right. We should go at first light."

Hell on Wheels

I glanced around the clubhouse. It was filling with more bikers and women in tight jeans with intimidating looks on their faces. Lights had gone on and someone had turned up the music. It looked like they were getting ready for something.

As if reading my mind, Chance explained, "Wednesday night is Fight Night. The clubhouse is about to fill up with sweaty bikers ready to bet on two men beating the shit out of each other in a ring. You might want to hang out in my room. It's going to get messy."

CHAPTER 14

CHANCE

I took her to my bedroom.

She was quiet. Preoccupied. And she'd gone pale.

But it wasn't because of what she'd told me back at the motel. Something had happened while I was in chapel.

"You want to tell me what's on your mind?" I asked, shrugging out of my cut.

She looked down at her phone and hesitated before handing it to me. On the screen was a message with a video link.

Pressing play, I watched a glossy politician talking at a media conference, begging for his daughter to come home. As I watched, I realized a giant part of the puzzle had just landed in my lap.

I looked up at her. "This is you he's talking about?"

She nodded. "Yes."

"You're Kerry Silvermane's missing daughter?"

Kerry Silvermane was an oil tycoon and politician. I didn't know much about him, but I knew his face.

Again, Cassidy nodded but said nothing.

"Is Cassidy your real name?"

She shook her head. "No. My name is Chelsea. But don't ever call me that, okay? She doesn't exist anymore."

I handed the phone back to her.

"Do you know who sent you the message?" I asked.

"No. But only two people know that number. Missy and my boss at the diner, Molly."

"You think either of them sent it?"

"I don't know. Maybe it's Missy fucking with me. She knows who I am now. She contacted my brother and told him where to find me. Maybe this is her way of getting back at me not telling her who my foster father is."

She could be right.

Missy sounded like a vindictive bitch.

She'd contacted Barrett and told him where Cassidy was, so it was more than likely she'd given him her phone number too.

Cassidy sat down on the bed, her glorious blonde hair tumbling around her tanned shoulders. She was quiet for a moment as she looked for the words. When she finally spoke, her smoky voice was heavy with sadness.

"Please don't let him find me." Her lips shook as she spoke, and I had an irrational desire to kiss them until they stopped shaking. "My brother is a very dangerous man."

I knelt down in front of her. "I think I can handle him."

All men fell down the same if you put a bullet through them. Dangerous or not.

"The best thing you could do is let me go. And forget you even met me."

I raised an eyebrow at her. "I'm balls deep in this now, so that's not an option."

She exhaled a rough breath, trying to stop her chin from quivering. "I ran away and my brother will stop at nothing to find me."

"And your father—"

Her eyes shot to mine. "He can't know where I am either. Chance, you have to believe me."

"I do." I wasn't going to push her. She was clearly traumatized, and if I pushed her for details tonight, she would probably flee. And from what she said, if she fled tonight, she could die.

So I was going to take her at face value. She needed help. So I was going to help her.

Tonight, the best thing I could do was reassure her, keep her safe, and do everything in my power to keep my fucking hands off her.

While Fight Night took off in the clubhouse, we ate a bowl of Red's chili and watched a Game of Thrones DVD.

Cassidy was one of the few people left on Earth who had never heard of the TV show, and after the first two episodes, she was fascinated. It was a good distraction. She seemed calmer.

"You know, you can sit on the bed with me," she said, her raspy voice alluring without trying to be.

"No, you have it. I'm fine." And I *was* fine, sitting on the incredibly uncomfortable chair well out of arm's reach of her.

"You're making me feel like Rose in Titanic," she said with a cute grin. "We all know Jack would've survived if he'd climbed on that damn door with her."

I couldn't help but laugh. But when an unfamiliar warmth poured into my chest, my smile faded. I didn't want that warmth. I had no business with it.

She turned her attention back to Game of Thrones.

"So let me get this straight," she said, getting comfortable on my bed. "She's married to the king, but that guy she's having sex with is her twin brother?"

"Yes."

"Hmm," she said, thinking about it. "And where is this set?"

Hell on Wheels

"It's a fictional world. The seven kingdoms of Westeros."

She gnawed the inside of her cheek as she thought about it.

"They're definitely kinky motherfuckers," she finally decided, reaching for an apple on the food tray next to our empty chili bowls. Peeling off the produce sticker, she rolled onto her stomach while I did everything humanly possible not to notice how peachy her ass looked as she lay across my bed.

"Darlin', you don't know the half of it."

She pointed to the TV. "And the blonde girl—"

"Daenerys Targaryen ..."

"I think she's going to be kick-ass. Although, she does kind of have a fiery look in her eye. Like she could get stabby at any minute." She bit into the apple. "Have you noticed how much her warlord husband looks like Maverick?"

"Whatever you do, don't tell Maverick that. He'll never get his head through the fucking door."

She smiled and took another bite of the apple. Juice ran down her chin, and it was all I could do not to lick it from her flesh.

"So you want to watch another episode?" I asked when the episode finished.

"I want to watch all of them!"

I raised an eyebrow at her. "There's eight seasons."

"Then we'd better start watching," she said.

She looked up at me from the bed and *damn* I was in trouble. There was no way I could stay in this room with her tonight.

Hell, there was no way I could stay in this room another minute without doing something stupid like kissing her.

Which was exactly what we *both* didn't need.

So while she dove into episode three of Game of Thrones, I stepped out into the hall and called my grandmother to let her know I was taking Cassidy to the cabin for a few days. Maybe a week. Maybe longer. She didn't ask any questions because

Grandma Sybil was no one's fool; she knew she'd only get the censored version from me.

Instead, she would find things out *her way*.

I had no doubt.

After speaking to Sybil, I checked in with Bull and let him know things were set for the following morning.

When I walked back into my room, Cassidy was sound asleep on my bed, on her side with her arms wrapped around my pillow. Her long blonde hair fanned around her face while her legs were parted with the just white satin of her panties visible.

Lust slammed into me, and I felt my blood rush south.

Not that I would touch her.

I was the last thing this goddess needed.

She was already rattled, and I didn't want to be another threat to her. And the plain and simple truth was I didn't trust myself not to be; I didn't know who I was turning into or what he was capable of. All I knew was that I didn't like him.

But I was still a living, breathing, red-blooded male, and it was impossible not to notice the sleeping beauty in my bed and all the magical things about her. Like the angelic face. The sweet curves of her luscious body. The tiny slip of satin between her firm thighs.

She was temptation.

But I was more than fucking tempted by her.

I was fucking *aching* to touch her.

And I hated that I was.

I reached down and covered her with the blanket, and it took all my will power not to touch her when she stirred and a small moan slipped from her parted lips. But I was a disciplined soldier and would die fighting the urge to touch her.

Instead, I kissed my fingers and pressed them against her shoulder. "Goodnight, California."

Hell on Wheels

I slipped quietly from the room, making sure the door was locked behind me.

She would be safe here.

And safer if I wasn't in the room with her.

CHAPTER 15

CHANCE

I headed out into the clubhouse. Fight Night was in full swing, and it was a full house. Tonight, Hawke and one of our newest club members, Animal, duked it out in the ring while girls in bikinis wandered through the small crowd of bikers, cheering on the fight. Around us, Led Zeppelin's "Trampled Under Foot" blared from the sophisticated surround sound system.

As I headed for the bar, Tiffani, one of the more popular club girls, stepped in front of me.

"Hey there, baby," she said, giving me serious fuck-me eyes as she slid a hand up my chest. "You've been back for months now and haven't bought me a drink. What does a girl have to do to get noticed around here?"

She pressed herself against me, and before I had the chance to stop her, she reached down between us and grabbed my cock. The cock that was still pissed at me for not doing anything about the half-naked goddess lying in my bed. The cock that was still hard and giving me a serious case of blue balls because just remembering that glimpse of white satin against the sleepy beauty's pussy was making me dizzy with lust.

Feeling my size and level of extreme hardness against her palm, Tiffani's eyes lit up with surprise. She gave the hard ridge a squeeze and whispered in my ear, "Let's go to your room and let me take care of you."

I untangled her from my body.

"That's a real sweet offer, darlin'," I said, sidestepping around her. "But it ain't going to happen."

Not tonight.

Not ever.

But Tiffani wasn't known for taking a hint. Or for her subtlety.

She pouted and batted her lashes at me. "You know how to break a girl's heart, Chance. Seems to me you could do with a little attention." Again, she stepped toward me. "If you take care of me, I promise I'll take care of you. I'll take care of you *real* good."

I gave her a wink. I didn't want to be a dick, but this wasn't going to happen. I simply walked away and went straight for the bar where I grabbed a bottle of Jack Daniel's from our barman, Randy.

"You doin' okay, buddy?" he asked as he slid the bottle of whiskey across the shiny bar top. Randy only had one arm but could mix a drink better than his two-armed rivals. Once a fall down drunk, he lost his arm after crashing his motorcycle into the back of a parked truck. He wasn't a King, but he was an employee, which made him as good as family. He was a good guy. A good listener. The girls all loved him and according to the rumors, he had a magic tongue. Which kind of had me questioning what he did that the rest of us didn't. Not that I'd ever had any complaints. But seriously. Club girls couldn't stop giggling about his sexual prowess like he was some goddamn magician.

"I'll be doing a lot better once I get some of this into me," I replied, unscrewing the cap. Randy placed a shot glass down in front of me, but I shook my head.

"I won't be needing that," I said, raising the bottle to my lips and taking a swig as I walked off.

I wasn't in the mood for company, so I climbed the fire escape leading to the roof and settled into a picnic chair I'd grown over familiar with in the last few weeks. I liked it up here, alone and under the stars. It was a good place to think. Under the expanse of a night sky littered with a billion stars, it was easy to rein in the self-loathing and guilt and let my mind roam free.

Tonight I was tired from the guilt and the shame of my past. I was tired of feeling hurt and let down by those I loved. And I was tired from fighting an attraction to a girl who was asleep in my bed in a very appealing state of near nakedness.

On nights like tonight, where my past nipped at my heels, the memory of my father's wickedness was heavy in my heart. It was hard to shake. People didn't know the half of what I had endured at the hands of him. When I left for the Navy, I was able to bury it, thanks to relentless training. But since my accident, my memories haunted me. Nighttime was the worst. And tonight was no different.

I took a swig from the bottle and stared up at the stars as another torturous memory from my childhood invaded my thoughts. My eyes closed and not having the energy to fight it, I let it sweep me away.

He led me down the long corridor toward one of the many bedrooms in the clubhouse.

"It's time you make yourself a man, boy."

I looked at the sad girl on the bed then back at my father. Swallowing hard, my voice was thick as I asked, "What do you mean?"

He didn't answer. Instead, he just shoved me through the doorway and into the room.

My guts twisted with dread. When he'd dragged me out of bed and brought me to the clubhouse, I had no idea what he was up to. His motivations became apparent the moment I saw the girl.

"Time you get a taste of pussy instead of hiding away in that room of yours, playing guitar and jerking off."

The girl on the bed drew in a deep breath, and I struggled to swallow. She was young, but a club girl nonetheless. She was broken in, probably by my father and other high-ranking members of the club. Dressed in nothing but a satin slip, she smiled up at me seductively.

"I'm not doing this," I said, turning away.

My father grabbed me by my shirt.

"You'll do what I goddamn tell you to do," he growled, shoving me closer to the bed.

The girl shifted uncomfortably. She was afraid of my father.

"Please, Dad," I pleaded.

I didn't want to do this.

And I doubted she wanted to either.

But my father wasn't having any of it.

He pulled out his gun and put it to my temple. "Go over there and fuck her."

Fear gnawed at my insides. He had never pulled a gun on me before.

I wanted to run. But you didn't run from Garrett Calley. It was so much worse if you did.

"It's okay," the girl said. She reached for me and gently guided me away from my father—and the gun pointed at my head. She nodded nervously at him, her eyes wide, her beautiful mouth turned up in a shaky smile. "It's not a problem, Prez. Chance wants to stay with me. Don't you, baby?"

I nodded and my father put his gun away.

"I'll just be on the other side of that door," he said, sauntering toward the doorway. "You kids play real nice now."

I watched him walk out and close the door behind him. I felt sick. Nervous.

The girl turned my face to look at her and began to undress me. As she lifted my shirt over my head, she whispered, "Don't fret. It will be over before you know it."

My heart pounded as she lay back amongst the pillows and parted her legs, slowly drawing me down to her warm body. Wrapping her legs around my hips, she started kissing me, her soft hands roaming up and down my back, her body moving suggestively beneath me. Desire filled my belly. And despite not wanting it to, my cock started to harden. I liked her lips. They were sweet and plump. And the feel of her tongue against mine was making me harder than I'd ever been in my whole life.

Kissing her was not like kissing the girls at school. There were no awkward fumbles and tight lips. Her mouth was juicy and sweet, and the way her little whimpers rose between us made me see stars. My hips started to roll, the ridge of my cock driving hard against the mound between her parted thighs.

My cock started to leak in my jeans.

"Do you have protection?" I whispered desperately against her lips.

"It's okay," the girl said, reaching between us for my zipper. "We don't need that. I'm clean."

"But what if I get you pregnant," I said, and for some crazy reason my cock throbbed at the idea of it.

"Oh, honey, you won't get me pregnant." She brushed my cheek. "Now relax. This is going to feel real good."

The moment she touched me and wrapped her fingers around my erection, my fears were vanquished. She released me from my jeans.

Hell on Wheels

"Are you sure?" I breathed, my balls already heavy with cum. I hadn't jerked off since the day before.

"I want to be your first," she replied guiding me to her pussy.

When the naked, slippery head of my cock touched her slick pussy, I let out a loud groan. I had never felt anything like it. The softness. The wet, smooth folds of flesh curling around me. Licking me. Caressing me. And when she guided me inside her, I cried out, and my brain spun with the dizzying delights of being inside a woman for the first time.

"Oh God," I rasped, clutching the headboard behind us.

Instinct took over me. Pure and primal. My body knew what it wanted, and it fiercely drove toward it with one thrust after another. There was nothing in this for her. This wasn't about pleasing her. I wouldn't know how to do that if I tried. No. It was about chasing the swell of the orgasm rising in my cock. That sweet tension building like a tightly coiled spring in my belly.

Possessed by the pleasure, I pushed her thighs further apart so I could thrust into her deeper. Harder. Faster. My cock pounded in and out of her tight pussy. A moment ago this was wrong. Now, I couldn't stop myself. My breathing quickened. I was going to come. But it was nothing like making myself come with my hand. This was something else. Something I had no control over. Her warm, wet pussy tightened around me, milking my cock, and it was blowing my mind.

I started to come and let out a loud moan. The ecstasy was intense. I gripped the headboard again, and with one last thrust into her body, I growled with lustful euphoria as I shot what was the most intense orgasm of my life into her.

I dropped to her body, lost in the afterglow of my climax and the soft satin of her slip against my cheek.

It was the clapping that brought me back to reality.

My father. He was standing in the doorway. He must've been listening through the door.

He walked toward us, a lit cigar between his teeth as he grinned.

"Finally, my boy is a man," he said.

I felt sick. My cheeks flamed with embarrassment.

I pulled out from the girl and my cum spilled out of her.

I tried to swallow but the shame and disgust formed a knot in my throat.

"I'm sorry," I rasped. But she just smiled up at me.

"You're a beautiful boy," she whispered.

I wanted to take her by the face and kiss her gently, and tell her that she didn't need to do these things. That she was beautiful and soft and how grateful I was that my first time was with such a sweet thing such as her. But then I saw my father and my feelings of appreciation and desire turned to darkness and hate.

He gestured to the girl to get out with a slight flick of his head. And just like that she was gone. My first time. My first lover.

Dismissed.

Regret poured through me, and I felt an overwhelming need to cry.

I rose to my feet and pulled up my jeans, thrusting my arms through my T-shirt and pulling it down over my head.

Turning to my father, hate heated up my veins. "Why did you make me do that?"

I felt so much in that moment. Shame. Hate. Betrayal.

"Why?" My father stepped closer, his dark eyes gleaming, his voice low and dangerous. "Because it was time you became a man instead of fucking around in that room of yours playing music and jerking off to the posters on your wall."

He sucked on his cigar and the smoke stabbed my eyes.

"I'm raising you to be a man. Not some wet fish. You gotta harden the fuck up, boy. One day you'll be the president of this club, just like your old man and your granddaddy before you, and you're going to need the balls to do it."

"Granddaddy would never have done this to you."

My granddaddy was Hutch Calley, the original president of the Kings of Mayhem. He was a quiet spoken man. Quietly formidable. Yet charismatic and likable. He was a good leader, whereas my father was abrupt and loud. He controlled and commanded, and he took from people.

Garrett Calley wasn't a very good man.

He grabbed me by my shirt and shoved me up against the wall. He bared his teeth and glared at me with a wild rage I'd never seen. *"Your granddaddy was lucky I was already man enough and not some little cocksucker who preferred jerking off to porn instead of fucking real pussy."* He thrust me harder against the wall. *"If I waited for you to become a man, I'd be dead in my grave before your fucking balls dropped. So you listen to me, you little punk, I'm going to harden you the fuck up so when I'm ready for you to fill my shoes, you'll be enough of a man to do it."*

He released me and let me drop to the floor.

It was the first time he'd forced me to do anything like that.

But it definitely wasn't the last.

A noise woke me. A helicopter overhead. I opened my eyes and realized the sun was just about to breach the horizon. I sat up and pain bolted through my brain. Shifting uncomfortably in the picnic chair, my boot kicked the near-empty bottle of Tennessee whiskey at my feet, making bells ring in my head.

I rubbed my heavy, fatigued eyes.

Remembering the sleeping beauty in my bed, I scrubbed my fingers down my face and let out a deep breath. I had deliberately left her alone because if I'd gone back into that room last night, temptation would've gotten the better of me. I wasn't prepared to let that happen, so sleeping on the roof seemed like the better option. She was safe here. No one was getting into that room without going through a lot of armed bikers first.

Climbing down the ladder, I entered the clubhouse and found a poker game still taking place in the far corner near the bar. Hawke, Vader, Joker, Cool Hand, and the new guys Yale and Animal were lost in a cloud of cigar smoke as they concentrated on the cards in front of them. Animal's face was bruised from an earlier bout in the ring with Hawke. A cigarette hung off his cut lip.

"You ladies know it's almost daylight?" I asked as I walked past them.

"Good. Must mean it's almost time to start drinking again." Hawke slurred as he raised his almost empty bottle of Patron to his lips and drank it.

Shaking my head, I headed for my room. In the hallway, Randy's door opened and he appeared in the doorway with two half-naked blonde women attached to his mouth. He grinned at me as I walked past. The handsome son of a bitch was a damn legend, and I couldn't help but grin back.

As I rounded the corner, I saw Matlock leaning against the corner while a redhead kneeled on the ground in front of him, her head bobbing up and down as she blew him. He dropped his head back, and I quickened my pace so I didn't have to deal with his sex noises so early in the morning.

It wasn't always like this in the clubhouse, but Fight Night usually brought out the worst of our behavior. I put it down to all the hard liquor and testosterone.

When I walked into my room, Cassidy was already awake and in the bathroom, washing her face. She looked up when she heard me walk in and patted her face dry with a towel she took from beneath the sink.

She looked stunning. Her hair was pulled back off her lovely face, and she wasn't wearing any makeup. She didn't need it. She was *beautiful*. A thought I quickly kicked to the curb as soon as it entered my head.

She wasn't beautiful. She was in danger.

"Did you sleep well?" I asked.

"Yes, thank you. Did you?"

"Yeah." I got the feeling we were both lying. "You ready to hit the road?"

She nodded and flicked her hair over her shoulders. "Always."

CHAPTER 16

CASSIDY

He took me to his grandmother's cabin in the pale light of morning.

It was on the outskirts of Destiny where the small-town charm and urban landscape of Civil War houses gave way to sprawling fields of green. It was a welcoming log home overlooking the river, with a wraparound porch and a small chimney on a shingled roof. To get to it, we drove down a long gravel driveway and pulled up under a towering oak tree.

Climbing out of the truck, the crisp morning air blew across my face and curled in my hair, sending goose bumps along my bare arms.

I drew in a deep breath and closed my eyes, letting the fresh air fill my lungs. Out here it smelled clean and fresh like...

Wait, was that weed?

I opened my eyes and looked around me, searching for the origin of the smell. After a minute of walking around in circles, I found it growing up the side of the cabin. A big fat cannabis plant.

Hell on Wheels

Chance walked up behind me. "They grow like weeds here."

"It's massive!" I said, in awe of the beautiful emerald green plant and the fuzzy, purple buds.

"Back in the sixties they used to grow it out here."

"They?" I asked.

"My grandma and granddaddy. This is their cabin. They used to harvest weed when they first started the club. Grandma used to grow them here because the plants love the soil near the water. After fifty years, they still randomly appear all over the property."

I couldn't help but smile. It was easy to picture hippies living out here during the Summer of Love, nurturing their fat marijuana plants while jamming out to Jimi Hendrix. This place had a good vibe about it.

I followed Chance up the front step to the porch where he found the key sitting under a pot plant. It was hardly a secure place to keep a key, but I figured most people in the county knew who this cabin belonged to and how unwise it would be for anyone to break in to it.

Watching Chance, I admired his broad back and the muscles of his powerful shoulders as he unlocked the front door and stepped inside.

Entering the cabin, I took it all in. The cozy living room with the plush couches and the worn rug spread out on the floor in front. The cedar-paneled walls and high ceiling. The river stone fireplace and the scent of freshly split wood coming from the log pile next to it.

It felt comfortable. Welcoming. *Safe.*

We moved into the kitchen where French doors opened out to a spectacular view of the river. Pale morning sunlight shimmered on the water, and birds took up song in the trees on the riverbank. This place was special.

"I don't know why you're doing this, but I really am grateful," I said, turning around to face him. "But you don't even know me. Why are you helping me?"

Last night I was frightened. Too frightened and in shock to think logically. But in the safe light of day, it seemed ridiculous that I hadn't asked him why he was putting himself out to help someone he didn't even know.

My question seemed to take him by surprise because he paused, his brow furrowed as he looked at me, weighing his words. "Because if I don't help you, you're going to get hurt."

I frowned. "What do you mean?"

He put the bag of groceries down on the kitchen counter.

"If you run now, you'll always be running. You need to take a moment to think about this with logic and not emotion."

"I *am* being logical. If Barrett finds me, he will make me pay for running away."

"He's one man, Cassidy. He isn't untouchable. The law—"

"The *law* has let me down more times than you could possibly imagine. Same with my parents. Believe me, if there was any other option I would explore it. But there isn't. No one can stop him. The only thing I can do is keep one step ahead of him."

"No one is invincible."

"He is."

"Then tell me about him."

I wanted to, but a cold lump lodged in my throat.

"I will. But can I have a shower first?"

His smile was devastatingly handsome, but the empathy in it made me want to cry.

"Come on. You can pick a bedroom and hit the shower. I've got a couple of phone calls to make."

We continued through the cabin toward the bedrooms. There were two of them. A big one with a king size bed and a view of the river and a second one with a set of bunkbeds and a double bed.

"Take whichever room you want."

I stepped into the smaller room and put my bags on the bed. Through the curtains, I could see an old shack across the river along the sandy bank.

"This will be perfect. Thank you."

He went to the kitchen to make coffee while I grabbed some toiletries and clean clothes from my bag, and disappeared into the bathroom. For a cabin, it was a decent size with a shower bath, toilet, a set of shelves with towels, and a porcelain basin beneath a big gleaming mirror. I set my clothes on the basin and turned on the shower. The pressure was good, and as the water warmed, I stripped out of my clothes and stepped under the hot spray. Immediately, I felt my body relax—probably for the first time since yesterday morning. Despite knowing I was safe in the clubhouse, even my sleep had been restless.

Safe.

It had been a long time since I'd felt it. And it was strange to think I found it in a clubhouse full of bikers drinking hard liquor while watching their own battle it out in a makeshift boxing ring.

And because of Chance.

Warmth poured into my chest when I thought about him; he was offering me a glimpse of an unreachable dream—to not have to run from my brother anymore.

I held up my hand and stared at the scar on my palm. The wound had been deep and long and courtesy of Barrett. *A reminder to not run away.* I was thirteen and it was my first attempt. I got as far as a bus station before a patrol car picked me up and took me home. Money was exchanged and nothing further came of the incident.

As punishment for running away, my parents sent me to my room without dinner and grounded me for two weeks.

Barrett's punishment was far worse.

That night he slipped into my room, armed with a hunting knife.

> "Scream and it will be the last noise you ever make."
>
> With his hand over my mouth and the other pressing the blade against my throat, I believed him.
>
> Barrett sliced his palm with a hunting knife and then held me down and cut mine.
>
> Mashing our palms together, he declared we were bound by blood. "My blood is in you and yours is in me. You are mine and I am yours."
>
> "I'm not yours. I will never be yours."
>
> His eyes narrowed as he squeezed our hands tighter and leaned in. "The sooner you accept it, Sister, the less it will hurt."

I shivered and closed my palm, shutting the memory back in its box.

Turning off the shower, I dressed quickly and wrapped my hair in the towel before stepping out into the hallway to the inviting aroma of freshly brewed coffee. Chance stood in the kitchen, his broad back to me as he talked on his phone.

"You can confirm you have eyes on him? And he is definitely in California?"

I paused to listen.

Was he talking to someone in California about Barrett?

I stared at the wide shoulders and the T-shirt straining over the muscular body. His arms were huge and the phone looked tiny in his large hand.

"Good, if that son of a bitch leaves town, you let me know right away. I want to be ready for him if he dares come here."

He was definitely talking about Barrett.

"What am I going to do to him if he does?" I noticed his fingers grip the phone tighter. "I'm going to break every bone in his goddamn body if he steps into this town."

CHAPTER 17

CHANCE

I hung up the phone and stood in the kitchen with a cup of coffee in my hand, staring out at the river. I refused to think about her taking a shower.

No. Fucking. Way.

My mind wasn't going to go there.

There being her taking off her clothes and stepping naked into the shower only a few feet away from where I was standing.

But fuck. I'm a guy. And when the girl of your dreams is taking a shower in the very next room, you go there. Not literally there. But you think about what is happening on the other side of the six inches of timber and drywall separating you.

Even if you can't touch her. Even if you swore off women because the wiring in your brain had short-circuited and touching another woman wasn't an option until you worked through the chaos in your head.

I drained my coffee and cursed the throb residing in my belly. I didn't need this. Or want it. But damn if my body had different ideas.

Hell on Wheels

Like I said... I'm. A. Guy.

Needing the distraction, I started to put away the groceries. Before we left the clubhouse, I'd grabbed a few supplies. Coffee. Creamer. Bread. Some of Red's corned beef. Mayo. Until I worked out what the fuck was going on, I couldn't gauge how long we would be staying at the cabin, so I'd grabbed a lot of random shit.

Bull told me to take some time off. Things were quiet for the club. He had it working like a well-oiled machine. Since the reopening of the cannabis fields and the supply alliance we had with the Knights, things were running smoothly between the two clubs. It had widened the channels of communications between us, making us allies and not rivals.

So while it was quiet, I was free to have some downtime.

To be honest, it was kind of perfect. I had neglected the fisherman's cottage over the last few weeks, and staying out here now gave me the opportunity to refocus some of my energy on the restoration.

I looked across the river to the old building. In three months I had cleared away all of the overgrowth and kudzu growing wild through the rotted wooden floorboards and broken brickwork. I had fixed the holes in the roof, but I still needed to re-shingle it. Thankfully the foundation was still solid, but the frame rot had taken me weeks to repair.

There was still a lot to do and taking some time away from the club meant I could focus on it.

The creak of floorboards told me she was behind me. I turned around and holy mother of God! Cassidy stood across the kitchen counter from me, damp from the shower, her hair wrapped in a towel, her Alice Cooper T-shirt doing very little to hide her very hard, perky nipples.

Christ and all things holy.

"Feel better?" I asked, averting my eyes from her rack.

"Yes, thank you."

I pushed a cup of black coffee across the island countertop toward her.

"There's creamer in the refrigerator and sugar in the cupboard if you want some."

She shook her head and took a hungry sip of the coffee. "This is perfect, thanks."

I watched her lace her fingers through the mug handle and take another appreciative mouthful.

"So what happens now?" she asked.

I poured a second cup of coffee.

"Now you tell me what happened."

A deep exhale left her body, and I could see her struggling with finding the right words. She nervously played with the necklace around her neck. Gold letters spelled the word *Hope*.

To help her relax, I asked her about it. "Tell me about the necklace. I've noticed you play with it when you're lost in thought."

"I do?" She looked surprised.

"Yeah. Last night while you were watching Game of Thrones and again the other night when …"

When you kissed me and it took every ounce of my discipline not to kiss you back.

She looked up at me coyly, her cheeks slightly flushed.

"When I kissed you?" An embarrassed smile tugged at her lips. "It's okay. We might as well address *that* elephant in the room."

This girl was a straight shooter. It was refreshing.

"I wasn't going to say that. And believe me, it took a lot for me to not kiss you back." I gave her an easy-going smile and gestured to the necklace again. "So tell me about it. Who gave it to you?"

She smiled softly but it was filled with regret.

Hell on Wheels

"My mom." She dropped her lashes. "My real mom."

"Right. That's why you were referring to Barrett as your *foster* brother."

She nodded. "When I was born my mother left me in a laundry basket next to the confessional box at a church just outside of Sacramento," she said, twisting the gold chain around her finger. "Besides me and a blanket, this was the only other thing in the basket."

"I didn't know. I'm sorry."

"It's okay. You don't need to apologize." She let go of the necklace and raised her coffee to her lips, taking a sip. "When I was little I used to think it was what my mother wanted to call me. But as I grew older, I started to think it was what she wanted me to always have. *Hope.*"

"Your mom really left you in a laundry basket?"

She tucked a lock of hair behind her ear and nodded. "For the first six weeks of my life I was known as Baby Doe—can you believe it? Made the news and everything. I lived in foster care until they could find the woman who had left me behind. But they never did."

"So what happened?"

"My story made the news and caught the attention of a prominent family in nearby Sacramento, and they decided to foster me."

"The Silvermanes."

She nodded.

"To those looking in from the outside, I suppose it was a godsend for the abandoned child to be adopted by such a rich and loving family. On the outside it was an idyllic match. A hugely successful businessman turned politician, a beautiful, stay-at-home wife and mother to a perfect little boy with a shock of dark hair and big brown eyes. When I came along, I was the cherry on top. Everybody thought we were the postcard perfect family all wrapped up with a big red bow. But that couldn't be further from the truth." She ran a finger around the rim of her coffee mug as she spoke. "Kerry Silvermane was an ambitious man. Fifthly rich and full of political aspirations. He was rarely home. And when he was, it was all about photo shoots at the house with his perfectly dressed children and immaculate wife. Everything was done as if we were on permanent public display. Kerry Silvermane wasn't interested in being a father for anything other than publicity purposes. And his wife was too bombed on vodka and pills to play anything other than the trophy wife."

I noticed how she didn't refer to them as her mother and father.

"It's important for me to have some kind of distinction between me and them," she explained when I asked her about it. "We're not family. I don't care how much they try to pretend that we are. We're not. It's the only way I can deal with what happened."

"Do they know about the rape?"

She frowned. "Can we talk about something else?"

I could see talking about it was affecting her, so I agreed. The rest would come out in time.

"Does your brother have the means to find you?"

She nodded. "And more. He's rich. And he knows how to get away with things. Worst of all, he will already have a plan in place."

I leaned down on the counter and raised my eyebrow at her.

"Then we'll just have to wreck those plans."

CHAPTER 18

CASSIDY

It was surreal, sitting across from a stranger in a cabin in the middle of nowhere, talking about running away from Barrett. It was out of character for me. I didn't usually tell anyone anything because people either wanted to help you or take advantage of you. And it was my experience that people were more likely to go for the latter when your surname was Silvermane. Case in point: Missy.

It took a lot for me to trust people. Yet here I was, sitting at a granite kitchen counter, drinking coffee with a *fucking amazing looking* biker called Chance, telling him more about my life than I'd told anyone in the past two years.

If anything, life was incredibly random at times.

"So do we wait it out? Wait for him to come here?" I asked.

"We don't know that he will."

"He will."

Barrett was already planning something epic. I was sure of it.

"I don't know what we're dealing with. I need a bit more time. Until then, you can stay here. We'll take each day as it comes, okay?"

Something told me this guy would know everything there was to know about Barrett come tomorrow.

Well, almost everything.

"You'll need to lie low. But you'll be safe here."

I stood up, wondering how to broach the subject.

"Listen, if I'm staying in Destiny, then there's something I really want to do," I spoke cautiously, knowing I was going to meet with some resistance. "I'd really like to go back to work at the diner tomorrow."

I couldn't explain it. I had only known Molly for five minutes, but I didn't want to disappoint her. There was something special about her. And despite my poor choice of friends, *i.e. Missy*, I was usually a good judge of character. Molly was kind and generous, and in some way she filled the motherless void in my heart.

But just as I suspected, Chance shook his head. "It's too dangerous."

"I know it could be. But I won't leave the diner, and I'll be surrounded by people all the time."

He frowned. "Yesterday you were leaving town, now you want to go back there. Why?"

"I know it sounds crazy, but I can't let Molly down. If she knew I was here and I didn't show up for my shift... she took a chance on me, and I don't want to repay her kindness with disappointment."

Chance did a good job at hiding his frustration. Well... almost. His eyes darkened as he thought about it.

"Fine," he said calmly. "But you don't leave the diner. Not for anything. And I mean for anything or for *anyone*. I'm not kidding. If Alice freaking Cooper is standing outside summoning you... you don't leave the fucking diner. Got it?"

I nodded. "Got it."

The look on his handsome face was stern. "And, California, if you want to beat this thing, we do it my way, okay?"

Our eyes lingered on one another for a moment before I slowly nodded in agreement.

Later, when the sun was getting low in the sky and the crickets came out to sing, we sat out on the veranda in two wooden deck chairs.

Chance told me about the fisherman's cottage he was remodeling. The old house with weather-beaten boards and a crooked porch was directly across the river from us. It looked like it had been abandoned for years and was only now seeing sunlight for the first time in a very, very long time.

I could see the overgrowth had been pulled back, and there were water lines staining the old timber where floodwaters had risen and receded over the years. The glass windows were still in place, and surprisingly unbroken, but the front door was missing. Once upon a time it would've been someone's pride and joy. Their house. *Their home.* I imagined babies sitting on the knees of grandparents who sat out on the covered porch and enjoyed the view of the river while the mother worked in the kitchen and the father worked out in the fields until dark.

But somewhere along the way it had been abandoned. Left to rot in the rain and the sun and flounder in the floods. Alone and unloved. Until Chance came along and decided to breathe life back into it.

Penny Dee

I wasn't going to even go there with the comparison between me and that house, because that was not only too cheesy, it was too damn sad to even contemplate.

Instead, I was going to sit here and play my guitar, which was always my go-to when I started to feel down.

"You're good. Who taught you to play?" Chance asked.

"Benji. Kerry's chauffeur. I was ten when he started driving me to and from school. We took to each other straight away. He was so funny. Friendly." Warmth collided with sadness in my chest when I thought about Benji. Warmth because Benji had been so nice. Sadness because of what had happened. "He used to drive me to and from school. He became my friend, I guess. After supper, I would sit with him and Mrs. Drinnan, our housekeeper, in the butler's pantry behind the kitchen, and he would teach me the guitar while Mrs. Drinnan got me milk and cookies."

They were the only fond memories of my childhood. Those evenings with them, learning guitar, while Mrs. Drinnan brushed my hair and Benji told us stories about growing up in New York. I looked forward to that time of the day. Being included. Being loved.

"This was his." I nodded at my guitar. "He gave it to me to practice with."

"He sounds like an alright guy."

"He was."

"Was?"

I put the guitar down.

"When Barrett ..." I paused. I hated recalling this time in my life, but I had to give Chance something to work with. He needed to know about the people he was helping me hide from. "When Barrett did what he did... I kind of confided in Benji. Asked him hypothetical questions. Asked *for a friend*. I told him things, *not everything*, just enough for him to realize something wasn't

Hell on Wheels

right. I'm pretty sure he already had his suspicions about Barrett. He knew something wasn't good with him." Absentmindedly, I started to play with my necklace. "One night I saw him talking with Kerry. I couldn't hear what he was saying but it looked tense. The next day someone new drove me to school. When I asked Kerry where Benji was, he curtly told me he had been relocated."

Years later I learned Benji hadn't *relocated* at all. He was made to disappear.

"I don't know what my father did. But it wasn't good. You don't question Kerry Silvermane. Ever."

Chance picked up the guitar, and to my surprise, started playing around with some chords.

"You play?"

He replied by playing the opening chords to Pink Floyd's "Hey You."

No. He didn't just play. He slayed. This guy was fucking good.

"Well, I'll be damned," I said, surprised.

He smiled and winked at me and everything inside me turned to liquid.

"I'm not just a pretty face," he joked, swapping Pink Floyd for the Beatles' "Here Comes the Sun."

I loved that song and started singing along to it. And slowly the bad feelings started to slip away. The darkness. The fear. The ache that swelled in me when I recalled my past. It all receded like the tide as we sat out on that deck under the stars and sang a Beatles' song together.

When the song was over, he put down the guitar and turned to me.

"I know what you were running from. But what was Missy running from?"

His question surprised me because it was so random. But then I realized he was trying to work out how Missy may fit in to everything. If she was somehow still a threat. That was when I understood that even when we were playing guitar and singing, and even though it looked like his attention was elsewhere, it wasn't. His mind was always on the task.

"She wasn't running from anything," I replied. "She just didn't have anywhere else to be."

CHAPTER 19

CHANCE

Much later, when I lay in bed, I couldn't get Cassidy's story out of my head. I knew how it felt to be raised by a man you couldn't trust.

As I struggled to fall asleep, another memory of my father invaded that quiet space between wakefulness and sleep.

I pushed her up against the wall and kissed her without control. It was wild and desperate. It had been days since I'd seen her, and I was crippled by the need to make love to her. Since she'd taken my virginity, we'd been sneaking around every chance we got. It usually meant I had to slip out at night and meet her somewhere no one could find out about us. She was a club girl, meaning she was at the beck and call of high-ranking club members. She took care of them and they returned the favor by ensuring her rent was paid, she had food to eat, and any medical bills were taken care of. It also meant she was untouchable to anyone but a King. Touching her would earn me a painful ass kicking. But I couldn't care less. I was in love.

One of these days I was going to take her away from the club. We'd hitchhike out of town or something. Go to New York to see the Statue of Liberty or west to California and dip our toes in the Pacific Ocean.

And I would be free to love her. Free to lose hours kissing those sweet lips and caressing that luscious body of hers without fear of retribution by the Kings of Mayhem.

Tonight was unplanned. It was a quick, clandestine kiss out back by the dumpsters while a barbecue took place on the other side of the compound.

A kiss that was roaring into so much more.

"I missed you," I rasped into the milkiness of her slender throat as I kissed a trail up to her ear. My fingers pushed through her long hair as I pressed my hips into hers. My cock ached. I wanted to slide into her warm pussy and embed myself so deep and hard inside her until we both couldn't stand it any longer. I wanted to make her come, first with my tongue then with my cock.

But there was no time.

Someone would realize we were missing if we were gone too long.

She lowered my zipper and reached inside my jeans to pull my erection free. I flinched and growled, hooking her leg up and pushing her damp panties to the side. She gasped when I entered her, her wet pussy surrounding me so tightly I was momentarily blinded by the pleasure. I pressed my forehead to hers as I started to rock into her. I wanted to savor it, but there was little time.

I was just about to come when the back door of the clubhouse swung open with a bang.

"Chance!" It was my father. "Chance where the fuck are you?"

He couldn't see us because we were hidden by the dumpster, but he knew we were out here.

Fuck.

I was about to come and my cock was begging me to keep going.

Fuck. Fuck. Fuck.

I pulled out of her and quickly shoved my erection back into my jeans. The best thing we could do was act as if there was nothing going on.

"I'm here," I said, stepping out from the cover of the dumpster.

My father's eyes gleamed like dark stones under the fluorescent light above him. "What are you doing out here?"

Before I could reply, the girl I was about to come inside of stepped out of the shadows and began walking toward him.

"He's helping me look for my retainer," she said nervously. "I left it in the bathroom and thought it might've been taken out with the trash."

She glanced at me and then looked back at my father.

"Did you find it?" he asked.

She shook her head as she made her way up the steps to where he was standing, her sweet ass swinging seductively in her tight dress. "No, but Chance was kind enough to help me look for it."

Whether my father believed her story or not wasn't clear. He waited for her to disappear inside, copping an eyeful of her sweet ass as she walked past him, before turning back to me.

"Come on. Come have a drink with your old man," he said to me before taking another look at her butt as she disappeared inside the clubhouse.

Resisting the need to adjust the front of my jeans, I met him at the steps and followed him inside.

He got me hammered on shots of Patron.

One after the other.

Down the throat.

Years later, when the scenario replayed in my head and I saw it with the perspective of an adult, I realized he had been a man with an ulterior motive. Shoving drinks my way. Getting me so drunk I could barely move while I sat slumped on an old couch. I was the perfect audience. Unable to move.

My father disappeared but then reappeared with the girl in tow. I watched as he led her across the room by the hand, a smug smile on his face, his eyes meeting mine before they disappeared into the kitchen.

In that moment I knew he knew about us sneaking around. He knew I had feelings for her. Of course he did. The great Garrett Calley missed nothing!

But I had broken club code. I had touched what wasn't mine to touch.

And now he was about to make his point.

I went to say something, but my lips couldn't form the words and my tongue was as useless as a dead slug in my mouth. It took all my focus to rise to my feet because I was so damn drunk. I stumbled across the room, pausing against the wall for a moment as my head swirled and my stomach churned with too much liquor. I belched and struggled to catch my breath before staggering through the bar to the kitchen.

It took a moment for my vision to focus.

To understand what I was seeing.

Then pain slammed into me with so much force I fell against the doorway.

Hell on Wheels

The girl my teenage heart was in love with was lying across the countertop, her legs wide open and her back arched in ecstasy as my father fucked her.

My heart shattered.

I watched, rooted to the ground, unable to look away.

My father was fucking her.

And she was fucking enjoying it.

Knowing I was there, my father turned his head and locked eyes with me, and an evil smirk slowly spread across his lips.

For my benefit, he rammed harder into her.

"Oh yes, fuck me harder, Prez," she cried out, throwing her head back.

"You like that, baby? You like it when a real man fucks you?"

She moaned, biting down on her lip. "I love it when you fuck me, Prez."

"Your pussy is so sweet. Tell me whose cock you like. Tell me whose cock gives you more pleasure than any other cock."

She gasped. "Yours. I love your cock, Prez. I love it when you fuck me." She gripped the sides of the countertop. "I'm coming, oh God, I'm coming!"

Her orgasm coincided with me vomiting Patron all over the floor.

I stumbled away, my father's growl ringing in my ears as he came inside the woman I was fucking only an hour ago.

Staggering through the clubhouse and out into the night, I fell to my knees and collapsed onto the grass in the playground. Rolling onto my back, I stared up at the starry sky and let my heart break in two.

I hated my father.

I hated my father, and I wished he was dead.

In less than three years, I would get my wish.

CHAPTER 20

CASSIDY

I lay awake in the dark, my thoughts tumbling over and over in my head. I was in a strange place with a man I didn't really know while running from my psychopathic foster brother. Call me crazy, but I was struggling to fall sleep.

Rolling over, my ears pricked when I heard the creak of a door hinge. It was slow and deliberate, not quick and random like a door being pushed open by wind. An out-of-place sound in the stillness of the night, followed by the quiet click of a door.

Foreboding tingled up my spine.

Someone was in the cabin.

Slowly, I pushed my hand beneath my pillow until I felt the hard metal slide under my palm. Out in the hallway, a floorboard groaned. I hadn't heard Chance get up, so it wasn't him. With blood pounding in my ears, my fingers curled around the handle of the gun just as the door to my bedroom creaked open. I sat up with a rush, threw the safety off and aimed my gun. When the shadow appeared in the doorway my finger jammed against the

Hell on Wheels

trigger and sent a bullet roaring through the darkness and into the wall across the room.

"Jesus Christ!" The light flicked on. "Are you fucking insane?"

I blinked, my eyes adjusting to the sudden intrusion of bright light. Across the room, Chance stood in the doorway, looking alarmed.

And rightfully so.

I almost fucking shot him.

I lowered the gun. "Shit, I'm sorry."

Chance stormed toward me and grabbed the gun out of my hands. "You could've killed me!"

"I'm so sorry," I apologized again. "I thought someone was breaking in."

"So you shoot first and ask questions later?" He looked at the gun in his hand. "Why do you have this?"

The yelling hit a nerve, and I glared at him. I didn't do very well when people yelled at me. It was that whole dominance and control thing.

"Hello, have you met me?"

He held up the gun, his eyes fierce. "This isn't a toy!"

"No shit!"

Despite the intensity of the moment and the fire in his eyes, I still managed to notice how tight his T-shirt was over his broad shoulders and thick chest. Not to mention how the pair of sweats he wore sat so low on his hips I could see the very defined V disappearing beneath the waistband.

The muscles in his arm bulged as he pointed at the door. "You almost shot me."

"I missed."

"By a stroke of fucking luck."

"No, not by luck. I aimed for the wall. It was a warning shot."

"I'm not kidding, Cassidy." He turned and stormed toward the door. *Pissed at me.*

"Neither am I." I climbed out of bed to follow him. "I've never miss a target."

He swung around so quickly I almost ran into him. His eyes blazed down at me. "This isn't a fucking joke."

"Don't you think I know that?" My eyes hardened against his, and for a moment it was a battle of wills as we stared at each other. But I was no match for those fierce blue eyes. "What were you doing creeping around in the dark anyway?"

"I wasn't *creeping around*!" he exclaimed with frustration "I heard something outside and I went to check. When I came back inside, I wanted to make sure you were okay."

"Why didn't you call out? Let me know you were there?"

"Because I thought you were asleep. Not in here toting a gun like Calamity fucking Jane! Why didn't you call out before shooting at me?"

"I didn't shoot *at* you. Like I said, it was a warning shot."

His mouth opened to argue with me but stopped as his bright eyes drifted down to my chest. His mouth closed and he swallowed thickly when he realized I was wearing nothing but a big, white T-shirt with nothing underneath. I saw his breath escape his slightly parted lips and felt it brush against my face. Under his gaze, my nipples turned to steel and goose bumps crept along my skin as lust ripped through me.

Around us, the air was dense with something raw and unsaid.

"What was it?" I finally asked, breaking the silence.

"What was what?"

"The noise outside?"

Still distracted by my state of undress, he frowned and shook his head to regain focus. "A raccoon out on the porch."

"I didn't hear you get up."

He raised an eyebrow at me. "Darlin', if I think someone is lurking around the cabin *no one* is going to hear me get out of bed and go check."

Hell on Wheels

Point taken.

I wrapped my arms around my waist. "Are you sure it was a raccoon?"

"I'm sure."

"Well then, now we can both get some rest. Can I have my gun back?"

"Are you serious?"

"As a heart attack." I put my hand out.

He glanced at it then looked back at me again.

"You really know how to use it?" he asked.

"You're still breathing, aren't you?"

He gave me a pointed look. Now wasn't the time for sass.

"Yes, I do," I reassured him.

His fierce blue eyes roamed my face as he took a moment to consider it.

"It's probably a good thing to have on you," he said finally and handed it back to me. "Tomorrow, after your shift at the diner you can show me exactly how you shoot your gun... in daylight."

I nodded. "Agreed."

His eyes lingered on me for a moment, like he was trying to work out what he had gotten himself into, before he turned away and walked to the door.

"Hey, I really am sorry," I said. "If I had known it was you, I wouldn't have shot at you."

"I should hope so."

"You know what I mean."

He half-turned and offered me a soft smile. "I know."

I smiled back at him. "Good night."

"Good night, California."

And with that he turned off the light and closed the door behind him.

CHAPTER 21

CHANCE

She shot at me.

That crazy, gorgeous, sexy as fuck woman lying half-naked in the room across the hall from me, fucking shot at me.

And now I was hard as fuck.

Despite, you know, almost taking a bullet to the face.

My mind ticked over with a hundred different things.

Why did she have a gun?

Where did she get it from?

Did she really know how to use it?

Was she wearing any panties beneath that T-shirt?

Damn.

I was wide awake with a set of aching balls and an urge to jerk off. I needed to get some sleep but that wasn't going to fucking happen when my body was so tight with need.

I let my hand drift beneath my sweats and my fingers stroked the engorged shaft before sinking lower to tease my balls. They were tight and full. *Throbbing.* When I closed my eyes, all I could see was Cassidy standing in the doorway, wearing that goddamn

T-shirt that clung so tightly to her body her nipples almost poked right through the fabric.

I groaned and slid my hand upward to tease the head of my cock with tight little tugs. Liquid pooled in the eye and slid downward to coat my fingers. I bit down on my bottom lip and imagined her removing her T-shirt and standing in front of me in nothing but a pair of tiny panties.

I pressed the back of my head deeper into the pillows. The pressure was building. I hadn't jerked off in days, so this wasn't going to take long at all.

I closed my eyes. In my fantasy, I dropped to my knees and pulled Cassidy toward me by her narrow hips and buried my face in the soft satin triangle of her panties. I inhaled the scent of her and let it engulf me, getting lost in the damp fabric against my lips.

Another moan left me as my hand worked up and down my cock while in my fantasy my mouth worked on her pussy through her panties. She moaned and just the thought of her moaning beneath my touch brought more pre-cum pooling to the crown of my cock. I ran my thumb over it and dragged it down the length of me, making it wet and slippery just as I imagined her pussy would be.

Back in my fantasy, I pulled her panties down her legs, and when she stepped out of them, I buried my tongue deep into her warm, wet flesh. She cried out and grabbed at my shoulders as my tongue lapped over her clit and teased the sweet spot until she came all over my face.

I came when she came. I pressed a pillow over my face to muffle the unbridled moans wild horses couldn't hold back because *goddamn* it felt good. My eyes rolled to the back of my head, and I gripped the pillow tightly as my cock pulsed with the violent release of four days' worth of arousal. With every throb, hot spurts of cum spattered across my hand until my orgasm receded, and I sank like a heavy weight into the mattress.

For a moment I didn't move. Every muscle drained of energy. I waited for my breath to even out and my pounding heart to slow to a steady, relaxed beat.

But even then I wasn't completely satisfied.

And I knew I wouldn't be.

Not until I could touch her.

But touching her wasn't a goddamn option.

CHAPTER 22

CASSIDY

I knew arriving on the back of Chance's bike was going to cause a stir when I turned up for my shift at the diner the next day.

Needless to say, Daisy lost her shit when she saw me on the back of a Kings of Mayhem motorcycle.

Thankfully we were busy pretty much as soon as I arrived, so I was able to avoid her rapacious need for details most of the day. But as soon as the diner cleared after the lunch crowd and we were alone, she cornered me.

What was I doing on the back of Chance fucking Calley's motorcycle? How did I know him?

"Have you fucked him yet?"

"No!" I exclaimed as if the idea hadn't been burning a hole in my head for the last two damn days. Especially last night, after he'd left my room and I lay in my bed with a body tight and hot with arousal. It'd only taken me a few minutes to bring myself to a mind-shattering orgasm with my hand.

"Are you insane? Man, I'd climb that man like a tree. Are you sure you're not fucking him."

I was pretty sure.

"He's just a friend."

"Friend? Uh-uh. The Kings aren't friends with women. They're either fucking them or helping them out." Her eyes narrowed. Damn Daisy and her expertise in all things Kings of Mayhem. She folded her arms across her big bust. "If you're not fucking him, then what is he helping you with?"

The less Daisy knew about me the better.

"Nothing. He's just being kind." I carried a tray of dirty dishes to the kitchen, but she followed me and sat down at the little table next to the walk-in pantry. She opened a packet of breadsticks while I started stacking the dishwasher.

"You know, you could do worse than Chance Calley," she said.

"I'm sure that's the case, but I'm not looking for anything."

I avoided eye contact with her because I knew I couldn't hide the lust in them. And it would be there. It was always there. Because every time I heard his name or thought about him, my skin tingled with heat and my head filled with crazy thoughts of kissing him until I was out of oxygen.

"Rumor has it, those boys are well endowed," she said, biting into a breadstick.

"Like I said, I wouldn't know."

"I bet it's true." She dropped her chin to her palm, looking at me dreamily, and said, "I bet he has a big—"

"Personality," Molly interrupted, walking into the kitchen and throwing her grand-niece a look. "If he is anything like his grandmother, then that boy is going to have a big personality."

"You know his grandmother?" I asked, putting the last of the dishes into the dishwasher.

"Oh, darlin', everyone in this town knows Sybil." She smiled fondly. "I used to work for her back in the sixties. I was a trimmer at the cannabis fields they had out by the river."

Hell on Wheels

"Oh my God, Molly! You used to cut weed for a living?" I couldn't help but sound surprised.

"I used to do a lot of things for the Calleys. I was twenty years old and they paid good money. I even babysat Griffin and Garrett Calley when they were just babes, running around butt naked out at the family cabin."

The cabin I now called home.

There was something comforting in that.

She smiled wistfully. "Had myself a summer fling with Hank Parrish. It was the Summer of Love, and boy did that man know how to love."

Daisy and I traded glances.

"Aunt Molly!" Daisy sounded shocked.

"What? I wasn't always a seventy-year-old woman, you know," she said, giving me a wink.

Daisy grimaced. "No details. Pleeeease!"

Molly ignored her and stared off dreamily out the kitchen window.

"He was little bit older than me, swept me off my feet, and gave me a summer I'd never forget." She sighed and shook her head. "It broke my heart in a zillion pieces when he fell in love with Connie and married her not long after. Quit my job at the cannabis fields and started hitchhiking across the country. Hitched all the way to California."

"You hitched to California?" Daisy sounded mortified. "Hello, Mr. Serial Killer. Yes, please let me climb in your car so you can murder me."

Molly waved it off. "We weren't worried about that kind of thing in those days. The term serial killer wasn't even coined back then. And no one knew about co-ed killings or psychopaths killing people at random. We were all about peace and love." She shook her head again, remembering the freedom of it all. "I hitchhiked up and down the California coast, stopping off at Woodstock along the way."

"Um... you know the Manson murders happened around that time, right? Same state. Geez, Molly. You're lucky you didn't meet yourself a young buck named Charlie."

Molly chuckled and began wiping down the benches.

"It's a shame what happened to Chance. He was always a nice kid. A real charmer. Always wore his heart on his sleeve." She shook her head. "Then he joined the Navy and got deployed overseas."

"He was in the military?" I asked. I was surprised because he had never mentioned it.

"Oh yeah, he was Navy SEAL," Daisy gushed. "And I've seen on the TV what they do. How hard they train. How fit they are. They're so dangerous and manly, I get all hot and bothered just thinking about it."

Daisy fanned herself while Molly looked at her as if she was crazy.

"What happened to him?" I asked.

"Got himself blown up," Molly said. "Barely survived. Spent months in a coma, burned and broken. It was real sad."

I knew he was injured somehow—the scar on his face was telling—but I had never asked him about it and he had never mentioned it.

When the growl of a Harley alerted us to Chance's arrival, we all went to the window and watched him turn on the street, all six-foot-four of him roaring into the parking lot and pulling up in front of the dinner. My heart did a double flip.

"If you haven't fucked him," Daisy whispered as she leaned in closer, "can I suggest that you do? A man like that doesn't cross your path more than once in a lifetime."

Hell on Wheels

Her words echoed through me as I rode back to the cabin on the back of his Harley, my arms wrapped around the wall of muscle taking me home.

Fucking him wasn't an option.

But letting him in was.

CHAPTER 23

CASSIDY

We sat on the porch. It was our second night out under the stars. Relaxing on the deck chairs, we ate leftovers from the diner while the pink dusk darkened into an indigo twilight.

When we finished eating, Chance took our plates inside and turned on some music. Stevie Ray Vaughan's "Texas Flood" cruised out of the speakers.

Chance reappeared on the deck with a couple of beers.

"Molly mentioned you were a SEAL," I said, accepting a beer from him.

He sat down slowly, his dark eyebrows drawn in. For a moment he didn't say anything, and I saw the muscle in his jaw begin to flex. This was obviously something he didn't like talking about. He took a gulp from the bottle before he spoke.

"Yeah, I was," he said. "Got medically discharged last year."

I wanted to ask what happened but didn't want to upset him. In the end, I didn't have to ask. Before I changed the subject, Chance offered me an explanation.

Hell on Wheels

"An RPG was fired into the building where my team and I were conducting a surveillance mission. I was the only survivor." He drew on his beer. "Got me put in hospital for some time. Got me medically discharged."

"I'm sorry," I said softly.

He looked at me, wearing his poker face, but I could see the pain in his eyes. I got it. You could mask the pain on your expression and in your body language, but in your eyes? Not a chance.

I wasn't going to push him. Just like he didn't push me.

Inside, Stevie Ray Vaughan changed to Katey Sagal's "Strange Fruit."

I put down the beer bottle. It was time to have the conversation I had avoided for days. It was time to bring down my walls and tell him everything.

"When my parents fostered me and brought me home, they let Barrett name me," I said, drawing my knees up to my chest and looking up at the stars.

Surprised, Chance turned his head to look at me. "They did?"

I nodded. "My foster mom said later that it was to help him cope with the change. A way to include him. Unfortunately for me he didn't see it that way. He saw it as ownership of me. Because in his warped mind, giving me my name made me his. I wasn't his foster sister. I was his toy. His *plaything*."

Chance was silent but his face was rigid, his eyes intense as he listened.

"When I was twelve and he was fifteen, he took me to an abandoned shack in the woods. He held me down and branded me with a branding rod he made in workshop at school." I slid the hem of my dress up so Chance could see the dark scar seared into my hip. It was in the shape of a B.

B for Barrett.

"Motherfucker." He exhaled, his eyes black.

"Like I said, he thinks I'm his." My heart started to thud in my neck when I thought about what came next. I paused, choosing my words carefully. "A few weeks later, just after my thirteenth birthday, he forced me to return with him to that shack. Our parents were at some charity gala in DC and had left us in the care of our elderly nanny. Later, he admitted he'd drugged her tea with something."

Chance shifted in his chair, his energy was changing, but he didn't say anything. He let me talk. I knew he was holding his reactions at bay because his hands were fists on his knees.

"I didn't want to go. I begged him not to make me. But he had his father's gun, and he said I had to do as he told me because if I didn't, he would kill me. And I believed him. I believed him because when he branded me, when he heard my screams and could see how much pain I was in, he showed no emotion. No remorse. No fucking fear for what he was or for what he was doing. So when he said he would kill me, I knew he would." I held my pain at bay with gritted teeth. "He made me drink some liquor. Then he forced me down onto the dusty floorboards. Even then I didn't really know what he was going to do. Not until he ripped my underwear off. Then I knew." I blew out a shaky breath as the memory rattled its way through me. "That was when he raped me."

Chance stood up with a rush. His jaw flexed and his nostrils flared as he struggled to contain his rage.

"Son of a bitch!" he snarled. He shook his head and smacked his lips together, unable to hide his wrath. Wild energy poured off him. "Did they know? Your parents? Did they know what he did to you?"

I nodded and his face lit up with barely contained fury. "Fucking sons of bitches!"

"At first they didn't believe me. They thought I was making it up. Barrett was an overachiever in school. Especially his senior year. He was good at everything he did. Sports. His classes. And boy was he popular." I shook my head and sniffed back the cold lump of pain that had lodged in my throat. "No one could believe that Mr. Popular would rape his foster sister. They thought I made it up. That I wanted the attention. So they refused to believe it. And that's what made it so easy for him. Because he didn't just steal it from me once. He kept stealing it for the next three years."

CHAPTER 24

CHANCE

Rage slammed into me.

Three years.

He sexually tormented her for three fucking years.

And don't get me started on that scar.

The sight of that scar made me want to go medieval on his ass.

I wanted to crush him. *Break him.* He branded her like she was cattle. Now I wanted to brand him repeatedly with my fist.

Little did I know, Cassidy was just getting revved up, filling me in on Barrett's depravity.

"When I was sixteen, he got me pregnant."

And just like that things got infinitely worse as she took me down to depths of despair I could only imagine.

"He knew he was in trouble. Up until then, he could charm his way out of anything. He could talk the talk. Convince you it was nighttime while you were standing in sunlight. But he knew he couldn't talk himself out of a pregnancy because there would be

Hell on Wheels

some kind of investigation." She paused. "If I had the baby, of course."

The air exhaled from my lungs in a rush. Her story was already bad, but I could tell it was about to get substantially worse.

"He waited for a night our parents were out. We lived on a big property just out of Sacramento. There was large pond on it. With reeds and lily pads. When I ran from him that night, he caught up with me right by that pond, and that's where he attacked me again. And while he was brutalizing me, he was laughing. He got off on the struggle. And that night I struggled more than I ever had struggled before. Because I knew what he was going to do before he even dragged me to the edge of that pond and tried to drown me."

Red-hot rage hit my brain like a shot of dope. And for a moment it blinded me.

What she had been through. What he had done.

I wanted to end him.

My hands curled into a fist at my side, and I could barely breathe. I had never wanted to end anybody as much as I wanted to end him.

"He would've killed me, if it wasn't for our parents arriving home when they did. He panicked and let me go." Tears swam in her eyes and her chin quivered. "I remember my foster mom calling out to me in the darkness. I remember climbing out of that pond covered in mud and reeds, staggering toward her voice. I remember the taste of pond water in my mouth as I stood in front of her, watery blood saturating my nightgown—"

"Cassidy—"

"I lost the baby." Tears dropped down her cheeks. "Finally, they listened to me. They couldn't live in denial and sweep his behavior under the rug anymore. They had no choice but to act. After all, we were the prominent Silvermane family. It wouldn't do well for Kerry Silvermane's son to be convicted of raping his foster sister. The one they made a big media circus about fostering. So they sent him away. Told me it was to some medical facility in Switzerland where they treated behavioral disorders. It wasn't until years later I learned there was no such place. That the *medical facility* they told me about was actually an exclusive college where rich boys got to enjoy the finest in away-from-home learning. He enjoyed his status. Wealthy friends. Trips to the Alps in winter and the French Riviera in summer. While I struggled and dragged myself out of the fire pit he threw me into when I was just a girl, he was living it up in Europe. He was never punished. My parents had too much money and social status. They couldn't afford the scandal. So they did what they did to protect themselves. They swept it all under the rug."

"I don't understand how they let him get away with it," I shook my head. Every inch of me was on fire with rage.

"My foster father was a very powerful man. He had access to the best spin doctors around. He knew how to avoid a scandal. Knew who to pay off or intimidate. He had a political career to protect. He couldn't let it get out that his son raped his foster daughter. And he was prepared to do anything to stop that from happening."

I couldn't stand what I was hearing. "So you ran away?"

She shook her head. "I graduated high school and went to college while Barrett continued to live his fabulous life overseas. After college, my foster father summoned me home. He was starting a new political campaign and wanted to sell himself as a family-orientated man. He needed Barrett and me to do that. He thought the time overseas had changed his son for the better, so he called us both back. That was when I learned the truth about Barrett—that he hadn't received any treatment, that he had been at college and not a medical facility." She swallowed thickly. "The moment I saw him, I knew he hadn't changed. Knew he was the same monster he was six years earlier."

She looked at the scar on her palm through the tears welling in her eyes. When she lifted her face, they spilled down her cheeks.

"He pushed me up against the wall that night. Told me he had been waiting six years to touch me again. So I ran. And I've been running ever since."

I pulled her into my arms and held her to my chest as she sobbed. I squeezed my eyes shut, feeling her agony as if it was my own.

"He won't touch you again." My voice was like glass on gravel. "You have my word."

"You don't know him," she murmured into the warmth of my neck. She pulled back to look up at me. "The moment he found out where I was hiding was the moment he started to plan what he was going to do to me once he found me. And don't doubt it, Chance. He *will* find me."

I cupped her face in my hands. "I won't let that happen."

"I wish I could believe that."

"That's the thing… you can." I wiped a lone tear from her cheek. "Because once he's in my scope, he's a dead man."

CHAPTER 25

CHANCE
Seventeen Years Ago

The door to my bedroom opened. My eyes snapped open just as the covers were ripped off me and a pair of hands hauled me out of bed.

It was my father.

"Get up. We've got somewhere to be."

A quick glance at the clock by the bed told me it was 11:27 pm.

"Where are we going?" I asked, now fully awake thanks to the dread pooling in my stomach. My father getting me out of bed at that late an hour told me nothing good was about to happen.

"Gotta take care of some business. Its time you get a taste for what it takes to run the biggest fucking motorcycle club in the south."

My mouth went dry and my skin heated, despite the cold whip of night air as he hustled me outside to where his pickup truck sat in the driveway.

Hell on Wheels

Twenty minutes later, we pulled up at a deserted warehouse on the far side of town. Fear coiled like a cobra in my stomach as we made our way through chain-link fencing and along the back of the building. A roller door went up, and two men in Kings of Mayhem cuts greeted my father, both clearly surprised by my presence.

"You sure this is a good idea, Prez?" the older biker with the beard asked.

"Kid's got to learn what it takes to lead," my dad replied.

We stepped inside and the roller door came down behind us. As we walked past the bearded biker, my father stopped. "And if you ever question me in front of my son again, I'll kill you."

His tone sent chills down my spine. I didn't doubt he meant it. And going by the look the two bikers exchanged, neither did they.

I followed my father down a poorly lit corridor that opened up to a large room. Massive industrial lights hung from the high ceiling, but they were off and the room was covered in shadow except for one small patch of light. And sitting under this dull light was a man gagged and bound to a chair.

I glanced at my father and then back at the man. As we neared, I could see he'd been beaten pretty badly. His head was hanging, and for a moment I wondered if he was unconscious. When he heard us walking toward him, he sat up straight and started to protest, which came out muffled because of the bandana shoved into his mouth.

"Do you know who this is?" my father asked me.

Terrified, I shook my head and struggled to swallow the knot of fear lodged in my throat.

My father grabbed the man by the hair and yanked his head back.

"This piece of shit is Miles Venables. You know who that is, boy?"

I nodded. Everyone at my school knew who he was. Once upon a time he was the school janitor. But that was before he raped Lily Reardon.

Lily was in my math class. Blonde and pretty, she was outgoing and friendly and popular with both the teachers and the entire student body. Three weeks earlier she was raped by Miles while walking home from cheer practice. He dragged her off the sidewalk and beat her unconscious with a rock. After raping her, he left her for dead in the scrub on the side of the road, her head caved in and barely alive. But she didn't die, and Wilson Robertson, a kid on the football team, found her when he walked home after practice.

But Miles Venables got off due to some bullshit legal technicality that had something to do with the evidence and how it was obtained, and he was released from custody. Now he was free to roam the streets and prey on whomever his deviant mind chose.

The town always turned to the Kings of Mayhem for these types of situations. They looked at the Kings as the town's guardians when the law failed them.

It had always been the way.

And the Kings never turned their back on their people.

My father would scare him out of town.

"Time to pop another cherry, Son," my father said with a deep baritone laugh dripping with evil.

I looked at the man tied to the chair, his mouth gagged, his face bloody, and my father's intentions became crystal clear. He wasn't going to scare him. He was going to fucking kill him.

"No, Dad, please! Let the police take care of it."

My father looked at me like I'd suggested he wear lipstick and a dress under his cut.

"The police?" He leaned in real close so I could see the seriousness in his eyes. "The police don't do shit to scum like

Hell on Wheels

this. You've gotta learn if you want real justice in this world, you gotta deliver it yourself."

He shoved the handle of the knife into my hands and fear ripped into me. He wasn't going to kill him... he expected me to.

"No," I rasped, barely able to get the word out. "Please. Don't make me do it."

My father grabbed me by the hair and painfully twisted my head so I had no choice but to look at Miles.

"Look at him. That piece of scum raped your classmate. Dragged her into the bushes and did what stinking pieces of filth do to a pretty girl when she tells him no." He released my hair but shoved me forward, making me stumble. "Now you show him what the Kings of Mayhem think about that kind of behavior."

"Please don't make me do this," I begged.

"You go on about your granddaddy being so damn righteous and justified, yet you do nothing to stand up for what he believed in."

"He would never do this."

My father leaned in real close. "He did do this. You think he let the man who raped his VP's wife get away with it? No. He took him to an abandoned car lot and when his VP couldn't do it, your granddaddy pulled out his revolver and planted a bullet right between his eyes."

The revelation spun through me.

"You're going to be a King one day, goddamn it. And you're going to have the balls to be a good one. Now go over there and show this raping piece of shit what happens to scum who come into our town and rape." Again, he shoved me forward until I was right behind Miles. We made eye contact. When he saw the knife in my hand, he started to struggle against his restraints, his pleas for mercy muffled by the filthy gag in his mouth.

I looked down at the knife in my hands and thought about Lily Reardon. She hadn't been back to school since the attack, and people were saying she was struggling to cope with what had happened to her. "Her light has gone out," her best friend told me. In that moment I thought about what she must've felt. The fear. The pain. The struggle. Those horrifying moments right before he drove the rock into her skull. My fingers itched around the knife handle. That thought alone made me place the blade against Miles' throat.

Licking my lips, I struggled to swallow as panic raced through my veins.

He deserved to pay for his crimes, yet he was free because somewhere someone had gotten something wrong and he couldn't be charged.

But I couldn't do this. I was a teenager. I wasn't a killer.

I dropped the knife and it clanged against the warehouse floor.

There was still a right way and wrong way to do things.

And this didn't feel right.

With a growl, my father reached me in three long strides and shoved me out of the way. I fell to the ground, my wrist slamming against the concrete as I hit it with full force. Pain shot through me, and I squeezed my eyes shut—but not before I saw my father run the blade across Miles' throat and a spurt of dark red blood hit the floor as the rapist died.

CHAPTER 26

CASSIDY
Present

It was a noise, something unfamiliar that woke me. My eyes flicked open. It was dark. *Middle of the night dark.* I could barely see anything but the shadows around me. Across the room, the curtain danced in the gentle breeze coming off the river. It was silent. Unease began to tingle at the base of my spine as I held my breath and strained to hear in the darkness.

Then it came again. A cry in the night.

"*No!*"

It was a male voice.

"*No, don't. Please.*"

I sat up.

"*I don't want to do it.*"

It was Chance.

"*There has to be another way.*"

And he was having a nightmare.

I ripped off the covers and padded across my room to the hallway.

"Let the police take care of it."

I pushed open his bedroom door and walked in. "Chance? Are you okay?" He was still asleep on his bed, the sheet pushed down around his narrow hips. His broad, muscular chest was shiny with sweat as he tossed his head side to side and continued to plead with someone in his nightmare.

Sitting on the edge of the bed, I gently shook him. "Chance?"

With a rush, he lurched awake and sat up, his breathing heavy and fast. His eyes darted around the dark room before resting on me.

"Is everything alright?" he rasped.

"You were having a nightmare," I explained.

"I was?" His brow furrowed and he struggled to swallow. He looked confused. *Concerned.* "Did I say anything?"

"You mentioned your dad then something about the police taking care of it."

He frowned, his eyebrows drawn together as he pinched the bridge of his nose. "I can't remember."

Sitting this close to him, I could feel the heat of his naked torso radiating around me and smell his subtle scent. It was deep and masculine and fucking intoxicating. I licked my lips, feeling the need take up in me.

I knew I should leave. Go back to my room. But the way he was looking at me sent all types of crazy spiraling through me.

"Are you okay?" I asked.

Maybe it was the lateness of the hour and the fuzziness of sleep still lingering on my brain.

"Yeah, I'm fine."

Or maybe it was the sight of that insanely chiseled chest and bare stomach thick with muscle.

"Are you sure?"

Or the knot of lust I felt every time I was in the same room as him.

Hell on Wheels

Maybe it was all of the above that made me lean forward and graze his lips with my own.

The move took him by surprise.

I felt him hesitate.

Felt his breath hitch in his chest.

Felt the violent thud of his pulse against his throat as I slid my hand up to his jaw.

My name fell from his lips but was stolen by me as I pressed another kiss to them. With one sweep of my tongue into his mouth, he moaned, and his lips moved with slight hesitation as he fought something inside him before surrendering completely.

He cupped my face between his giant hands and kissed me hard and deep, like a man starved. His lips were masterful and his tongue skillful in the way it danced with mine, taking the lead and making me see stars behind closed lids.

I reached for him, my hands sliding over the bulk of his broad shoulders and down his spectacular chest. I felt him flinch beneath my touch as my hands brushed over thick abdominal muscles. He groaned—a desperate, primal sound that made my skin tingle with lust and my body ache for more.

A throb took up between my thighs. A hot, achy pulse wanting to be filled. Stretched. A need to feel him stroke in and out of my body.

Rolling us, he covered me with his bulk, and I could feel his cock, stiff and big in his boxers, pressing into me. I shifted beneath him, welcoming the hard ridge between my legs, rubbing me in exactly the right place. His breathing came quick, and he groaned as I rocked against him. I was lost in a dizzying storm of sensations. The bulk of him on top of me. The heat of his breath on my skin. The kiss he seared into my lips. The friction of his hardness against my clit. I gasped again. I wanted him. All of him. I wanted him naked. I wanted to see and touch his cock. I wanted to feel the fullness of him as he thrust deeply and slowly into me.

I wanted him to make me forget.

Just. For. One. Night.

Engulfed in his heat, I moaned into his open mouth as his pelvis began to grind harder into me while his lips kissed a trail up my throat and along my jaw. I wrapped my legs around him, knowing I was only moments away from an earth-shattering orgasm.

Then, just like that, the heat was gone as Chance suddenly roared backward as if he was pulled away by some invisible entity. Goose bumps rippled across my skin where the coolness of the night invaded the warmth of where his body had been. He knelt backwards and looked alarmed.

No. He looked fucking mortified.

"I'm sorry," he breathed, his chest heaving, his lips wet with my kiss.

He climbed off the bed, which only gave me a better view of the outline of his erection.

"For what?" I asked, confused, my clit aching at the sudden loss of friction, my orgasm abandoned.

"We can't do this."

"Why not?"

He ran the palm of his hand up the back of his neck. "It would be a mistake."

His words stung like a slap to my cheek, and it was hard not to show it.

"Not to me."

In the pale moonlight, I could make out every dip and groove of his impressive abdominals as he stood in front of me looking like he'd just made the biggest mistake of his life.

A slow realization began to trickle through my veins, and I climbed off the bed.

"Please don't do this," I said, unable to hide the chilliness in my voice. "Don't pull away because of what happened to me."

"Cassidy—"

"I'm not defined by what he did to me," I cut him off. "Yes, he keeps me running. But he hasn't taken away who I am. That's one thing he can't take away from me."

"It's not about that. It's about keeping you safe." His chest still rose and fell with heavy breaths. "And this isn't keeping you safe."

"It *is* about that. Now that you know what he did, you don't want to touch me."

One second we were facing each other in the dim light, my hands fisted at my side, my heart pounding with rejection. The next he was backing me up against the wall, caging my head in his big arms and pinning me there with his hard body, his eyes blazing into mine.

"I want to touch you more than anything in the whole fucking world. Do you understand me?" His hands came down to cup my face. "I want to kiss you more than I want fucking oxygen. I want to bury myself so deep inside you and make you cry out my name it makes me hard just thinking about it. But I won't. Because if we're up against what I think we're up against, then I can't afford the distraction. And you, California, are a big fucking distraction."

He pulled away, taking the heat and hardness of his body with him. In the shadows he pulled on a T-shirt and sweatpants while I stood boneless and cold against the wall. Then, with his kiss still burning on my lips, I watched him walk out of the room and disappear into the bathroom, closing the door behind him.

Feeling breathless, I went to my room and after an hour of tossing and turning, finally fell into a disturbed sleep.

CHAPTER 27

CHANCE

I escaped to the fisherman's cottage before Cassidy woke up. I called the prospects to come over and watch her while I was gone. Despite being safe out here, I wasn't going to risk leaving her alone.

But I needed the alone time to put things in perspective. Needed to untangle the chaos in my head, and working on the fisherman's cottage was a good way to loosen the knots in my mind and find the clarity I needed.

Working with my hands was a good distraction. It kept me from doing something rash, like climbing on my bike and riding to California to show one raping son of a bitch what real men thought about rapists.

When I thought about what he had—*what he was*—putting Cassidy through, I saw nothing but a white-hot fury. I wanted to hurt him. I wanted to take all of this raging energy and punch it into his face until he stopped breathing.

But that wasn't a possibility.

Hell on Wheels

I also needed the distraction from my feelings for her. I thought I was able to control myself around her, keep her at a distance, but last night was just proof that I was losing that control.

And fuck, part of me wanted to lose control just so I could drink from those sweet lips and sink my cock deep into her luscious body.

Which was exactly what I shouldn't want.

So I worked hard, hauling drywall off the back of my pickup and fixing it to the walls inside the cottage. Since the floorboards had been put down, things seemed to be coming together quickly inside. The rundown cottage was finally taking shape around me.

But at lunchtime, I put down my tools.

I had made up my mind.

All morning I had imagined all the unpleasant ways I was going to inflict revenge on Barrett for what he did to Cassidy. But they were just fantasies. Because there was only one way I could handle this.

I was going to put a club hit on Barrett.

Being a part of a club as big as the Kings of Mayhem, there were ways you were expected to handle things. In this case, going up to the son of a famous politician and shooting him in the face for what he did was not in the best interest in the club. If it was, believe me, I'd already be on my bike.

But taking the asshole out quietly *was* in the best interests of the entire fucking world.

It would also mean Cassidy would be free. No more running. No more looking over her shoulder.

So, my only option was a club hit.

Taking my truck, I drove to the clubhouse. But just as I pulled up and parked, my phone rang.

It was Wyatt in California. He rang every day at 12:30.

"Just letting you know your boy is still in town," he said.

Wyatt was a few years older than me with a beard and a beer belly. Originally from Texas, he had a deep, western drawl. He and his two brothers ran a small private investigation business outside of their involvement with the Kings of Mayhem California chapter. His brothers used technology to find and track people, using things such as phone hacking and vehicle tracking, while Wyatt provided the eyes on the ground. He often boasted they could find anyone no matter how hard they tried not to be found.

"I'll tell you, Barrett Silvermane is one kinky son of a bitch. Followed him to Club Throb last night. Stayed for about three hours. Do you know what Club Throb is, Chance? It's a fucking BDSM club. You know how I know that, Chance? It's because when I agreed to this gig, you said I had to follow him into any bar, club, or public place he went to. Guess who now holds a five-hundred-dollar membership to fucking Club Throb. This very straight, very not-interested in men in gimp outfits with balls in their mouths getting fucked by a man in an executioner's outfit man! Three hours, Chance. Three hours of all that and more. That was some eye-opening shit." He sighed. "This guy doesn't just like women. He digs the men too. I'm telling you, this guy is greedy."

"I'll reimburse you the membership costs."

"Hell yes you will. But can you reimburse me those three fucking hours back? No, you can't. That is some shit I'm going to have to live with for the rest of my life."

"Was it really that bad, Wyatt?"

To answer me, he hung up in my ear.

Wyatt wasn't into that shit, but I knew him well enough to know he would've found it fascinating. Like a car wreck. Or a plane crash. No one actually liked those things, but fuck me it was hard to look away when they were happening.

Hell on Wheels

Inside the clubhouse, I found Bull in a booth, talking with Red, our cook.

"I need to talk," I said.

Going by my tone, he knew I meant right away. He took me into the room we used for chapel.

We were barely in the room before I said, "I want to put a club hit on someone."

Surprise rippled across his face as he closed the door behind us.

"Who?"

"Barrett Silvermane."

It took him a moment to recognize the name.

"You mean, *the* Barrett Silvermane? As in the son of Kerry Silvermane?" He took off his glasses. "Are you fucking kidding me?"

"He's a raping psychopath."

Bull moved to the wooden cabinet across the room and poured two shots of Patron. Handing one to me, he downed the other one himself then moved to the head of the table and sat down.

"You'd better tell me the story. And don't leave out any of the fucking details."

I sat down and told him everything. About Cassidy being fostered. About her foster brother's obsession with her. The branding. The rapes. The violence. The ongoing torment. The threat to her life.

"You're telling me Cassidy is actually the missing daughter of one of the most prominent politicians in the country?"

"Yes. But this stays between you and me. A club hit doesn't require the vote of the other members. It only needs the approval of the president and VP. I know Cade will approve it."

My brother was our VP. He had already put two bullets in a murdering rapist a few years ago when a psychopath kidnapped Indy.

"That may be right, but as president I have the governing power to veto it before it goes any further."

"Is that what you're doing? You're going to veto my request?"

He nodded. "This isn't a club hit you're after, Chance. Barrett Silvermane has got nothing to do with the Kings of Mayhem. This is a personal matter, son, and you know we don't do club hits for personal affairs."

"He's a piece of scum rapist who doesn't deserve to live."

"I don't disagree. But if you put a hit out on everyone who hurt someone good and decent, then you'd be putting a hit on a lot of fucking people."

"She's not just anyone—"

"What is it with this girl?"

His question surprised me. "I'm trying to protect her."

"No, it's more than that. And whatever it is, you're letting her cloud your judgment."

"This guy is bad news, Bull. Look at how much he's been able to get away with. He's fucking untouchable." My fist collided with the table, and it rattled. "With his parents' protection he's been able to keep torturing her."

"We're not fucking taking out a politician's son. Not the club. Not you. I mean it, Chance. Don't get any stupid ideas about taking matters into your own hands. You murder Barrett Silvermane and the feds will be all over you—and this club— like fucking ants at a picnic. So you stay away from him, got it?"

I left the clubhouse frustrated as all fuck. I couldn't go against the wishes of my president. My only option was to leave it in the hands of fate.

If Barrett came after Cassidy, I would be waiting, ready, and only too happy to put a bullet in his smug face.

CHAPTER 28

CASSIDY

It hurt to wake up and see he was gone.

It hurt when he was gone all day.

But nothing hurt like offering myself to him and him backing away.

Again.

Being knocked back once was bad enough, but offering my nearly naked and horny body to him on a silver platter and being rejected was mortifying.

Throughout the day I bounced from embarrassed to hurt, confused to frustrated.

Reject me once, stupid you.

Reject me twice, stupid me.

I had feelings for him. For the first time in my life, I had feelings for a man, and it gutted me that they were one-sided.

I had dated a little in college, but it had never amounted to much. It was more about finding a way to enjoy sex. Because I refused to let Barrett take that away from me.

I met Logan one New Year's Eve at a college bar. We spent one night together, and he showed me what it was like to make love to someone. Showed me how a real man pleasured a woman. Taught me how good it felt to be touched and kissed and licked. He gave me multiple delicious orgasms—orgasms I asked for—with his magnificent body. I didn't know his last name. Didn't know anything about him. Only that he took a scarred, young woman and showed her what the other side could look like, in that little motel room under a neon sign that blinked VACANCY.

Not long after him, I met Travis, a six-foot wall of muscle who played hockey for our college. We dated for six weeks and shared a lot of naked time before he accepted an overseas placement, and we broke up. He gave me sex on tap, and with every encounter I felt myself move further and further away from the shadows of my past.

The next was a cowboy in Texas, who was as gentle and giving as he was tall and broad. We spent three days together before Missy and I hit the road again. And in those three days, a little more of me healed beneath his tender caresses and whispered words of lust.

But I had never had any deep feelings for them. Not like the ones I felt for Chance.

Old habits came to the surface, and my instinct to run was hot in my veins. I wanted to pack my shit and flee, but my angry little heart wanted to confront him first. To know why. To hear him say it.

Reject me because of me. Not because of what he did to me.

I unfolded my fist to look at the scar on my palm.

Yeah, I was done with running. Oh, I was leaving alright. But I would walk out that door, *not run*.

Before that, though, I needed to stay and talk to him.

Hell on Wheels

Despite being mortified by his rejection, I felt better for telling Chance about Barrett and the things he did to me. It felt liberating. Just as it had when I'd vented it all to a psychiatrist back in my college years. For three years I'd maintained a weekly appointment with an amazing doctor named Michelle, who helped me work through my past.

Thanks to Doctor-patient confidentiality, I knew my secrets were safe with her. And if anything happened to me, at least someone other than me knew the truth.

Of course, Michelle tried getting me to go to the authorities, just like Chance did. And just as I had explained to him, I had told her that Kerry Silvermane's reach was too far and too wide for me to ever be able to do that safely. There was some push and pull, but once we got over that and she stopped trying, she focused on helping me through the trauma.

It took me a while, but I finally climbed out of the deep pool of grief and confusion to understand it simply wasn't my fault. And when the understanding hit, it was so freeing. Because for years I wrestled with thinking the fault lay with Barrett and his psychopathy while at the same time questioning if it also lay with me. Did I let it happen? Did I fight hard enough? Scream loud enough. Run fast enough.

But the truth was plain and simple.

None of this was my fault.

The fault lay with Barrett.

He took what wasn't his to take.

Because he was evil and vile.

Right through to the bone.

CHAPTER 29

CHANCE

I left the clubhouse and visited Caleb at Sinister Ink. He was surprised to see me in his studio. Unlike my younger brothers, I didn't have tattoos all over me. I only had a small SEAL team tattoo on the inside of my wrist and the date I joined the Navy on my left forearm.

"Everything okay?" he asked.

I pulled my T-shirt over my head and turned my back to him so he could see my scar. It was the first time he'd seen it. And the first time I'd ever shown anybody. He stood still, his vibrant eyes sparkling as he absorbed what he saw.

"Can you tattoo it?" I asked.

His brow creased. "Why?"

"Because I want it gone."

He stood up and came over to get a better look. With him, I didn't feel so exposed. He was the closest person in the world to me, and I knew there would be no pity there. No judgment. No repulsion.

Hell on Wheels

"You can but I wouldn't. Not yet anyway. It's too fresh." He studied it like a doctor would study a wound. "And there's a lot to consider. The depth of the scar tissue. The possibility of nerve damage. Scar tissue holds onto the ink differently."

"So that's a no?" I said, pulling my T-shirt back on.

"Definitely not right now while it's so new. And I'll be honest, Brother, I'd be hesitant to do it in the future. But let me look into it." He looked at me, trying to work out what was going on in my head. "Why do you want it gone?"

I raised a brow at him. "Wouldn't you?"

"I don't know. I guess it depends on what I went through to get it, I suppose."

"I'm sick of the reminder," I said. And then it happened. In a moment of weakness, I felt the emotion of the past year knock down a few of my barriers. I leaned against the tattoo bed, feeling the need to let some of the pain out to ease the pressure in my skull. The words fell out of my mouth before I could stop them. "It reminds me that I killed my girlfriend."

Caleb's eyes darted to mine. "What do you mean?"

"I was seeing a girl over there." I let myself picture her in my head, and for the first time in a long time, thinking about her didn't make me feel like a giant hole had been blown out of my chest. "We got close. I wasn't in love with her, but close to it. Close enough that I thought about staying back after my tour was done and seeing where it went."

Caleb looked shocked and sat down on his desk. "I didn't know. What happened?"

I blew out a deep breath. "Turns out we were working for opposing sides."

"She was a—"

"Yeah, she was one of the bad guys."

Even to this day, I still couldn't believe it. When I think about the time we spent together, sharing our dreams while we shared our bodies, it still seemed so surreal. I was trained to spot a threat a thousand yards away, yet I couldn't even see it when it was lying right beside me in my bed. That part still ached. And I don't know if I would ever forgive myself for that.

"I didn't know until I saw her in my scope. Didn't know until my commander was telling me to take the shot," I explained.

"And did you?"

I thought about those last few seconds.

I thought about seeing her in my crosshairs and the sound of my commander's voice in my ear, telling me to take the shot.

I thought about my bullet ripping open her chest and blowing her back three feet just as an explosion sent my world into a tailspin like a fucking tumbleweed.

"Yeah, I did." I glanced down but then looked up. "I put a bullet in my girlfriend. Tell me, what kind of man does that make me?"

He stood up and came toward me. "It makes you a soldier. You did your job. You served your country."

"I want to forget."

If I forgot, then maybe I could move forward. Maybe then I wouldn't run when a beautiful woman was beneath me. Kissing me. Wanting me.

I thought about Cassidy and the look on her face last night, and it fucking gutted me to know I'd hurt her.

I was tired of fighting my feelings. I wanted to kiss her and more. I wanted to sink every inch of my rock hard cock into her sweet pussy. I wanted to make her cry out my name. I wanted to feel her writhe and whimper beneath me. I wanted to make her come all over my cock and get drunk on the sound of her moans, knowing it was me making her crazy with pleasure.

But how could I touch her after what I had done and everything she had been through?

Hell on Wheels

Caleb studied me, his eyebrows drawn. "Are you worried that you're some kind of psycho because of what you did overseas?"

Bingo, Baby Brother.

When I didn't reply, he huffed out a deep breath. "Jesus, Chance! You did what you had to do."

"But if I was capable of killing the woman I was falling for ..."

"It was war."

I told him about the girl in the shower. He ran a hand up his bare neck, his eyebrows pulled in as he listened.

"Have you been with anyone since?"

"No, and I'm not going to until I unpack all this shit in my head."

"What about Cassidy?"

"She's been through hell, Brother. I'm not about to drag her through mine."

"But you like her?"

"Yeah," I growled. "More than I fucking should."

CHAPTER 30

CHANCE

When I arrived back at the cabin, the prospects were smoking and playing cards out on the porch. After a few minutes of small talk with them, I sent them on their way.

Cassidy was waiting for me inside the cabin, her bag packed.

I looked at it sitting by the front door then back to her and an uncharacteristic panic shot into me.

She was leaving.

"Don't," I said, my pulse suddenly thumping against my throat.

Tension hung in the air around us.

"Give me one reason why I shouldn't." Her voice was calm and low, but full of hurt.

"Because you're safer here." I struggled to swallow. "With me."

She shook her head. "I need something more than that. Tell me something. Anything. Make me stay. And if you can't, then you need to let me walk out that door."

I didn't want her to go.

Hell on Wheels

Not for her sake.

For mine.

But she was going to leave if I didn't give her another reason to stay.

It was time to step off the ledge and fall toward her.

I stared across at her, knowing she was everything I had ever wanted.

"You make me want things I gave up wanting a long time ago," I said finally.

My words crackled in the air around us. I had just taken my heart out of my chest and handed it to her.

Across the room, her face softened, and she closed the distance between us.

"Then why have you pulled away from me?" she asked. "I know you feel something for me. Why won't you let it happen?"

I took her beautiful face in my hands, aching to kiss her.

"It scares me how much I want you because you deserve so much more than this."

"Then why did you walk out? Why were you gone all day?"

I thought about the club hit and Bull's refusal. I thought about the things Cassidy told me about Barrett.

Fuck, just thinking about it made me want to kill him.

"Barrett deserves to pay for what he's done to you. I want to destroy him. Do you understand me? I want to hunt him down and fuck him up for what he did to you. I want him to beg and cry for mercy. I want him to feel the same pain you did and more. And when I am breaking him, I want him to know why he is being broken." I took a step back from her, as if protecting her from the darkness pouring out of me. "But I can't. Because the club has a code that prevents me from doing all the shit I want to do to him. So I asked Bull to put a club hit on him, and he refused."

Her eyes widened. "A club hit?"

I briefly explained the rules to her before adding, "So my hands are fucking tied. I have to wait for him to make the first move."

Thinking about it made me white hot with rage and I knew it was written all over my face.

But Cassidy didn't look afraid. She looked confused. Pain filled her big blue eyes, and I was consumed by a sudden need to remove every drop of it as a fierce protectiveness swept through me.

All of my walls were down now.

I curled my fingers around her jaw. "You're a fucking angel. You deserve a man who knows how to love you right. I've never truly loved anyone. Maybe as a kid I thought I did, but I didn't. Not really. And it's been so long since I've made love to someone I've forgotten what it's like. I've had plenty of sex, but sex is nothing. And you... Christ, Cassidy, you deserve to be touched with respect and tenderness, and love. And until I work out how to—"

Her eyes were fixed firmly to mine.

"But I want you to touch me," she said. She stepped back and started to undo the buttons to the front of her dress. "I want you to make love to me."

Her words struck me hard. And not in my dick. They reached up deep inside of me and wrapped themselves around my heart.

"Angel—" I breathed, fighting every goddamn urge in me.

Her dress slid to the floor. And just like that she was standing naked and tanned in the lounge room, looking so fucking perfect it stole my breath away. She was a goddess. So soft. So sweet. So irresistible. I closed my eyes and swallowed thickly. When I opened them again, she was moving toward me, her glorious blonde hair a stark contrast against her tanned skin, her eyes shining like sapphires. In the late afternoon light, she glowed like an angel, and every cell of my body roared at me to let this fucking happen.

"Touch me," she said.

Reaching for my hand, she placed it against her breast and my knees went weak.

"You don't want this," I rasped.

War raged inside me, because I had never wanted anything so much in my life as much as I wanted to touch her right now. It went against all the barriers I'd put up to protect myself, *to protect her*, from the harm I could do.

But Cassidy ignored me and pressed her beautiful body into mine.

"I want you," she whispered. She lifted up on her tiptoes and brushed her lips against mine.

In my mind, little pinholes of light were breaking through the darkness. But the darkness was resisting them, reminding me that she deserved better than this.

That I was the monster to her angel. The beast to her beauty.

I'd always thought my darkness was the most powerful force I'd ever known.

But it was nothing compared to the power of her allure.

Her lips brushed mine again, and when she whimpered, it was my undoing.

Light shattered the darkness completely, and I growled as I surrendered and kissed her until we were both breathless.

Her cool fingers slid to the back of my neck, and I stiffened. Her hands. They rubbed over my scars, and even though I still had on my T-shirt, there was no way they couldn't feel the lumps and bumps of rough skin beneath the fabric.

She hadn't seen my scars on my back.

Hadn't seen the layers of rough, melted skin.

The ugly side of war.

But not the ugliest side of me.

For a moment I had forgotten.

I'd been so lost in her, I'd forgotten the ugliness inside me.

I looked down at her, my heart aching.

She needed to know who she was dealing with.

"I came back from war… different," I rasped out. "I'm not the same man I was when I left."

She took a tiny step back so she could look up at me. "What do you mean?"

"My body was broken over there, Cassidy. The scars are pretty horrific. But not all the scars are on the outside." I slid the pad of my thumb across her lips. I needed her to understand what was growing inside of me. "I'd never forgive myself if I hurt you."

She thought about it for a moment, looking up at me, her eyes glittering. Then she reached up and tenderly touched my face. "You talk like you're a monster. But you're not."

There was an infinite gentleness in her eyes, and again my heart ached with longing.

"You don't know me, you haven't seen…"

I frowned. I couldn't tell her about taking the shot.

"Let me see you," she whispered. "All of you."

She stepped back and with her eyes firmly riveted to mine, found the hem of my T-shirt. My abs flinched beneath her touch, and my breath hitched in my throat as she lifted my shirt over my head and let it drop to the floor. I was powerless against the intensity of the moment. Rooted to the spot. My heart pounding like a jackhammer against my ribcage.

Her gentle fingers whispered my abs as she slowly walked around me. They trailed across my bare chest and over my shoulders, curving around my bicep until they reached my back. I winced when they left the smooth plane of my shoulder blade and touched the puckered, scarred skin of my back.

I closed my eyes. I felt exposed. Open.

Hell on Wheels

Vulnerable.

I held my breath and felt the disgust tremble through me.

I waited for her to recoil. But she didn't falter. She kept trailing her fingers along the rubbery skin as she slowly moved around me.

When she faced me again, she rose up on her toes, and I felt her breath against my ear.

"You're so beautiful," she whispered in my ear.

"I'm not—"

She cut me off with her finger on my lips then replaced it with her sweet lips. Warmth burst through me, ripped from my heart by her tenderness. Her lips were sweet, the stroke of her tongue slow and seductive.

She broke away and took a step back. When she reached for my belt, I was utterly mesmerized by her. Unable to move and at her mercy, I let her unbuckle it and slowly pull it through the hoops of my black jeans before she dropped it to the floor. She went for the button, her eyes still secured to mine, and I didn't stop her. I waited, my heartbeat thumping against my throat as she slowly lowered the zipper and reached inside. My eyes closed at the touch of her delicate fingers against my flesh, and I shivered, my breath slipping from my lips. Every cell of my body longed for this. Begged for it. Ached for it.

She took my hand in hers and placed it against her naked breast, and everything inside of me ignited into a powerful inferno.

With a hiss of breath, I swept her up in my arms and kissed her wildly. She weighed nothing in my arms as I carried her through the cabin to the bedroom, where I let her down on the bed and kicked off my boots and jeans. Covering her tiny body with the bulk of my own, her legs tightened around my waist, and she moved beneath me until my cock was right where she wanted it.

"I don't want to hurt you," I breathed, painfully restraining myself from pushing into her. I wanted this to last. I wanted to savor every morsel of it.

"You're not going to."

She rolled us on the bed. Crawling across me, covering me in her warmth, every inch of her perfect, naked body feeling so fucking perfect against mine.

She slid her thighs open and placed them on either side of me, her eyes filling with the wildfire of lust as she took me in her hand and guided me to her. I watched, spellbound, as she rose up and then very slowly sank down on my throbbing, rigid cock.

My eyes rolled backward, mind blown by the sensation. Stars danced in the darkness, and my breath left my lungs in a wild rasp. My pulse roared through me when she repeated the move, rising up and slowly lowering herself back onto me again.

In that moment I shed my fears and lost myself in her. Lost myself in a haze of euphoria as I watched her ride me, her hips slowly rocking back and forth, her tight pussy gripping me and building the sweet tension. Sweat gleamed on her skin like a golden sheen. She dropped her head back, and her long blonde curls brushed my thighs as she rode me, moaning and grinding.

She was perfect. Every fucking inch of her.

I gripped onto her hips, driving my pelvis upward to bury myself deeper and harder into her. A low moan spilled from her parted lips, and her eyes closed as her orgasm began to roll through her.

"Angel …" I rasped out.

Tight muscles curled and squeezed around me, milking me, taking my arousal and making me its bitch. She cried out just as my own climax hit me full force, and I held her thighs still, shuddering beneath her, pulsing my release deep into her body.

She fell forward, her hair falling against my chest, her eyes gleaming between the curtain of blonde.

Hell on Wheels

"See," she said breathlessly. "You're not the beast you think you are."

Later, she lay in my arms, all warm and soft, her pulse a gentle rhythm against my chest. We had just made love again; this time I took the lead, slowly grinding into her body, making her cry out, making her come with my name on her lips. Now I felt drunk on it. Heavy and hazy. Addicted.

Outside, the stars were out and the crickets were singing. Twilight settled across the river, it was a still night, with the warmth of spring in the air.

We fell asleep, entwined in each other, our bodies spent, our minds hazy in our post orgasm glow, and the warm flicker of hope burning in our hearts.

CHAPTER 31

CASSIDY

I woke up to the sound of the shower. Stretching my limbs in the large bed, I smiled contently, thinking about the night before. Thinking about Chance and how crazy spectacular he was. The more time I spent with him, the less afraid I felt. When I was in his arms, I was untouchable. For the first time in my life I was safe.

The shower turned off and I heard the door open and close. I sat up, my hair tumbling about in a big blonde mess. I brushed it out of my face and settled against the pillows, my pulse already quickening at seeing Chance this morning.

Post sex.

Post taking him in my mouth and sucking him.

Post him giving me several delicious orgasms.

He appeared in the doorway, a towel hanging low on his hips, and every womanly part of me lit up, like it was on crack, at the sight of the muscular arms and chiseled chest. His shoulders were huge. His abs ridiculous.

"Good morning," he said, slaying me with his boyish grin.

"Good morning." I started to throb.

"How are you feeling?"

My inner bad girl roared out of me, brought on by the sexiest man alive standing near naked in front of me. I smiled seductively.

"Turned on," I said huskily, my eyes dropping to the tight V disappearing beneath the towel. I was already wet. Swollen and slick.

He gave me a heated look. A wicked smile. His tongue slid across his bottom lip as he tugged on his towel.

It slipped away and holy cow!

Chance's body defied all reasoning. It was hard and strong. Warm and golden. Godlike, even. I drank in the image of him, absorbing it to memory, my body trembling with anticipation as he approached the bed with an almost predatory look on his face.

My eyes dropped to his manhood. It was long and thick, and it swayed at half-mast as he climbed onto the bed. He knelt before me, his broad chest gleaming like it was cut from granite. But despite how spectacular his chest and abs were, I couldn't tear my gaze from his enormous cock.

I walked across the bed on my knees and took it in my hands, marveling at its size and thickness as it grew harder between my palms.

He trembled beneath my touch, and a thrill rolled through him when I slipped my lips over the wide head and drew him deep down into my throat. He threaded his fingers through my hair and gently rocked his hips. I released a soft moan, the taste of him consuming me as I suckled and licked and sucked him hard. He was salty and warm and so virile I could taste his strength as he slid in and out of my mouth.

With a husky groan he pulled away.

"You keep doing that baby and there's no way I'm going to last."

He gently guided me down to the pillows and settled between my open thighs. His eyes shone brightly in the low light, and I was surprised by the affection I saw reflected in the deep blueness.

He fit himself to me and very slowly pushed in.

My breath left me as his left him, because of how fucking amazing it felt when he was inside me.

"You're so wet, baby. So tight." He began to move slowly into me. His eyes were darker now. Filled with heat and lust and all the promises of what was to come. "I never want to lose this."

Joy lit up inside me, flicked on by his words. I shifted beneath him so my clit met the friction of every stroke into my body. I gasped and it was husky and desperate because *dear God* the pleasure was almost too much to handle.

I never imagined we could fit so perfectly together. But we did. Like our bodies were made only for each other.

He pressed harder into me, grinding against the most sensitive part of my sex. I flexed and tightened around him, and he groaned. He quickened his pace, each stroke coming harder and faster than the one before, his breath coming quick, his brows drawn together. I raised my hips to meet every thrust, my legs shaking as the pleasure grew and grew until it erupted through me like a fucking star bursting. I cried out his name, my mind leaving my body and drifting up toward the heavens.

I was only vaguely aware of his moans until they grew louder and his controlled thrusts quickened. He started to come and his face shimmered as he stilled, his cock buried so deep I could feel it ejaculating into the very depths of me.

We lay heavy in the sheets. After a while he rolled onto his elbow and looked down at me. His fingers drew a gentle trail down my side and around my belly button.

"No regrets?" he asked.

"Not one. You?"

"I might be slightly fucked-up, but I'm not completely insane." His smile was beautiful. "Letting you walk out would've been my only regret."

Outside, clouds covered the sun as a morning thunderstorm rolled in, shattering Chance's plans to work on the fisherman's cottage.

So we spent the day lost in each other instead as the rain hammered into the roof above us. We took a shower together. Made sandwiches in the kitchen and then made love on the granite counter top with such emotion and frenzied energy we sent two plates to their demise, crashing on the floor, and I somehow managed to break a nail.

It was a nothing day but an everything day all at the same time.

Because here Barrett didn't exist.

And I wasn't running for my life.

CHAPTER 32

CASSIDY

The following morning, I woke up high on emotion, tangled in the sheets with my beautiful beast. Without words we made love again, slow and warm, our bodies speaking what we were feeling, our early morning moans breaking the stillness of a blue dawn. It was blissful. Erotic. And through it all, I felt a little more of Chance's wall come down. With every breath. With every stroke of his glorious cock. With every brush of his lips and tongue against mine, he took another step toward me, and I took another step away from the shadows where I'd hidden for so long.

And that was how it went for days.

We cocooned ourselves in his cabin. Nestled amongst the trees and the sparkling water of the river. Spring was here, and it was all around us in the greenness of the riverbank and the blueness of the sky. Birds sang of promise, cicadas chirped in the pale warmth of a March sunshine, and the air was warm with the sweet scent of blooming flowers and the marijuana plants that dotted the riverbank.

Hell on Wheels

Neither of us knew what was happening. Only that time had stopped as we lost ourselves in the comfort and ecstasy of each other's bodies.

We didn't speak about our feelings. Didn't talk about what was happening. Didn't make plans. Because despite the euphoric bliss of our lovemaking, we were both realists and we still wondered if this was something that could ever last. We were too broken. Too jaded by our past. And too frightened of our future.

But it was a break from the darkness.

A break neither of us were in a hurry for it to end.

When I had to work, we rode into town on Chance's bike, and he would kiss me passionately as we parted, his lips and tongue speaking promises of what was to come when I returned home. When my shifts finished, he would be waiting for me, casually leaning up against his motorcycle and looking so damn hot it was inevitable I would tear his clothes off as soon as we stepped into the cabin.

Nights were spent in bliss. Early morning hours spent in ecstasy as he woke me up with his commanding hands, luscious tongue, and hard body.

But like they say, all good things must come to an end.

And it's true.

Our happiness was short lived.

Because that's when the body washed up.

CHAPTER 33

CHANCE

A jogger found her. Half submerged on the sandy riverbank, nude except for a sock on her left foot.

She had been shot in the head.

Her name was Vander Quinn, and she was the wife of our town mayor.

By mid-morning the riverbank was crawling with law enforcement.

By lunchtime, I was sitting in our clubhouse with Bull, Cade, and Ruger, across from Mayor Quinn and his assistant. Quinn looked distraught.

"On behalf of the club, I'd like to offer you our condolences for the loss of your wife," Bull said, giving him a sharp nod of his head. He knew the pain of losing the woman you loved. For seventeen years it had kept him from having anything serious with another woman. But while he was empathetic toward our mayor, it didn't stop him from being suspicious. "What I don't understand is why you would ask the Kings for help."

Hell on Wheels

Within hours of his wife's body being discovered, Quinn had reached out to Bull and asked for a meeting.

"I want to find out who did this, and I want them to pay," he said through gritted teeth.

"That's to be expected, but you have the sheriff's department and the state troopers all over this."

Quinn leaned forward to rest an arm on the table. "Everybody in this town knows that if you want something done, you reach out to the Kings. I want who did this. And I don't want to wait."

"Buckman is a good sheriff."

Quinn cocked an eyebrow at Bull. "Come on, he's so corrupt he'd sell his own grandmother's soul for the right price. Don't think for a second I don't know about the things he does for your club."

Bull's expression didn't waver. "He's a good investigator."

"That may be the case, Bull, but I want the person responsible for this to be found and dealt with in the most appropriate manner."

"Meaning?"

"Meaning, I want it dealt with outside of the law. Going to prison would be too good for the son of a bitch. I want him cold and stiff in the ground."

His words crackled in the air like electricity.

"We're not murderers for hire, Quinn," Bull finally said.

"Oh, I don't expect you to murder anyone. I just want you to find him and leave the rest to me."

Bull's eyebrows rose above his sunglasses, but he said nothing. Quinn nodded to his assistant who pulled out a thick yellow envelope from of his briefcase and slid it across the table.

"There's twenty thousand. You'll get another twenty thousand when you deliver whomever was responsible to me."

I leaned forward and looked inside the envelope. Sure enough it was fat with cash. Bull turned his head in my direction, and I nodded, letting him know it was full of money. He gestured for me to give it back.

"I'll say it again. We aren't murderers for hire, but we'll find out what piece of shit came into our town and murdered one of our own." He rose to his feet. He was tall and formidable, and the dark sunglasses added more intimidation to his already imposing figure. "And I'll trust that this act of *loyalty* will be remembered by our prestigious mayor in the future. Do we understand one another?"

Quinn looked at the yellow envelope on the table, weighing up his options. He rose to his feet and stretched out a hand to Bull. "You have yourself a deal."

"Good."

Twenty thousand dollars was a lot of money to turn down, but I understood why Bull did it. Currency like the one Quinn was offering could be traced back to the Kings and could become a headache for us further down the track if things went pear-shaped with the investigation. A future favor and a handshake was far less incriminating than a pile of cash.

The two men sat back down.

"Can you think of anyone who might want to hurt you or your wife?" I asked. As Sergeant at Arms, Bull would rely heavily on me to help find out what happened to Vander Quinn.

"My wife had a lot of friends. She was a people person. They gravitated to her like bees to pollen." He paused, his face marred by sadness. "I can't think of anyone who would want to hurt..." His voice trailed off as he remembered something. "A couple of weeks ago she started getting phone calls from a number she didn't recognize. She told me about it over breakfast one morning. But then she never mentioned it again. Do you think that might have something to do with it?"

"It could but I would say the sheriff's department would have already sent a request to her phone provider for access of her records," Ruger said, meaning we'd be able to get them off Buckman later. "Can you think of anything else?"

Mayor Quinn paused, thinking.

"There is one other thing."

We waited.

"My wife was having an affair."

"An affair?" I asked.

Mayor Quinn waved it off. "It was nothing serious. Just like all the others."

Seeing the confusion on our faces he elaborated.

"My wife and I had an arrangement. We've been married thirty years this June, gentlemen, and I'm man enough to admit that marriage can get a bit boring once the shine of new love wears away and you're faced with the day-to-day monotony of real life together. My wife enjoyed a few trysts here and there, and I understood them. She was a good looking woman with time on her hands and a healthy sexual appetite. We had a great sex life, believe me. But that didn't stop her wanting to eat pork chops instead of sirloin steak every once in a while."

Ruger glanced at me, his eyebrows raised, while Bull's expression remained unchanged.

"You really expect us to believe you were okay with her having an affair?" he said.

"I don't expect you to understand, Bull. But you need to realize that not all relationships are cookie-cutter. Vander and I grew up together. Went to college together. Trusted each other. I accepted her and she accepted me. That's why we are... *we were*... celebrating thirty years together." Sadness swept across his face. "She was the love of my life."

"This guy she was having an affair with... you think he had anything to do with her murder?" Ruger asked. "Perhaps he wanted more and took out his frustrations on her when she refused to end her marriage."

Mayor Quinn stood up and his assistant quickly did the same.

"I don't know. That's what I expect you to find out. All I know is my wife is dead and her red mustang is missing." He looked at Bull. "Start with those bikers that have been hanging around town. Satan's Tribe, if I recall correctly. Saw them just outside of town at Coota's Bar & Grill."

"She has a red mustang?" I asked.

"It's a limited edition. Royal crimson. Find her car. She won't be far behind."

We watched him and his assistant leave before we spoke.

"You think he's involved? Or knows who is?" I asked Bull.

"I don't know. But his suggestion about the Tribe isn't unreasonable." He pulled his phone out from the breast pocket of his cut. "I'm going to give Behemoth a call."

Behemoth was the president of Satan's Tribe. His real name was Balthazar Julius but he was known as Behemoth in the MC world. Bull put him on speaker so we could hear the conversation.

He answered on the third ring. "Who is this?"

"You know who it is or you wouldn't have answered," Bull said.

"What do you want?"

"I want you to tell me why three of your men are in Destiny?"

"Fuck you," Behemoth snapped and hung up the phone.

Bull's face barely registered his wrath, but his eyes glowed with it.

Hell on Wheels

Putting his phone on speaker, he dialed the number again. When Behemoth answered he yelled into the phone, "Fuck me? Fuck you, motherfucker. Now this can go one of two ways. You can either tell me why your men are in my town, and I will hang up feeling very appreciative of your cooperation. Or you can tell me to fuck off again, and I will ride all the way down to Gulfport *just* so I can beat some motherfucking manners into you. Now for the last fucking time, why the fuck are your men in my town?"

There was a pause as Behemoth probably thought about the consequences of hanging up again. He would be stupid if he did. Bull didn't make idle threats. If he said he would ride down to Gulfport, he would ride down there and shove his fist so far down Behemoth's throat he'd be able to feel his kidneys.

Behemoth wisely decided to help.

"They got some job to do up there. Don't ask me what. Those boys are brothers, and they do a lot of moonlighting. They can do what they like when it's not on club time." His voice was gruff. "Happy, Mr. President?"

Bull grinned to himself. "See, was that hard?"

Behemoth replied by hanging up.

Bull looked at me.

"Holiday is over. I need you back working on this."

CHAPTER 34

CHANCE

I wasn't happy about my time with Cassidy being cut short. But I was the SAA. It was my job to stand by my president and be the enforcer in the investigation.

I spoke to Wyatt on the phone on my way back to the cabin.

"What is Barrett up to?" I asked. "Has he done anything out of the usual?"

"The guy is a douche, there's no denying that, but is he coming your way? I don't think so. This guy is balls deep in a pretty indulgent life out here in Cali. Money. Cars. Flashy clothes. Women. Men. This guy is too busy being a rich prick and fucking his way through the population of SoCal to worry about anything going on two thousand miles away in Mississippi."

The reports were promising. Consistent. So far, Barrett hadn't made any moves to suggest he was planning anything.

Likewise with Kerry Silvermane. There was nothing to suggest he was even aware Barrett knew where Cassidy was.

Which was a relief.

But at the same time troublesome.

Hell on Wheels

Unfortunately, only time would tell. Until then, I would stick to Cassidy like glue, and when I couldn't be here because of club business, I would make sure one of the prospects was with her.

Cassidy was in the kitchen when I got home, still dressed in her waitress uniform, chopping vegetables for dinner. I walked in and stood behind her at the kitchen counter, the scent of her immediately driving me wild.

She turned around in my arms and kissed me like she hadn't seen me in weeks.

"I could get used to this," I groaned against her lips.

I liked what was happening between us. I wanted to explore it some more. Vander Quinn's murder investigation couldn't have come at a worst time.

"Want a beer?" she asked, walking to the refrigerator.

When I nodded, she handed me one and I gave her a wink. "I could *definitely* get used to this."

We took our drinks out onto the porch just as the sun began to set. The sky was red and orange with hints of pink.

As we sat sipping our beers, I filled her in the murder investigation.

"Any idea on who might have killed her?" she asked.

I told her what Mayor Quinn said about his wife having an affair.

"So we visited the guy who was supposedly her lover, but it was a dead end. They were only friends. Met at the tennis club where he works and she plays. They became close but nothing intimate."

"Can you be sure he was telling the truth?"

"When we met him, he was with his boyfriend. It's a well-kept secret. Apparently the tennis committee is old school and have a thing about homosexuality." I shook my head. "Judgmental sons of bitches."

"So what now?"

"Tomorrow, we're checking out a few more leads." I ran a finger up her bare arm. "This means I'm going to have put in some long hours with the club."

"I thought as much."

"You okay with that?"

She put down her drink and gave me a seductive smile.

"It just means we'll have to make the most of our time together," she said suggestively.

Her tongue slid across her bottom lip, and my cock lurched to life behind my pants.

"Ever made love outside?" she asked, kneeling down in front of me and reaching for my belt buckle. She raised an eyebrow as she slowly lowered the zipper.

I was at her mercy.

And there was no other place I wanted to be.

She reached in and took me in her soft hand, her beautiful blue eyes closing as she leaned down and slid her plump lips over the broad head of my cock. A deep groan tore out of my mouth, and my head fell back in pleasure.

Her mouth and tongue were insatiable, sucking and licking, building the tension. I rasped her name and tangled my fingers in her hair.

As her fingers curled around the base, her other hand found the tight skin of my balls and I almost filled her mouth when she began to massage them. I growled, my mind so crazy with euphoria it left me almost intoxicated by the pleasure.

She looked up at me with lust-filled eyes, her hand continuing to stroke me, her skillful tongue licking through the pearl of pre-cum pooling in the eye of my cock.

The urge to come was violent, tightening like a rubber band getting ready to snap. But I fought it, breathlessly, holding back my climax so I could enjoy the torture of her mouth for a little bit longer. Because goddamn this woman knew what she was doing, and I wanted her to keep doing it.

"I love your cock," she whispered against the engorged head. I released a rasped moan trying to hold back from blowing it—excuse the fucking pun—and coming on her face.

Christ, that thought was almost my undoing. I ran my hand through my hair, my breathing growing ragged as the most beautiful woman in the world sucked my cock like it was a goddamn lollipop.

Her name fell from my parted lips, and she looked up at me, her eyes heavy with desire as she drew the full length of me into her mouth. That was it. There was only so much a man could take. I closed my eyes and tossed my head back, giving in to the ecstasy, my moan low and ragged and ripped out of me by a climax so powerful my hips shot upward off the chair. My eyes half-open, I gripped the armrests as cum roared out of me in pulsing white threads, landing on the smooth plane of her waiting tongue. I watched, mesmerized as she took it all and swallowed, my cock and my mind blown by the beauty kneeling before me.

I drew her up to me and kissed her. I was so fucking under her spell it was ridiculous.

Later, we walked to the bridge and crossed it, taking the small dirt path to the fisherman's cottage.

"So this is where you go," she said as I led her along the trail to the newly built covered porch.

I walked her through the bright and airy cottage, and she gazed around in awe at the new interior. The freshly painted walls. The crisp white baseboards. The restored crown molding. The new cabinetry in the kitchen and the granite island.

It wasn't quite finished, but it wasn't far from it.

"This place is incredible," she said breathlessly, turning around and taking it all in. She reached out and ran a delicate finger over the polished brass doorknob. "You've done such an amazing job."

She made me smile. Watching her admire my work. Seeing that incredible smile on her face.

As she stepped through the French doors to the little porch out back, I pulled her back to me and in one maddening moment let down every damn wall I had.

"Stay here with me," I said, gutting myself open and exposing myself completely to her.

Her brow wrinkled and for a moment she looked confused. "What?"

"After this has all passed. Stay here. With me." I held her fingers tightly in my own. "Because you want to, not because you need to."

Her beautiful blue eyes shone up at me. "Chance, I'm not here because I have to be. Not anymore. I'm here because I've never felt anything like this in my entire fucking life."

I kissed her then. Hard. My heart completely and utterly surrendering to her.

"This can be our home," I said against her warm lips. "We can have a good life here."

Her smile was breathtaking as she looked up at me. "Do you mean that?"

I took her face in my hands. "I meant it when I said you make me want things I had given up wanting. I want this. Us. *Here*."

Happiness tugged at her lips, and she nodded, her voice barely a whisper as she said, "Me too."

Hell on Wheels

We left the cottage with our fingers entwined, feeling high from the sudden realization that we had a future. As we walked across the bridge back to the other side of the river, the sky rumbled with thunder and cracked open, sending a fast and furious downpour onto us. But instead of making a run for it, we stood under the pelting rain and kissed like lovesick teenagers. I held her rain-soaked face to mine, consumed by the sweet taste of her, my chest filling with all the feelings I'd trapped in my heart for so long.

When lightning lit up the sky, we ran back to the cabin through the mist rising up from the river. Already soaking wet, we stood at the back door kissing for a ridiculously long period of time as fat raindrops soaked our skin and ran down our faces.

Finally tumbling through the back door, I peeled Cassidy's wet clothes from her luscious body before pulling off my own, and we showered together, soaping each other's bodies beneath a warm stream of water. And as she kissed me passionately with her slippery body pressed up against mine, I wondered how the fuck I had ever existed without her.

CHAPTER 35

CASSIDY

That night it rained. Hard. It pounded into the river and rattled against the windows as Chance laid me down on the plush rug in the living room and made love to me with excruciating slowness. It was easy to forget the outside world when I got lost beneath his touch and the things he did to my body.

Afterward, we ate ice cream out of the tub and drank neat whiskey as we smoked his cigarettes and talked.

For the first time in my life, I was free.

Really free.

And I didn't want the feeling to end.

We talked about a future, and as we got drunk on whiskey, we got more intoxicated on our plans.

Here, wrapped in our own little universe, it was easy to forget the outside world and all the darkness I was running from.

When we lost power, we lit candles. And in their soft, muted light, we began to make love again.

Chance slid over me, moving slowly as he parted my thighs and covered me in his delicious warmth. With one purposeful push, he was inside me and the sudden fullness sent my eyes into the back of my head. I ran my hands down his powerful and muscular back, my hips tilting to meet every slow and controlled thrust. He nuzzled into the crook of my neck, and his breath was hot and comforting as we fell into a deeply erotic rhythm.

I bit down on my bottom lip, more aware of every thick hard inch of him pushing in and out of me. I lingered on the edge of an orgasm, my body surging forward to take it but not quite reaching it.

Frustration prickled at my nerves. Sensing my need, Chance pulled out of me and slung my legs over his shoulders. Light and stars danced before my eyes as his velvety tongue found my clit and the swollen wet flesh of my sex.

I clawed at the plush rug beneath me, my hips driving up to meet every tormenting lap of his tongue.

It was pure torture. The slow build. The shallow dips. The teasing licks. His heated groans against the most sensitive part of me whenever I moaned. I felt my body tighten. Felt the tension knot and pull until it snapped and my climax spread through me like wildfire. I cried out and arched into him, blindly grabbing the leg of the sofa behind us as the ecstasy consumed me.

I sank, boneless and spent, into the floor. I was liquid. Done for.

Chance rose up from between my thighs and crawled along my body.

"That was …"

"The best head you've ever had?" he asked, his eyebrow cocked with confidence.

"Dreamy," I sighed, teasingly.

"And the best head you've ever had," he repeated.

When I didn't reply, he gave me a dark, fiery look. He had my head caged between two muscular arms, and the look on his face was dark and masculine, heated by the molten fire in his eyes.

When I still refused to give him the answer he wanted, he drove his hard cock into me, his eyes riveted to mine as he pulled back, only to thrust back into me harder and deeper.

If he wanted me to tell him he was the best, then this was the worst way to go about it. Because I didn't want him to stop what he was doing.

As if reading my mind, he pulled back again. Instead of driving back into me, he dragged his cock all the way out so just the tip brushed against my slippery clit. Slowly, he started to tease me with it, swirling through my wet flesh, dipping into me but not enough to satisfy my body's craving for him. I squirmed against him. Wanting more. Needing all of him.

"Please," I begged, wanting all of him inside me.

He grinned down at me, flooring me with the most devastating smile. His wet hair fell over his forehead, and he brushed it back with his free hand while the other tortured me with his cock.

"Say it," he commanded.

"It was the best head I've ever had," I breathed desperately.

Leaning down, he kissed me. "Baby, you haven't seen anything yet."

Rewarding me for my good behavior, he slowly pushed into me and detonated my orgasm, sending me into outer space for the second time that night.

CHAPTER 36

CASSIDY

I woke up to Chance kissing me goodbye.

He leaned down and planted a long kiss on my mouth, the warm scent of him engulfing me. He was freshly showered, and I could smell the sexy combination of his heat, deodorant, and soap on his skin.

I had been in such a deep sleep I hadn't heard him get up or have a shower.

"I won't be long. Only a couple of hours. The prospect is on his way."

The sun was out. It was a perfect morning to get some time in at the fisherman's cottage.

He pressed his lips to my forehead, but I didn't want him to leave. I had woken up needy and aroused. Even after a night of crazy love making the night before, I was still looking for more.

I pulled him to me and kissed him hard and long so there was no misunderstanding about what I wanted.

"Really?" He raised a sexy eyebrow at me. "I wish I'd known this half an hour ago."

"Are you turning me down?"

"Merely asking for a rain check, darlin'," he leaned down and kissed me again. "I have more drywall being delivered in about fifteen minutes."

I grabbed him by his T-shirt and held him to me. "I can be real quick."

"And Hawke has organized some bedrock for the fireplace to be delivered today."

"Drywall. Bedrock. Keep talking sexy like that, baby. You're driving me wild."

He grinned against my lips. "Anyone tell you you're greedy."

I dragged his hand under the sheet so he could feel just how much I wanted him while my other hand slid up his thighs, to where his jeans were beginning to tent at the zipper, and he rasped out a breath.

"You're going to kill me," he groaned when I started on his zipper.

"Are you complaining?"

He kicked off his jeans and ripped his T-shirt over his head so all I saw was a wall of muscles in front of me.

He nestled his bulk between my thighs, and I began to tingle.

"Baby, the day I can't make time for this is the day they should bury me," he said, driving a hard thrust into my body and making me gasp.

Kissing me fiercely, he began his encore performance from the previous night, his hard body turning mine to mush for the next hour and leaving me well fucked and spent in the tangled sheets when he left.

Hell on Wheels

I was still lying in the sheets with a smile on my face when I heard the front door open and a woman's voice announce her arrival. I sat up abruptly and patted down the bed covers to find the T-shirt and panties Chance had ripped off me the night before. Quickly putting them on, I hunted for my denim cutoffs and found them on the floor. Shoving my legs into them, I hurried out of the bedroom to find and an old lady with bright red hair and even brighter red lips unpacking groceries at the kitchen counter. She was wearing a dazzling multi-colored caftan covered in tiny crystals, and in the sunlight she glowed like a prism. She was unpacking two grocery bags and humming.

"Hi there," I said, doing up the button to my denim shorts as I walked in.

She looked up when she heard me, and her face broke into a big smile. "Well, hello there."

She breezed across the room to me, her caftan sparkling like a disco ball as she walked through the rays of sunlight spilling in through the windows.

"You must be Cassidy," she said, her eyes wise and bright as she looked at me.

"I am," I replied. "You must be Grandma Sybil."

She seemed impressed that I knew who she was.

"Why yes, yes I am." Her eyes gleamed mischievously. "Well, aren't you just a beauty. I always knew my grandson had good taste."

"Oh, um... it's not... you know... to be honest..." I stuttered under her gaze. I didn't know what was happening with Chance. I knew I was falling for him. Hell, I was bat-shit crazy falling in love with him. But as far as his feelings... I wasn't sure if he was ready to tell the world.

"Well, I know my grandson. You must be pretty special for him to bring you here."

I couldn't stop the goofy smile from spreading across my face, because her words and her kindness had just turned my heart to mush.

"Thank you for letting me stay here for a while," I said.

"You're so welcome, sweetheart. When Chance mentioned he was bringing you out here, I thought to myself, *Sybil, this girl has got to mean something to your sweet boy. She's going to be something pretty special for him to do this.*"

I didn't know what to say. I shoved my hands into the back pockets of my shorts because I was suddenly feeling all gooey inside like a lava cake.

"Now, you come with me," she said, taking my hand and guiding me into the kitchen. "You can help me bake my brownies."

"Sure. But I have to warn you, I pretty much suck at baking."

"Not after today you won't, my gorgeous girl. Because I'm going to show you how to make the *perfect* brownie."

I watched as she took an apron from the pantry and put it on over her caftan. She found a second one and handed it to me.

"Ready?" she asked with a glittery sparkle in her eyes.

I nodded. "Ready!"

"Right. Get me a baking pan out of that drawer over there and turn the oven on to 325 degrees."

I did what she asked and placed the baking pan in front of her. "What's next?"

"I'll just whisk these together and then we'll get to the secret ingredient," she said, measuring flour, sugar, and cocoa powder to a glass bowl.

"What's the secret ingredient?" I asked, watching her add a pinch of salt to the mix.

She reached down and pulled a second bowl from the cupboard beside her.

"Cannabutter," she said as she cracked an egg into the new bowl.

I looked at her blankly.

Cannabutter?

Then it hit me.

We were making cannabis brownies.

Laughter tugged at my lips. "Are we making brownies with *weed*?"

The old lady with the wild red hair, face full of makeup, and crazy colorful nails leaned in and gave me a wink. "Are there any other kind?"

I started to laugh.

I was falling crazy in love with this old lady.

"I bake them out here because I have nosy neighbors," Grandma Sybil explained, adding a splash of milk to the egg mix.

Grandma Sybil didn't seem like the type to let a neighbor force her to do anything. Hell, Grandma Sybil didn't seem like the type to let *anyone* force her to do anything. I was pretty sure this whole thing was a charade just to check me out. The girl staying with her grandson in *her* river cabin.

I didn't blame her because I'd want to check me out too.

And I couldn't help but smile at her ruse.

Cannabis brownies.

Grandma Sybil was fucking hilarious.

For the next twenty minutes she showed me how to make a marijuana pouch using grounded up marijuana and a muslin cloth, and how to double-boil butter and water on the stove.

"The perfect cooking time for potency is two hours," she explained as she pulled a container out of the grocery bag. "That's why I've brought some already made. We can let this simmer while the brownies bake. Means we'll have plenty for next month's batch."

I watched her heat the pre-made cannabutter in the microwave and then mix it through the batter.

"So what do you do with special brownies?" I asked.

She tipped the batter into a baking dish, scraping it off the sides with her spatula.

"I belong to a ladies' circle. *Ladies of the River,* we're called. A ridiculous name, I know. Makes us sound like we dress in togas and sacrifice animals to a water god. But they are a fun bunch of women. We meet once a month at the town hall. Have been going on forty years now. We used to meet to swap recipes and support one another. Now we catch up with bottles of wine, my brownies, and Led Zeppelin playing on the radio."

She ran a spatula over the mix to smooth the top layer before shoving it into the oven. "I'll tell you what, sweetheart, it's a lot more fun at my age. You get away with a lot more than you do when you're young!"

I thought about my foster grandmother back in California. She was cold and impersonal, immaculately put together with an over-sprayed bouffant, Chanel suits, and gold jewelry. She wasn't fun or colorful like Grandma Sybil. We never received a hug from her. Children weren't her thing. They annoyed her.

How different my life might have been if Kerry Silvermane had been raised by someone as cool and as fierce as Grandma Sybil. It might have given him some balls.

I was just about to ask her what else they did at this *Ladies of the River* circle when the front door burst open and two very large men appeared in the doorway.

At first I thought they must be friends of Chance. They were big, *biker big*, although there was something a little less sophisticated about them than the other Kings of Mayhem bikers I had met. One had a long mullet and looked like he'd stepped out of a nineties redneck movie while the other looked scary with beady eyes and a heavily pock-marked face.

Hell on Wheels

A cold chill ran down my spine.

They weren't friends of Chance.

They were there for something very different.

My panic started in my bones. I thought of my handgun in the nightstand next to the bed, but I knew I had zero chance of reaching it before one of these brutes put their hands on me.

"Well, well, well, what do we have here?" The tall, beady-eyed one said as he sauntered into the lounge room. Grandma Sybil stepped in front of me as if to protect me.

The one with the mullet raised his chin and inhaled the aroma of baking weed.

"Seems to me these lovely ladies are baking up some ganja brownies," he said with an ugly grin.

"Mmm, I love me some weed brownies," his gross friend said as he walked around the kitchen counter toward me, peeling the clothes from my body with his horrible eyes.

"What do you want," Grandma Sybil demanded calmly.

"What do we want?" our unwelcomed guest said as he reached out and touched my hair. He made a sound. A vile, aroused sound that sent a tremor of terror rolling through me. He licked his lips. "I want a *taste* of that brownie."

I knew that look in his eye. Knew what the suggestive leer on his lip meant.

"Take whatever you need and get the fuck out of my house," Grandma Sybil said.

Beady-eyed man snickered. "Oh, lady, it's going to take a little bit longer than that."

I eyed the knives in the knife block on the counter. If Beady Eyes got any closer to me, I was going to grab one of them and put it in his chest.

"Where's the weed?" the man with the mullet demanded.

"I used it all in the brownies," Sybil replied.

"I don't mean that weed." Mullet Hair joined us in the kitchen. "I mean your stash. I know who you are. Bet you got pounds of the stuff stashed everywhere."

"I sure hope you're not a betting man, son, because you're wrong. There ain't no more weed here. Just an old lady and her grandson's girlfriend is all. Now I suggest you boys leave before my grandson comes back and kicks both your asses so hard you'll be tickling your assholes every time you brush your teeth."

Both men snickered.

"We got ourselves a feisty one here," Beady Eyes chuckled. He turned his attention back to me. "What about you, baby, are you feisty like the old lady? How about you and me go into one of those bedrooms and you can let your feisty flag fly?"

He looped a finger through another lock of my hair, and I gritted my teeth.

"You touch me and I'll break every bone in your goddamn hands."

Our eyes met and I realized I was looking into a greasy pit of hell.

He leaned in closer and moaned. "Oh yeah, you're a fighter. I like it when they fight."

I was seconds away from lunging for one of the knives in the knife block when Mullet Hair interrupted.

"That's not what we're here for," he reminded him. "We got no time for that."

But Beady Eyes wasn't deterred. He kept his eyes riveted to mine as he said, "Yeah, but I'm willing to make time."

"I need to pee," Grandma Sybil said suddenly.

It was so random it caught us all by surprise.

"Hold it," Mullet Hair demanded.

Hell on Wheels

Grandma Sybil remained calm but gave him a very direct look as she said, "Son, when you get to my age and you gotta go, it ain't a suggestion."

The intruders looked at one another before the one leering at me shifted his eyes to her and jerked his head, indicating for her to go. "Make it quick."

Grandma Sybil dusted off her hands and slowly made her way to the bathroom while I stared off with the beady-eyed man.

I shifted uneasily. I wasn't wearing a bra and my fear had puckered my nipples so they poked through the thin fabric of my shirt. I watched Beady Eyes lick his lips, and goose bumps spread across my skin with a cold chill.

I was seconds away from lunging for a knife when the sudden boom of the shotgun reverberated throughout the little room and sent my ears ringing.

Across the room, glass exploded and timber splintered as the crystal cabinet was blown apart from the shotgun blast. I swung around and saw Grandma Sybil brandishing a 12-gauge shotgun.

"Jesus Christ!" Mullet Man yelled.

"Crazy old bitch!" Beady Eyes growled.

When she shot a second round into the wall behind them they jumped and scrambled toward the door.

"Yeah, you'd better run you little twerps!" She yelled after them as they ran out the door and down the driveway. "Next time you set foot in my house, I'll blow a hole in you the size of fucking Texas, you pussies!"

If I wasn't so freaked out, I would've laughed.

Grandma Sybil was one gun slinging badass.

"Are you okay, sweetheart?" she asked, turning back to me.

Gob smacked, I watched her walk to the kitchen and load more rounds into the shotgun. She was calm and collected, moving about as if nothing had happened, while I remained frozen to the spot like my feet had grown roots and had burrowed into the floorboards.

"What the fuck just happened?" was all I managed to say.

"That, my darling girl, was a home invasion."

I glanced around me.

"Do you think they'll come back?"

"Not if they don't want their innards being used for dog food!" she said, digging into her apron pocket for another round and jamming it into the shotgun.

My mouth dropped open again.

"I'm just kidding," she said, waving her comment off. "It's much easier burying a whole body than a body bleeding guts all over the floor."

I stared at her, still dazed.

"Where on Earth did you get the shotgun?" I asked.

She gave me a sweet old lady face. *"Son, when you get to my age and you gotta go, it ain't a suggestion."*

"You mean to tell me you keep a shotgun in the toilet?"

"And a handgun behind the refrigerator." She gave me a pointed look as she rammed another round into the shotgun. "This is the MC world, darlin'. If you want to survive, you need to expect the unexpected and make sure you got enough firepower to cope."

CHAPTER 37

CHANCE

I saw him when I was hammering the last of the roof shingles onto the fisherman's cottage. He was standing on the riverbank, staring across the water at me. A man dressed in black. But he was no ordinary man. He radiated darkness and bad news, and wore a skull bandana that covered half his face.

I rose to my feet, but he didn't move. He remained rooted to the spot just fucking staring up at me like an intimidating ghoul.

When the sound of a shotgun blast rang out across the river, the shock of it violently crashed into me. Another blast only seconds later sent me shimmying down the outdoor plumbing to the ground below. But still *Skull Face* didn't move. He continued to watch me from across the water, only glancing over his shoulder as two men raced out of the cabin and ran toward the driveway. When he looked back to me, our eyes locked and stayed riveted to one another before he slowly turned away and walked back up the riverbank toward his companions.

I ran to my truck and chewed up the gravel getting back to the cabin. By the time I got there, *Skull Face* and his friends were gone. I didn't pass them on my way because they had probably parked their bikes further down the road and made their way through the trees on foot.

In a plume of dust, I skidded to a halt at the front door. Inside, I was surprised to see Grandma Sybil crouched down and looking on in dismay at the remnants of a shotgun-blasted glass cabinet. My eyes darted to Cassidy, who was as pale as a ghost, standing as if she was frozen to the floorboards.

I crossed the room to her and ran my hands up her bare arms, my heart pounding. "Are you okay?"

I knew my feisty grandmother would be unfazed.

Cassidy nodded, her gaze glued to the mess on the floor. "Her gun is much bigger than mine."

If I wasn't so pissed at the situation, I would have smiled. Hell, I would've laughed. Because this woman. This angel. Christ, she was amazing.

The stuff queens are made from.

I wrapped my arms around her and pulled her to my chest, pressing a kiss to the crown of her head.

"I'm sorry I wasn't here." I was also fuming that the prospect hadn't shown up.

She shook her head and gently pushed away from me. "Your grandmother scared the hell out of them."

"Pussies," Grandma Sybil said over her shoulder as she rose to her feet and walked to the kitchen.

It was only then I noticed the aroma of weed hanging heavy in the air. Grandma Sybil was simmering cannabis butter on the stovetop. I raised an eyebrow at her, putting two and two together, and was about to say something when the prospect stumbled through the front door looking banged up.

"Where the fuck were you?" I growled at him.

Hell on Wheels

"Motherfuckers ran me off the road a few miles back," he panted. "Fucking Satan's Tribe. Three of them. Took me twenty minutes to get my bike out of the ditch and started again. I made it as far as the end of the driveway before it gave out on me."

"Call Bull, tell him the Tribe has paid Grandma Sybil's cabin a visit," I said to him. "He'll organize a tow for your bike."

Twenty minutes later, Cade, Bull, Ruger, and Maverick roared up the driveway, with Animal and Cool Hand not far behind in the tow truck. As the six of them surveyed the scene, Grandma Sybil filled them in on what happened while I did my best to comfort Cassidy. I felt fiercely protective but utterly useless at the same time.

Thankfully, the color had returned to her cheeks.

"A bit extreme, isn't it?" Cade said, holding up an oil painting peppered with shotgun pellets.

"You didn't see them. They were trying to intimidate us, so I intimidated them right back," Grandma Sybil replied.

"Are you sure it was Satan's Tribe who did this?" Ruger asked.

I was sure it was.

"They said they knew who lived here," Grandma Sybil explained. "Said they wanted the weed."

If Satan's Tribe bikers were in town moonlighting, perhaps they were after some free weed while they were here.

But the million-dollar question was *why were they here?*

Behemoth had said they were working for someone. Was that someone Quinn? Or worse... was it Barrett?

My head did the math.

Quinn had ties to Gulfport. But what involvement could Barrett possibly have with a biker gang thousands of miles away from California?

I also had to consider it was possible they were working for someone who wasn't even on our radar yet.

"You think this has something to do with the weed fields?" Cade suggested.

"Maybe." I wasn't convinced, though.

I heard gravel on the driveway as Sheriff Buckman pulled up to the house. A minute later, he appeared in the doorway. He took off his hat and shook his head at the pile of kindle that used to be Sybil's glass cabinet.

"Any idea who did this?" he asked us.

"You're the police," I snapped. "Shouldn't we be asking *you* that?"

I was angry at myself for not seeing this threat coming at us. If it wasn't for my gun-toting grandmother, things could've gone south real quick.

"A few people out here on the river have reported B & E's. We weren't sure if it was kids or not. But there has been a spate of them in the last week, so they are more than likely related."

"You've had reports of B & E's along the river, and we're just hearing about this now?" I growled.

"It's police business, son."

"We pay you to make it our business," I barked at him. Christ, if anything had happened to Cassidy. "And when I have someone I'm protecting, I should know about this... *fuck*!"

"You're protecting someone?" Bucky stepped closer. "And why am I just hearing about this now?"

Touché.

Bull put a hand between us, and I stepped back. I was beyond frustrated. I should never have left Cassidy alone before the prospect got here. I was distracted by my feelings for her. If I hadn't been, I would've seen this coming.

"Think it's time we had a word with those boys from the Tribe," Bull said. "Quinn said they've been hanging out at Coota's."

Hell on Wheels

Coota's was a bar just out of town. Far enough for Bull not to worry about them lingering too close to our territory.

"Just don't make it a bloody word," Bucky said wearily. "I don't want the paperwork."

"Relax, Bucky," Cade said. "Coota's isn't in your jurisdiction. Sheriff Pamela would get this particular headache, and I'm pretty sure she will see it from Bull's point of view." He gave Bull a raised eyebrow. Bull's affair with Sheriff Pamela from our neighboring county was the worst kept secret in both counties.

"I'm coming," I said. "I've got a few things I'd like to say to them."

With my fists. Over and over until they get the message.

"No, you take Cassidy back to the clubhouse until we get this mess sorted," Bull said. His eyes told me to not fight him on this. "You take care of her."

I nodded and turned to Cassidy. "Go pack your things and we'll head back to the clubhouse."

When she disappeared into the bedroom, I turned to Grandma Sybil.

"Let's get out of here. The prospects can clean this up."

"You go on right ahead. I'll just take care of the brownies and then I'll be right behind you," Grandma Sybil said.

I shook my head. "We're not leaving you here alone. It's not safe."

Grandma Sybil waved me off. "Those babies aren't coming back. Probably gone home to change their shorts. Little punks."

"I'll stay and help Grandma Sybil with the brownies," Maverick said with a grin. "And if those freaks come back, I'm sure Ma Baker and I can handle it."

CHAPTER 38

CASSIDY

"You okay?" Chance asked as we walked into his bedroom at the clubhouse.

I dumped my bag on the bed and turned around. "Do you really think those men were there for stashed weed. I mean, they knew whose house they were breaking into, but I get the feeling there was something else going on."

He drew me into his arms. "I know it was scary for you, angel, but you're safe now." He wiped my cheek with the pad of his thumb. "I'm sorry I wasn't there. I'm sorry I didn't see this coming. If Bucky had told me earlier about the break-ins along the river, I would never have left you."

"It's okay. Your badass granny kicked their butts." I couldn't help but chuckle as I remembered the old lady and her shotgun.

Chance grinned and that warm gooey feeling came back again.

"I'm all yours for the rest of the day. What do you want to do?" he said, pulling me to him by the hips.

I knew the perfect distraction.

Hell on Wheels

I reached up on tiptoes to kiss his beautiful lips. "I know exactly how I want to spend the afternoon."

He grinned into our kiss. "I have a feeling I'm going to like what you're suggesting."

Two minutes later, we were lying on the bed with another episode of Game of Thrones playing on the TV.

"This isn't exactly what I had in mind," he murmured against my shoulder. He lay behind me, my body resting on his broad chest, my arm spread across his solid abs. Here I felt secure. Safe and hopeful.

I reached up and felt for my necklace. But it wasn't there.

I sat up abruptly and looked around me.

"What are you looking for?"

"My necklace." I frowned, peeling back the layers of memory to when I had it last. I took it off before I went to bed and hadn't put it back on. It was still in the cabin.

I started to put on my boots.

"Whoa, what are you doing?"

"I have to get it. It's too important to leave out there."

"We can't go back out there tonight," Chance said calmly.

"But you don't understand, it's the most important thing I own in this world."

"I know how important it is to you." He laced his fingers through mine. "But it will be dark soon, and it's too risky to go now. We'll go tomorrow, okay?"

It wasn't okay. But what choice did I have?

I lay back down and pulled his arms around me, letting the warmth of his massive body thaw the frost of my anxiety and eventually lull me into a peaceful sleep.

CHAPTER 39

CASSIDY

I woke up much later in the dead of the night to find Chance sitting on the edge of the bed. In the low light, I could see he was leaning forward, his broad shoulders hunched, his forearms resting on his knees. He was lost in thought. Troubled.

I sat up and slid across the bed, moving behind him to rest my chin on one of his big shoulders. Something was up. He was somewhere else.

Finally, his deep voice broke the shadows.

"When I was deployed, we were sent to a little town in the middle of nowhere to set up camp." In the dead of the night, his words hung heavily in the air around us. "When you stay in one place long enough, you meet people. You develop friendships." I heard him swallow. Felt the regret coming of him. "I met someone over there. It was months before anything happened. But when you're lonely and you're missing home... war is a different place. She was offering comfort. Something I hadn't felt in a long time. Something I didn't realize I was missing so badly."

"Did you love her?" My voice was not my own. It came out of me before I had a chance to stop it.

He shook his head. "No, I didn't. At one stage, I thought I might be able to if I gave it time." He turned to look at me, his jaw tight. "Turns out, she was someone we were looking for. Someone capable of some pretty fucked-up shit. I didn't know until I saw her in my sights and my commander was telling me to take her out."

In my head, I was picturing him lying on his belly, his face lowered to the scope of his gun, his heart breaking when she came into view. I couldn't help but wonder what she looked like. Was her hair long? Was it dark? Did he look at her the same way he looked at me?

"Did you?" I asked, my voice just a whisper. "Take her out?"

He looked back to his hands in front of him. "Just before the missile hit the building we were in, I shot and killed her."

I stiffened involuntarily and he noticed. His brows drew in and his torment was a dark shadow on his face. My heart ached for him. This big man, with his broad shoulders and strong body, was in pain from the leftovers of war.

"Everyone in my team was killed." He dropped his head. "Everyone except me."

"Because of your involvement with her?"

He was quiet for a moment. "At first, I thought so. But there was an investigation, and they cleared me. Intel confirmed she and her brothers didn't know we were there. An insurgent was alerted to our position when one of my team dropped his canteen, and it hit the rubble three stories below and landed beside him. He was the one who fired the missile." I heard him swallow. Felt his body get rigid. "Another SEAL team was with us. Seven, of their team of eight, survived."

I ran my hand over on his shoulder. "I'm sorry."

"I should have told you earlier," he said.

"Why?"

He turned to look at me. "So you knew who you were getting involved with."

This right here... this is why he thinks he's a monster.

I slid my legs on either side of him and wrapped my hands around his thick waist. I pressed my cheek to his scarred back and exhaled deeply against his warm skin.

"I wish you could see me as I see you," I said softly.

I could feel the violent thump of his heartbeat. Felt his abs tremble when my hands brushed over them.

"I'll never hurt you," he rasped out.

"I already know that. I just wish you did."

He twisted around to face me and reached up to cup my jaw. "I will do anything and everything to protect you. That's my word."

I smiled at him, my heart warmed by the gesture. I scooted back across the bed and reached for his hand, pulling him toward me. He settled on top of me. Easing my legs apart, he effortlessly pushed into me.

He kissed me and it was slow, his hands moving purposefully as they slid down the length of me. I sank back into the pillows and got lost in what he did to me. But then he stopped rocking. Stopped the delicious friction of his stroking to look me in the eye. He pushed his fingers through my hair.

"I love you," he whispered.

Magic lit up inside of me.

I opened my mouth to tell him that I loved him too, but he pressed a finger to my lips. Torment registered on his face and I watched his throat work as he swallowed thickly.

"You don't have to say anything." His eyes searched mine, reaching deep, and I realized now was not the time. I relaxed beneath him, and as I looked up into his handsome face, drew his finger into my mouth.

Hell on Wheels

I felt him flex inside of me, felt the shallow rock of his hips become a deeper grind, heard the pleasure in his moan as he began to make love to me again.

But this time it was different. The L-bomb had exploded and hung in the air around us, fusing emotion to every movement, every moan, and every lip-searing kiss. He entwined his fingers through mine and pinned them to the bed as he moved deeper into me, grinding against my clit until the pressure became too much, and I came hard beneath him.

"You're so beautiful when you come," he moaned against my neck. "I want to hear it again."

He thrust my arms above my head and held them there with one hand while the other kneaded my breast. The touch of his tongue on my nipple sent electricity zipping through me, but then his mouth closed over it and joined in the torment with luxurious agony. All of this while his gloriously hard cock continued to thrust into me.

It was an assault against all my senses. A sweet torture. A mind-blowing ambush that sent raw pleasure streaming through every vein. My second orgasm roared through me with no warning. My back arched and I clawed the bed sheet, crying out into the dim light of his room. Because I was clenching him tightly, Chance groaned against my throat, his breath hot, his skin slick as he came with a violent shudder, his cock pumping his release into me.

With a growl, he collapsed against me, and I basked in the heat and the comforting pressure of his naked body blanketing mine.

I love you.

His whispered declaration of love settled through me, bringing warmth and happiness.

But it was as unexpected as it was wonderful, and I couldn't help but wonder if it was too soon. If it was said in the bliss of sex. Or if it was felt because of the high intensity of the situation.

My fingers slid across the tight skin of his scar and he didn't flinch. That, in and of itself, spoke volumes.

What we had.

It was real.

CHAPTER 40

CHANCE

The following morning, we were finishing up chapel when Bull received a phone call from one of his informants on the street.

"We've got a lead," he said, shoving his phone into his cut. "Apparently Vander Quinn had a drug problem and talk on the street is she owed her dealer a lot of coin."

"Who's her dealer?" Ruger asked.

"Laurent de Havilland."

"Do we know where Laurent is?" I asked.

"He's missing."

"Of course he is," I replied.

"According to my sources she liked playing around with meth. Namely, *sapphire meth*."

"You thinking she got her gear from the Swampers?" Maverick asked.

"The Swampers?" Animal looked confused.

"Lowlife rednecks who cook meth and still think it's 1959 when it comes to civil rights and women's liberation."

Bull was being diplomatic.

The Swampers were racist, chauvinist pigs who knocked up their sisters.

They also cooked swamp-meth. Nasty, vile shit that chewed out your teeth and took your soul. It was also a very recognizable due to its bright blue color. Hence the name *sapphire meth*.

Fortunately, they kept to themselves. They destroyed their own lives and those of their kind with their swamp crank. It never made it into our town. They had tried peddling it in Destiny once. A while ago now. Back when the president's rank was new to Bull's cut and the death of his wife still lingered in his bones as fresh as the day she died.

He had paid the Swampers a visit and showed them what happened when people came into our town and tried peddling teeth-chewing drugs. Blood had thickened the backwaters of the border into Louisiana that afternoon, and no Swamper had been to our town since.

They didn't like the Kings of Mayhem cut, and Bull intimidated the fuck out of them. So it was no wonder our arrival was met with a convoy of dilapidated pickups and men in trucker caps carrying shotguns.

Three men approached while seven hung back. Right away, I could see the weird looking motherfucker with the handlebar mustache and ginger sideburns was some kind of leader of the group. Despite being a good head shorter than the others, and with a voice usually saved for jockeys, he exuded crazy like it was pheromones.

"Whataya doing here, Bull?" he whined, squinting his eyes against the midday sun as he looked up at our prez.

"I want to talk to Snake," Bull said, straight to the point.

"And what business you got with our mayor?"

Just as we all were, the Swampers were governed by federal law and local law enforcement, but that didn't stop them

Hell on Wheels

creating a sovereign government within their community. They were led by a slimy guy appropriately named Snake.

"That's for me to discuss with Snake," Bull said.

Ginger Fuzz and Bull stared off for a moment before the little man spat a wad of wet tobacco out of his foul mouth. "Guess I better take you to him."

"You guessed right," Bull replied.

Ginger Fuzz and his associates led the way as we headed into the swamp and crossed a rickety wooden bridge toward a house buried deep in the water oaks and Spanish moss.

"Man, this is real *The Hills Have Eyes* shit," Maverick muttered, all six-foot-six of him looking squeamish.

"It smells like decomposing bodies 'round here," Vader said. "Do they bury their dead above ground in this part of town?"

"Bury? Once a Swamper dies, they're gator food," Ruger replied.

"*Pet food.*" Maverick grinned. "Just another way of keeping it in the family."

Despite smiling at the conversation, Bull said, "Keep your focus, boys. Not to mention your eyes on the greenery. You can't be too sure what's lurking in them."

The wooden bridge gave way to a mud path leading up to the house. It was an eerie place. Despite be open and seemingly harmless from the outside, there was a heavy sense evil in the air. And *weirdness*.

Not to mention decomposition of some kind.

"Well, well, well, if it isn't Michael Western and his band of merry men," came a voice from a hammock hanging between two water oaks.

We all turned to see Snake lying casually in the afternoon sun. He had sunglasses on and was wearing dirty jeans and a T-shirt with a near-naked woman on the front.

He sat up and swung his legs over the side of the hammock, slowly rising to his bare feet. "So what do I owe the pleasure of the mighty Michael Western darkening my doorstep?" He chewed a toothpick with his rotted teeth.

Bull held out his hands. "You don't pick up your phone, you don't call, how else am I going to know how my crazy Swamper friend is doing?"

Snake removed the toothpick from between his lips. "Friend? I don't think so. We stopped being friends the day you came in here and blew holes in my family."

"They shot first."

"You killed my cousins."

"You brought drugs into my town and wouldn't listen to reason. You forced my hand. Their blood is on yours."

Snake's jaw ticked. He removed his sunglasses. "What do you want?"

"I want to know where Laurent de Havilland is hiding out."

Snake's eyes shifted to a pocket of trees to the side of the house then back to Bull. It was so quick I wasn't sure anyone noticed. But I did. And there, just through the leaves, I could make out a flash of bright red paint.

My wife is dead and her red Mustang is missing.

"Name isn't familiar," Snake said.

"Cut the shit, Snake. We know he's on your payroll. So stop wasting our fucking time. Where the fuck is Laurent de Havilland."

"And why would you be looking for him?"

"We're investigating the murder of Vander Quinn."

"Name's not familiar."

"Just like Laurent de Havilland wasn't familiar, huh?" Maverick said.

"If you're not familiar with Vander Quinn, why is her car parked through those trees?" I asked, stepping forward.

Hell on Wheels

Brandishing a shotgun, one of Snake's buddies stepped between us, the stony look on his face telling me he didn't have a problem blowing a hole in any of us.

"I think it's time you boys leave," Snake said, replacing his toothpick between his teeth and walking back to his hammock. "And next time you think about wandering into these parts again... do yourself a favor and don't."

On the ride back to Destiny, we stopped at a roadhouse a few miles before the state line. After ordering, we sat at a counter by the window. Just as our food was ready, I noticed a woman make her way through the crowd of diners toward us. She was tall and beautiful and all kinds of sin wrapped up in a tight body. Long blonde hair flowed like satin down her back. She wore a tiny pair of denim cutoffs with cowboy boots and a top that did little to hide her ample rack. As she walked through the roadhouse, she had the attention of every man in the room and knew it.

Sauntering up to Bull, she leaned an arm on the counter and offered him a small smirk.

Up close, there was no denying she was real pretty.

Until she opened her mouth.

And there they were, broken, jagged teeth that had been rotted away by years of poor oral hygiene and meth abuse.

She was a Swamper.

Despite her bad teeth, she still oozed sex. The body language. The slow blink of seductive eyes. The lick of her tongue across plump lips. She gave Animal an interested smirk before turning to Bull.

"My name is Vicki-Marie. I'm Snake's sister."

Bull nodded but said nothing.

"My brother is a stubborn mule. Too damn stubborn for his own good. He don't want to back down in front of you on account of your past. But I don't have no problem with the Kings." She winked at Animal and kept her lusty, hooded eyes on him as she added, "I'm all about keeping things real *friendly*."

While she and Animal made eyes at each other, Bull remained focused.

"You want to tell us what you know?" he said. "What you think it is that your brother didn't tell us."

Vicki-Marie dragged her eyes away from Animal long enough to answer.

"Your Vander Quinn got herself into financial trouble with Laurent on account of her not paying for her *product*." Vicki-Marie was careful with the words she used. *Product* was code for meth. She was only going to give us enough to get us off the Swampers backs and wasn't going to incriminate herself or any of her family in the process. "She gave him her car as a down payment on her debt, which he in turn sold to my brother. That was why you saw her car there. It was paid for fair and square."

"You expect me to believe that?" Bull asked.

"It's true. They brought it to Snake and offered him a good price."

"Now why on Earth would Laurent do that?"

"Said he needed the money."

"After he killed Vander Quinn?"

"You misunderstand me, Bull." She said his name so seductively even I felt it hit my cock. "She was with him."

You could feel the realization settle over all of us at the same time.

"*She* came with him to sell her car to your brother?" I asked, surprised.

Hell on Wheels

She nodded. "Wanted to sell it real quick too. Didn't say why."

"Now why would Vander come with Laurent to sell the Mustang to Snake? The car she'd just given him?" Ruger asked.

I had a feeling I knew why. It was slowly starting to piece together.

She shrugged like she couldn't care less.

"You know the sheriff's department is looking for that car, and it's only a matter of time before they find out it's there," Bull said.

Vicki-Marie looked at him suspiciously. "Oh really? And how so?"

"A bright red limited edition mustang rolling into town?" He raised an eyebrow at her. "You don't think someone noticed it?"

She leaned her elbows further back on the bar. The move pushed her boobs out, and Animal's eyes almost fell out of his head.

"Probably," she said. "But by the time I get back, that pony will already be in pieces and sold."

That didn't surprise me.

"This guy Laurent, is he the murdering type?" Ruger asked.

Vicki-Marie fixed him with her own raised eyebrow. "Oh, honey, in the swamplands, you do what you gotta do to survive. Probably everybody got a bit of murder in them."

"So where do we find this Laurent?" Bull asked.

"Oh, you won't find him now. Let's just say, when you piss off the wrong people, you get up close and personal with the gators."

"You say it like you know someone was out to make him disappear," Ruger said.

She shrugged. "Let's just say he's been acting shady lately. Hadn't been around as much. He was one of Snake's best *salesmen*, and then all of a sudden he wasn't as available."

Salesmen was another one of those carefully chosen words.

"Did your brother think he was selling someone else's product in town?" I asked.

Drug kingpins and dealers were territorial. You didn't peddle anything in town that was direct competition to their product. If Laurent had gotten entrepreneurial and started selling the competition's product, it would be a good reason for Snake to feed him to the gators.

And if Vander was witness to any of this, it was no surprise she ended up dead in the river.

CHAPTER 41

CASSIDY

Chance gave me explicit instructions to not leave the clubhouse. But the idea of retrieving my necklace from the cabin chipped away at me until I was completely convinced it was the right thing to do. If I took his truck, I could be there and back before he was any the wiser. And like Cade had suggested, maybe the home invasion had nothing to do with Barrett and everything to do with the cannabis fields. That would mean I wasn't in any danger at all, which meant my little excursion out to the river was hardly dangerous.

Plus, according to Chance's sources, Barrett was still in California as late as yesterday morning.

So weighing up the odds, I decided to go. I took Chance's truck and sped out of the clubhouse parking lot, heading in the direction of the cabin. It was a perfect spring day, warm and alive with promise. I wound the window down and let the sunny breeze blow through my hair and across my skin while I sang along to the radio. Today my heart felt light. Almost free. And that thought alone had a big smile spreading across my face.

Approaching the outskirts of town, a figure sitting at the bus stop caught my eye. As I got closer, I was surprised to see it was Missy.

Just keep driving, I told to myself. *She threw you out on your ass and didn't care that you had no place to go.*

But as I passed the bus stop, I could see the misery on her face and the packed bags at her feet. Something bad must've happened to put her at a bus stop with all her belongings.

Damn it.

With a skid of breaks, I swung the truck around and pulled up to the curb. When I got out, Missy looked up, her face dropping when she saw me. Cautiously, I walked toward her but stopped a few yards away.

"What happened?" I asked, doing little to hide the betrayal in my voice.

She looked away and I watched her throat work as she swallowed hard. She looked resigned to her predicament, whatever it was.

"I'm skipping town," she said quietly, avoiding eye contact with me.

"Why?" My voice was sharp. *Hard.* Because the pain of what she did to me was still very raw.

She shrugged and stared down the street. "Things didn't work out."

"What about Johnny and the baby?"

She closed her eyes briefly and exhaled, obviously hurting.

"I honestly thought I was pregnant," she said. "When I told him, he seemed so happy. Said he would leave his wife. Said we'd start a life together. He said his wife couldn't have babies, so us having a baby meant everything to him. I was so happy, Cassi. Thought I could finally put down some roots, have a home and a man by my side." She scoffed sadly as if the idea had been ridiculous. "But then I got my period, and I didn't know how to tell him. I was so scared he would stop loving me. So I pretended I was pregnant until I could work something out. I thought maybe I could get pregnant and he would never know. But then he caught me buying tampons, and I had to come clean about it." Tears streamed down her cheeks. "He fired me first. Then he dumped me."

I didn't know what to say. I didn't want to empathize with her, but it was hard seeing her so upset.

"But why leave town? You can get another job."

"I had nowhere to go," she sniffed.

"What about Craig, and your mom's house?"

The look she gave me told me another revelation was coming.

"It's not my mom's house and he's not really my brother."

I stared at her, mouth agape.

You have to be fucking kidding me.

"My mom dated his dad. They both died in a car accident a few years ago. I was tired. I needed to stop moving. So I contacted him, and he said we could stay for a while."

I had no words.

That was why she was protective of him. He wasn't her brother and the house wasn't hers. He could throw her—*us*—out at any time.

I shook my head and exhaled slowly, letting the knowledge drain from me. There was no point getting upset.

I looked at the packed bags sitting at her feet.

"Why did Craig throw you out?"

"He came into my room. Saw me crying. Tried to comfort me by forcing his tongue down my throat. When I pushed him away, he told me to get out," she scoffed bitterly. "He didn't have to tell me twice."

I considered telling her about him jerking off with my underwear but decided against it because just remembering it made my stomach want to throw itself out of my mouth.

Instead, I asked, "Where are you going to go?"

She shrugged. "The 409 bus will be along in a minute. It goes to the station." She looked down the street... I assumed to see if the bus was approaching. "Guess I'll catch the next bus out of town. Leave it to the gods to decide."

God, how many times had we done that?

She stood up so we were eye level, clutching the smallest of her bags in her hands. She looked apologetic. Innocent. Younger than her twenty-three years.

"I'm sorry I told your brother where you were," she said. "What did he say when he caught up with you?"

Missy still had no idea what Barrett would do if he found me. He wouldn't *say* anything. He would *do*. And it would be brutal. But there was no point explaining it to her. She was leaving town, and I would never see her again.

"He never showed up," I said.

"He didn't come and see you?"

"He never came to town."

"What are you talking about? I saw him yesterday."

And just like that all the air left my lungs.

"What do you mean? Are you sure?"

She nodded. "I was in the post office when a big black town car pulled up at the curb, and he climbed out. I recognized him from the Internet. It was him. He's here, Cassi."

Dread spread through me like the shockwaves of an atom bomb. Blood drained from my face, and my mouth went dry. I swung around, my eyes darting about, searching for any sight of outsiders. A strange vehicle. A big black town car. *Him*.

"Are you okay? You've gone as white as a ghost."

I couldn't breathe.

He was here and he was going to kill me.

And while Chance was physically powerful, he didn't have what Barrett had.

Hell on Wheels

Psychopathy.

Barrett was violent and insane.

I would never forgive myself if Chance got hurt because of me.

As I stood there struggling to breathe, my thoughts raced and my heart pounded violently against my ribcage. I should never have involved Chance in this mess. It was selfish and irresponsible. He had his own demons. He'd walked through Hell and still felt the flames on his skin. I had no business getting him caught up in this. Because there would never be an end to the nightmare.

Barrett was right. I would never be free of him. He would always find me and bring hell with him.

It was suddenly crystal clear.

I had to leave.

Run.

"What are you doing?" Missy called out after me as I stormed toward the truck.

"I'm doing what I always do," I said, opening the door. "I'm running away."

I climbed in and gunned the engine.

"Well, hey! Wait!" The passenger door opened. "Take me with you!"

I paused, my foot ready to press down on the gas. I owed her nothing. And I would never trust her again. But two sets of eyes would be safer than one while I was getting out of town.

I looked at her, my mind frantically weighing up my options. She could keep watch while I drove; she knew what car he was driving. When we were safely out of town, I could drop her where she wanted to go.

"Climb in," I said.

Within seconds, I was swinging the car around, the tires screeching as we took off toward the cabin. I would take the car and leave Chance a note. Whenever I could, I would wire him money as payment.

CHAPTER 42

CHANCE

The thing about riding your bike on the open road is that it was meditative. Calming.

Being so free, you drop your ego and let your mind slip away. It gave you the clarity to see things for how they really were.

Unfortunately for me, it was also an easy way for the memories to worm their way into my head.

As we crossed county lines and headed into Destiny, we passed a playground with a small basketball court, and I was rocked by a powerful memory that almost sent me off my bike and into a ditch.

We pulled up to an outdoor basketball court at the neighborhood playground, and my father killed the engine. Across the grass, two men were shooting hoops.

"See that piece of shit in the blue T-shirt?" my father asked.

I looked at the man. He was tall and built well with broad shoulders and strong arms. He intercepted the ball from his friend, lined up the shot, and then sent it straight into the hoop. When he smiled, I saw rows of straight white teeth.

"Who is he?" I asked.

My father's eyes sharpened with meanness.

"He's the man who's been sticking his dick in your mom."

At first I thought I'd misheard him. "What?"

"He's been fucking my wife behind my back. And now I'm going to show him what I think about that."

He waited for the game to finish, for the man to say goodbye to his friend and walk away, before he got him alone in the deserted parking lot. I watched from the front seat of the car as my father approached the man. He was unlocking his car and didn't see my father storming toward him. For a split second, I wondered if I could warn him somehow. Catch his attention. Make a sound. Anything to get him to look up in time. Because I knew what my old man was capable of, and something told me that this man was going to receive the full force of Garrett Calley's wrath.

Fear ripped through me, and I was about to "accidentally" lean on the car horn to catch the man's attention when my father increased his pace and started to run toward his target.

He must've said his name, because the man looked up just in time for the tire iron to catch him in the face.

Blood splattered into the air, some of it landing on the windshield.

The next strike sent him backward, a third into a heap on the concrete where my father laid into him with his boots as well as the tire iron.

Terrified, I hit the horn. I didn't care if I got a beating off my old man. I had to stop what was happening in that car park.

The horn grabbed my father's attention and stopped another kick of his boot into the man's ribs. He looked down at

Hell on Wheels

the bloodied mess, his face twisting with rage as he leaned down and spat on him.

When he returned to the car, he was covered in blood.

"And that is how you deal with men who think they can put their hands on your wife." He was breathing heavy and sweat trickled down his temple, mingling with the blood on his face. He didn't look at me, just kept his mean eyes on the man stirring on the concrete.

"Is he... dead?" I asked, terrified.

My father shrugged as he started the car. "If not now, he will be in a few minutes."

He didn't know I had called 911 from my cell phone. Now I prayed an ambulance wasn't far away.

As if on cue, the sound of a siren cut into the quiet Sunday afternoon air.

"Time to go," my father said as he put the car in reverse and drove away.

We didn't speak on the way home. I stared out the window, trying not to think about the man lying in a crumpled bloody mess on the ground.

Instead, I thought about how much I hated my father.

And how, given the first chance, I would run as far as possible from him.

When we arrived home, he pulled into the driveway but didn't move to get out. As I went to open the door, he stopped me.

"Best you don't say anything to your mom," he said calmly. I looked at him. He'd wiped the blood from his face while we waited at a set of lights, but there was still a drop of blood in one of his eyebrows.

I struggled to swallow. "Okay."

He nodded and then added, "And, Son, if you ever honk my horn again, I'll cut your fucking hand off."

Feeling the terror of his threat, the last vestige of my childhood burned to ash and broke apart because I didn't doubt him. He would hurt me if it somehow suited him.

I said nothing as I climbed out of the car and followed him solemnly into the house, wondering how I was going to keep this from a mother who knew everything just by looking at me. But the moment he walked through the front door, my mother stormed up to him and slapped him so hard across the face it left a bright red handprint on his skin.

She already knew.

The second slap to his face was with equal force and probably hurt my mom's palm, but she was so wild with emotion I doubt it even registered.

"You monster!" she screamed at him. "You cock sucking monster."

Rage lit up my father's face as he squared his shoulders and walked toward her. "Let's not kid ourselves here, Veronica. I'm not the one who's been sucking cock! It's just a shame you weren't sucking the right cock."

My father was an intimidating man, but my mother was fierce. "Like you don't get your cock sucked by every whore who visits the clubhouse," she yelled. Tears streamed down her face. "Why? Why did you hurt him?"

I wondered how my mom knew.

She was holding her phone in one hand. If he was okay, maybe the man had called to warn her.

My father towered over her, his teeth gritted. "Because that cunt stuck his dick in my wife. And no one..." he grabbed my mom by the arms "...no one gets to fuck my wife but me."

My mom's face brightened with white-hot fury.

She shook herself free. "I want a divorce!"

Hell on Wheels

He snarled and walked her backward until her back was against a wall. "There's only one way you're leaving this marriage and it's in a body bag. Do you understand me?"

"And what would your precious club think about that?" she seethed, her eyes full of loathing, her voice calm but hateful. "They will disown you."

He leaned in. "They'd have to prove it first."

"I'm not frightened of you, Garrett."

Evil was bright in my father's eyes. "You should be."

Swerving off the main street, I steered the Harley toward the playground and killed the engine. Realizing what I'd done, Bull peeled back and signaled for the others to keep going before pulling into the playground car park and parking next to me. He climbed off his bike and walked over to where I was standing.

"You remember Joey Atwood?" I asked him.

"Name sounds familiar."

I kicked the concrete with my boot. "This spot right here is where my old man beat the fuck out of him with a tire iron."

Recollection crossed Bull's face, and he nodded.

"He lost all his teeth and sight in one eye," I said.

"I remember."

"Yet he never pointed the finger at my father."

"Your father could be an intimidating man."

Yes, he was. But he never intimidated my mother enough for her to leave. They patched things up not long after and came to some kind of weird mutual agreement that strengthened their relationship rather than tore it apart. She never divorced him. She didn't need to. He made her a widow a few years later.

"I never understood why she didn't leave him. But I was kid. I didn't understand how complicated their relationship was. I guess I still don't. But I do know they loved each other in their own fucked-up way." I shook my head. "They loved each other despite knowing what the other was capable of. I don't doubt my father would've killed her. And I don't doubt my mother would have killed him for trying."

I looked toward the horizon. It was late afternoon, and the sun was slowly making its way lower in the sky.

"Mayor Quinn murdered his wife," I said calmly. "And then he hid it with a series of distractions, including using the Kings of Mayhem to find the supposed murderer."

"What do you mean?"

"A murder victim's spouse is usually the first suspect. Quinn wasn't eliminated by Bucky or the Kings. *He* told us he didn't do it. And then he did everything he could to portray himself as the grieving husband."

"Then why tell us she was having an affair?"

"Because he knew it would come out and throw suspicion on him. Remember, the best defense is offense, so he addressed the evidence before it became a motive." I could see Bull doing the math. "He pointed us to Satan's Tribe because he knew they were in town. But they're not involved in Vander Quinn's murder. They're here for Cassidy. I know it. You need to wrap this up without me. I need to get Cassidy out of town."

"You can't be sure about this—"

"I am sure about this," I cut him off. "Those men were hired by Barrett Silvermane. So I'm stepping down as SAA, and I'm taking Cassidy as far away from here as possible. He knows she is involved with the Kings."

I walked back to my bike and climbed on.

"Ruger should be your SAA." I ignited the engine, and the Harley came to life with a rumble. "Also, Laurent wasn't Vander's drug dealer. He was her lover. And I'm pretty sure they sold the car for money so they could leave town, not because she owed him money. Keep digging. Laurent's body will wash up soon. If you keep looking at Mayor Quinn, you'll find out I'm right."

And with that I rode off. I had to get back to Destiny.

To Cassidy.

Because she was right.

Barrett was after her.

So far he'd just been toying with us. Using Satan's Tribe as his eyes and ears in Destiny and feeding Cassidy's fear of him. Tormenting her from afar by using her own fear against her was all a part of his sick torture.

He was a sick motherfucker.

And I was going to kill him.

CHAPTER 43

CASSIDY

"We can go anywhere we want, Cassi. Anywhere at all. It will be just like old times." Missy talked at a hundred miles an hour, but not even her relentless chatter could distract me from the violent panic taking hold of me.

Barrett was here. Probably watching. Waiting.

As soon as I entered the cabin, I felt heartsick. I was already missing Chance, and I hadn't even left yet. That was when I realized, for the first time in my life, another emotion overpowered my fear of Barrett—the fear of losing Chance. I couldn't get him out of my mind. Couldn't help but feel him in every room I walked through. This little cabin held so many wonderful memories of us together, even for such a short time.

I glanced down at the rug on the floor, the one where we'd made love for hours during the storm while the rain beat down on the roof and rattled the windows—and then to the kitchen counter, where he'd made me come with such ferocity I'd broken a nail against the granite.

Hell on Wheels

Walking into the kitchen, I looked out the window to the two deck chairs sitting side-by-side, overlooking the water, and thought about the nights we'd spent under the stars, getting to know one another. Both of us slowly letting down our walls as we grew more comfortable, *more trusting* of each other.

A wave of heartache crashed through me. How could it be the end?

How could it be that I would never see him again?

Swallowing hard, I stared out past the sparkling river to the fishing cottage and felt tears well in my eyes. I recalled my first few days here and how we would sit on the deck, how every part of me was already fully aware of his intensity. Of his prowess. How I had lusted after him without even realizing what I was lusting after. That he was so much more than what I could ever have imagined. I began to physically ache and thought about how he would react when he found out I was gone. How deeply hurt he would be, especially after what he'd shared with me last night.

I love you.

This was going to hurt him.

I will do anything and everything to protect you.

My heart hurt. No. I couldn't do that to him. And I couldn't do that to *me*. Not anymore. It was time to stop running. I was ready to banish my fears to make room for a chance at happiness.

Missy walked up behind me. "You're not leaving are you?"

I paused long enough to let her know she was right.

I couldn't see her but somehow I knew she was nodding.

Turning around, I looked at her. "No. I'm not."

She didn't ask me why because she already knew. She could see it written all over my face. I was in love with him. But it went beyond that—I couldn't imagine life without him now.

"Come on," I said. "I'll drive you to the bus station."

After grabbing my necklace from the bedroom, we left the cabin, and I drove Missy to the bus station in town. She didn't say much, and I could feel her disappointment fill the cab of the truck. But she accepted it and wasn't going to try to talk me out of staying.

She paused before climbing out.

"We had some good times, didn't we?" she asked sadly.

I wish I could say that we did. But she threw them all away the moment she contacted my brother. I really didn't have much to say to her about any of it.

But there was one thing I needed to know before she left.

"Why did you kick me out?"

I didn't need to ask her why she sold me out to Barrett. That part was easy. It was greed. But why throw me out of the house? Was it a guilty conscience?

She looked surprised at the question, but then her expression softened. "Because I didn't want him to find you."

Her words hung heavy between us.

"Because you knew I was running from him."

She nodded regretfully. "You never told me anything. I just knew you were running away from something. Or someone. Then when Craig found out who you were, I figured your dad must've done something bad to you."

The only thing my foster father did was fail to protect me from his son.

"I knew if I contacted them, I would be sending you back to the very thing you'd run away from for two years."

Yet you did anyway.

"I didn't want them to find you. But you have to understand, Cassidy, I needed that money."

I couldn't look at her because hearing her say it made her betrayal cut a little deeper into my heart.

"Was it you that sent that video link to my phone?"

Hell on Wheels

"Craig sent it. He was pissed because you were out of his league. He said you thought you were too good for him. Stupid ass." She sighed. "You know I really am sorry. I made a mistake. I want you to know that I will regret what I did to you for the rest of my life."

I appreciated her honesty. And in some warped way I could appreciate that her selfish actions led me to Chance. But I would never forgive her for contacting Barrett and selling me out for a paycheck.

"Well, I guess this is it," she said.

I nodded. "Take care, Missy."

I had nothing left to say to her.

Without another word, she climbed out of the truck and walked away. She didn't look back. And as I watched her make her way toward the ticket counter, I knew I would never see her again.

Feeling the door close on that chapter of my life, I pulled out into traffic and headed back to the clubhouse, my heart feeling a weird sense of closure.

I got as far as the gas station down the street. That was when something moved behind me and the shadow rose up from the backseat. I felt the evilness before I saw it. Felt the fear drill into me before I felt the cold metal of the gun against my temple. Felt my world slip into hell as he leaned closer and whispered in my ear, "Hello, Sister."

CHAPTER 44

CHANCE

She was gone. And so was my truck.

I tried her phone but it went to voicemail.

Damn it.

I tried it again but got the same thing.

Desperation funneled through me.

Had she had run away because of what I told her the night before? That I was in love with her? That I had killed the last woman I was with? I growled with desperation. If she had, then I only had myself to blame. Last night I'd dumped the mother of all revelations on her, and in the cold light of day she'd probably decided it was better to run from me than to hang around to find out if she would one day meet the same fate.

I was a killer. She knew it. And now she was fucking gone.

Except...

Her white dress, the one she loved, was in a pile on the floor by the bed, and the tiny thong I'd peeled from her body last night was still tangled in our sheets. I walked to the closet. Her clothes

Hell on Wheels

were still in her bag and her guitar was leaning up against the back wall.

I tried her phone again, but it went straight to voice mail.

Cassidy hadn't run away.

But she was fucking missing.

I ran out into the clubhouse and found Hawke leaning up against the bar talking to Animal.

"Have you seen Cassidy?"

"Yeah, man. She left here an hour or so ago sayin' somethin' about a necklace."

A mix of relief and alarm spiraled through me. She had put herself in danger by going to the cabin, but at least I knew where she was heading.

I started running for my bike but my phone rang. It was Tommy, the VP from the Kings of Mayhem California chapter.

"Tommy!"

"Hey, brother. Thought I should let you know Wyatt disappeared yesterday afternoon."

I stopped walking. "He's missing?"

"We found him about an hour ago. Unconscious and beat up pretty badly in an alleyway."

"Is he going to make it?"

"Doctors think so."

"Any idea who did this to him? Did he say anything?"

"He hasn't regained consciousness yet, but I suspect whomever you had him tailing didn't want him tailing him no more."

Fucking motherfucker.

Fuck.

Fuck.

Fuck.

When I asked Wyatt to follow Barrett, I didn't think he'd get hurt. It was a simple tail and report job. Now he was unconscious in hospital.

Barrett did this.

It meant he probably knew about the tail all along. Probably found it amusing.

But worse, it meant he was on his way to Destiny.

He was coming for Cassidy.

"Keep me posted. I want to know if he wakes up or if his condition changes."

"Will do, brother."

I tore out of the parking lot like a bat out of hell. Panic ignited every cell. I weaved in and out of traffic with skill, my mind focused on one thing and one thing only—getting to Cassidy and taking her as far away from here as fucking possible. I would stop at nothing to protect her. I had already walked through hell once before, and I would crawl through it on my hands and knees if it meant protecting her from harm.

Hitting traffic, I roared up the middle and then took my chances through a red light. There was less traffic on the road to the river, and I took the Harley off the chain and let her roar like a wild cat as we tore along the wide-open road.

Coming to the small township just before the turnoff to the cabin, I slowed down. There was more traffic here. A cab. A family sedan. A station wagon towing a caravan. A black van.

I overtook them and tore out of the little main street and back onto the road, toward the turnoff.

That was when I noticed the black van behind me.

Something wasn't right, but the realization came too late.

The black van roared passed me but then swerved at me, running me off the road and into a ditch, catapulting me off my bike. I hit the ground with a dusty thump. It knocked the wind out of me and made me see stars. Winded, I struggled to inflate my lungs with oxygen, my breath only coming in short, sharp rasps. A short distance away, I heard car doors slam and the sound of boots on asphalt. I couldn't move, but I knew I would probably die if I didn't because whoever ran me off the road wasn't done with me yet.

Still struggling for breath, I hauled myself up onto all fours because I had to find Cassidy. And *goddammit*, I wasn't going to go down without a fight. Whoever those motherfuckers were, they were going to pay.

A twig snapped behind me. I wasn't alone. And before I could even register it, I was hauled to my feet by one very unattractive man with a heavily pock-marked face while a redneck who looked like Billy Ray Cyrus circa his "Achy Breaky Heart" era slammed a heavily ringed fist into my mouth. I barely had time to taste the blood before a second punch to the side of my face made me see stars and sent me to the ground again.

If I was winded before, then it was nothing compared to being kicked in the stomach with a set of steel-toe boots. No. Wait. It was nothing compared to being slammed in the gut by *two* sets of steel-toe boots. Excruciating pain spread from my stomach, and blood sprayed out of my mouth, followed by the sudden eruption of air from my throat as a second blow got me right in the groin.

When Billy Ray decided I deserved a third blow, I grabbed his ankle and yanked it out of under him, making him lose balance so he stumbled into the dirt beside me. Before his sidekick could derail me with another blow to the head, I broke Billy Ray's arm in two places and gave him his own galaxy of stars with a powerful hit to nose.

With him in blinding pain and distracted, I kicked the legs out of the other man, and he hit the dirt with a ground-shaking thud. From there it was easy. I got up onto my knees and swung at him with an almighty fury. Blood spattered across his face, and my knuckles, followed by more when I broke his nose and sent him to the ground unconscious.

I dropped to all fours, exhausted. Blood filled one eye, and there was a ringing in my ears, but I was alive. When Billy Ray wouldn't quit with his crying, I crawled over to him and with barely any air left in me, I sent him to sleep with an angry smack to the head.

Leaning back on my heels, I looked skywards. My lungs gasped hungrily for air. Every nerve and fiber in my body ached. Blood dripped from my mouth, my nose, and a deep cut through my eyebrow. It spilled into my eye and trickled through the dust and dirt on my face.

Ignoring the pain, I went to stand but was sent lurching forward into the dirt by a fucking hard kick to the back.

Rolling over with a groan, I looked up, and the last thing I saw before everything went black was a pair of menacing eyes and a face half concealed by a skull bandana.

CHAPTER 45

CASSIDY

"Please," I begged. "Don't do this."

My pleas were forced out with so much emotion they were nothing more than a wheeze.

But Barrett only laughed at me. He pushed me up against the wall and held me there with his body, pressing his palm against my throat. He leaned closer so I had no choice but to feel the heat of his breath on my cheek. "Hurting you is what I live for."

His eyes roved over me, soulless and full of evil. But there was also a burning fire in them. A dark light so hot and needy and raging with lust.

I didn't know where we were. A warehouse somewhere. He'd made me drive for miles before we pulled up outside the abandoned building. I didn't know what was going to happen, only that it was bad.

"You're the only thing in this world that drives me crazy," he moaned, his voice low and husky. *Aroused*. When he pressed his hips into mine and I felt the hardness of his erection, my strangled sob burst from my lips and died in the space between us. "I've missed you," he breathed desperately. "I've missed you so much."

"Let me go," I pleaded.

His eyes glittered over my face. "I can never let you go again. Do you know what torture it's been? Waiting. Wanting. Needing to see you. Smell you." He drew in a deep breath as if he was capturing my scent to memory. Then his hand slid between my thighs. "Touch you."

"Please," I sobbed.

"I love you," he whispered against my lips.

With a yank, he ripped open my jeans and shoved them down to my hips. I knew what he was looking for. His initial. The one he branded into me when I was twelve.

"It's still there," he breathed out. He raised his head to look at me again, and a triumphant smile curled on his lips. "See. You belong to me."

He kissed me then. Hard and rough. His hands holding my face still so I couldn't turn away from him, his moan torturing me just as much as his tongue and mouth did. I bit down on his bottom lip and tasted the coppery taste of blood on my tongue. But this only turned him on more. He laughed against my lips. "Do it again, sweet Chelsea. Oh baby, do it to me again."

Sick fuck.

He went for another kiss. But I brought my knee up and got him right in the balls. He growled and stumbled backward, the pain registering on his face before slowly morphing into anger. He stormed forward and whipped his hand across my cheek then squeezed my chin. His eyes glowed with anger and evil. *And madness.*

"Why do you always have to fight me? Why don't you understand that you are mine?" His fingers tightened on my chin and I winced. "What's it going to take to stop you from running away from me?"

He smashed his lips to mine. Hard and mean. But the sudden rap on the door ended the kiss abruptly.

"What?" He barked over his shoulder.

The door opened and a man with a skull bandana hanging around his neck appeared in the doorway.

"It's done," he said. "He is in the warehouse."

Barrett let the information register and then smiled. "Excellent. I can take it from here."

The man looked at me and then back to Barrett. There was hesitation before he added, "You should know, Clint and Billy Joe are in the hospital. He fucked them up pretty bad."

Barrett shook his head with a chuckle. "Of course he did." He gestured to the man. "Leave."

The door closed and Barrett turned back to me. "Looks like it's showtime."

"What have you done?"

He smiled evilly. "You'll find out soon enough, sweet Chelsea."

"If you've hurt him…"

His head snapped in my direction, and he glared at me, his face bright with rage. He thrust me up against the wall again, his gloved hand crushing my throat. "He touched what wasn't his to touch, and now I'm going to make him pay. But the best thing about this is making you watch while I destroy him." He leaned in so close his lips were almost touching mine. "Killing him quickly won't be an option. Be ready. This is going to be torture."

Terrified, I watched him walk toward the small desk across the room. He picked up a cloth then crossed the distance between us. I backed away from him and moved around the room until he pounced on me and smothered the chloroform-soaked cloth over my face, sending me to sleep.

CHAPTER 46

CHANCE

When I came to I was zip-tied to a chair. I raised my head and blinked to shift the fog from my brain.

I tasted blood.

I was in a small warehouse, lit only by one industrial light above us. Shadows crawled out from the walls. I couldn't see anything.

Then he appeared.

Barrett.

His sinister laugh reached me before I saw him.

"Welcome. It's a pleasure to finally meet you."

I didn't say anything.

"You made a mess of poor old Clint and Billy Joe," he said, amused.

I gave him a murderous look.

"It's nothing compared to what I'm going to do to you."

He chuckled as he walked over and flicked a switch, sending a beam of light over an unconscious Cassidy slumped in a chair only a few feet from me.

A growl ripped out of me.

Was she breathing?

Had he killed her?

Relief flooded me when I saw the beat of her pulse in her throat.

Barrett walked back toward me, pleased with himself.

"See that? You and your club did that. I was happy to watch from afar. For the meantime, of course. It was all part of the game, you see. I knew her silly little friend told her about what she'd done because the stupid girl called me, said Chelsea had skipped town. I don't know if she was trying to throw me off her scent or what. In all honesty, the girl is a fruit loop. But I already had eyes on Chelsea by then. I knew she hadn't skipped town. Knew she was hiding out somewhere. And it added to the excitement, knowing how frantic she would be. How panicked. Wondering when I would show up. What I would do to her." An ugly smile curled his lips.

"You were using Satan's Tribe to watch her."

"It was like we were fighting fire with fire in our little love dance," he replied theatrically. "She had the protection of an MC, while I used their rivals to watch her every move until I was ready." His face darkened. "But then you and your club had to go and get involved. Threatening to run them out of town." He tsk-tsked as he crouched down in front of me. I glared at him, realizing I was staring into the face of a madman. "Not very neighborly of you."

He sighed and rose to his feet again.

"You won't get away with this," I said darkly.

Barrett looked at me as if it was the most ridiculous thing he'd ever heard.

"Oh, but that's the thing... I always do."

Cassidy woke up then, and she freaked out, lashing out with her legs and screaming.

Her pain became my pain.

"Baby, I'm here," I rasped.

She stared at me with wide eyes, her brow furrowing, her chest heaving. But hearing my voice seemed to calm her down.

"Aww, *baby*," Barrett mocked. He glared at Cassidy. "Is that what he calls you? *Baby?*"

He inhaled deeply before crouching at her feet and looking up at her with an evil glint in his eyes. He reached out and trailed a finger slowly up her exposed thigh. She flinched, and I felt a stronger, more murderous rage take up inside of me.

"What do you think, Chance? You like this? You like the way she squirms beneath my touch? The way she trembles. What do you think she will do when I force her legs open and force myself inside her."

"Let her go," I growled. "Let her go or I will—"

"Or you will what? Tell me, tough guy. What will you do?"

I looked up at him through my brow. My eyes dark. My face the mask of a man who would rain down fire and brimstone if he hurt her. "Make no mistake. I will kill you."

Barrett feigned surprised. "How," he challenged, "when you're tied to that chair?"

Pleased with himself, Barrett grinned and returned his attention to Cassidy, tilting his head to the side, his eyes gleaming with wickedness.

"I know what she likes. I know how to make her... *respond*. Isn't that right, Sister?" When I snarled with anger, he swung back to me. "Oh, you didn't know? You mean, she didn't tell you how I made her come? How her mouth said one thing but her body said something completely different."

He launched himself so he was almost on top of her, pelvis to pelvis, chest to chest, his lips whispering against her ear as he added, "Not just once... not just twice... tell me, Sister, will you come for me again when I defile you in front of your boyfriend?"

Hell on Wheels

Cassidy whimpered, and I unleashed a roar straight from my soul. I rocked the chair side-to-side, desperate to get my hands free.

Barrett stood up, a nefarious gleam in his eyes as he looked down at Cassidy.

He shook his head as he circled her slowly, thinking, planning, enjoying the fear he saw in her wide, frightened eyes.

"Nah," he said suddenly, and the sinister look on his face forced me to fight the binds tying my wrists together. "I think I'll just kill you."

Before I could blink he was behind Cassidy with one hand clamped over her mouth and nose and the other wrapped around her neck

She screamed but they were muffled. She fought against him, kicking out and rocking the chair, desperate to break free, gasping for air.

Fear ripped through me. I struggled frantically, my muscles fighting the ties, my teeth gnashing together as I roared with determination, fear, and rage. I rubbed the zip ties against the wooden armrests to weaken them, but it was no fucking use. It would take time to break them down. Time I didn't have.

"Stop!" I yelled desperately. "Tell me what you want."

Barrett didn't move his hands and looked almost amused as he asked, "I'm sorry, what did you say?"

Cassidy's wide eyes begged me for help.

"Whatever you want... kill me. Take me."

Barrett looked pleased with himself. He thought for a moment and then grinned. But his hands remained on Cassidy, slowly taking the life from her.

"Oh, I don't want to kill you yet." His voice was smooth and calm, and he barely seemed to notice that Cassidy was slowly dying beneath the palms of his hands.

"What do you want?" I roared.

Darkness swept over his face. "You will succumb to me."

My eyes met Cassidy's.

"Anything you want."

She started to go limp, her eyes beginning to close.

"I said anything you want!" I yelled at him just so he would take his damn hands off her. She was about to die and there wasn't a fucking thing I could do about it but this.

Relief ripped through me when he removed his hands from her. Cassidy's eyes widened, and she gasped, desperately gulping in oxygen.

He crouched down, and I felt the sharp stab of understanding

He looked up at me from between my jean-clad legs.

"I want you to submit to me, just like she did." He licked his lips, his eyes gleaming with perverse pleasure, the front of his pants already growing. He slid up my body to whisper in my ear, "I'm going to make you come and it is going to torture you later because you will be filled with the shame of how much you enjoyed it. But only for as long as I let you live, of course."

He trailed his fingers across my chest, and I flinched at the intimacy of his touch.

"Such a powerful body," he whispered, biting his bottom lip as his fingers traced a line down my stomach and over the front of my jeans. He pressed his palm against my crotch and desire slithered across his deranged face. "I'm going to make you hard. Do you understand me? I'm going to take you in my mouth and suck you, and then, when I'm fucking you, I'm going to wrap my hand around your hard cock and jerk you off until you come with the pleasure." He ran his hands through my thighs. "And you will remember it, always. The way my touch felt on your skin. The way my moans whispered in your ears. The way my cock felt inside you, filling you, making you come."

He exhaled with a shiver, lost in his fantasy.

"You sick fuck," I spat.

Hell on Wheels

But he just laughed and rose to his feet, adjusting his erection.

Slowly walking behind me, he bent down and whispered, "You'll try to forget. Try to tell yourself it wasn't what you wanted. But your body will betray you. It will succumb to me, and it will ache for the things I'm about to do to you. And you will let me do them... or she dies."

His laugh was wicked. Deep. Low. *Evil*.

He walked back to crouch down in front of me again.

"And I'm going to make her watch." He nodded toward Cassidy, who was staring at us with terrified eyes, tears rolling down her cheeks as he leaned forward and undid my belt buckle. Her eyes were riveted to mine.

Look at me, they pleaded. *Don't look at what he is doing to you.*

They sent a silent apology as his hand slid across my thigh. I felt his hand on my zipper and heard the trembling breath he took in anticipation.

"Oh you are such a beauty," he whispered, his voice hoarse with lust.

He bent his head as he lowered my zipper but realized his mistake in not tying my ankles to the chair when I drove my knee upward into his chin and thrust my foot into his chest.

He fell backwards and I used the little time I had to start on the zip ties again, rubbing them back and forth along the chair arm to create enough friction to weaken them. With a ferocious wrench of both arms, I was able to snap both my wrists free.

But Barrett was already climbing to his feet. Blood spilled from his broken nose and when he roared at me, I could see his blood-stained teeth were broken.

He pulled out a knife and came at me. But even armed, he was no match for my years of military training. To his credit, he tolerated the right hook to the face, but the second took him down. He slumped to the floor, dropping the knife.

Picking it up, I was able to get Cassidy free.

But Barrett wasn't done.

Lost in his psychosis, he rose to his feet, laughing.

"Well, ain't that a bitch," he said as he wiped his sleeve across his bloody mouth.

Cassidy and I stood a few yards away from him, watching him sway on his feet as he continued to laugh. I was anticipating his next move. He was maniacal. Capable of anything. When he reached for the gun in his holster, I ran at him and thrust the knife into his shoulder. Spinning him around, I rammed him into the wall.

Winded, he dropped the gun and slumped to the floor.

I kicked the gun over to Cassidy.

And then I lost my mind.

I wailed into him. Over and over again. Blood and spit splattered across his face and the brick wall behind him as I kept going and going. Pain radiated in my knuckles, but even then I kept going. For all the terror, for all the torment, for all the raping and torture he subjected Cassidy to, I let it take over me until my angel stepped in and pleaded for me to stop.

I straightened, breathless and wild.

She had stopped me just in time.

Because one more punch and I would've killed him.

CHAPTER 47

CASSIDY

I had to stop him before he killed Barrett.

I saw the fire in his eyes.

Understood the rage on his face.

"He's done," I said, putting my hand on his arm to stop the punches.

He straightened, rope-like veins bulging in his forearms, sweat mingling with blood on his forehead as he caught his breath.

Our eyes met and I saw him come back from the dark place he'd lost himself to as he'd pounded into Barrett.

I reached up and touched his face, and his eyes filled with tenderness as he drew my hand to his lips and kissed it.

Barrett's baritone laugh reverberated around the room; it was dark and sinister, and it sent shivers up my spine.

Blinded by a sudden rage, I dropped to one knee in front of him and shoved the muzzle of the gun under his chin.

"You're pathetic," I spat. "Look at you. Bloody and beaten. Not so tough without your zip ties and biker buddies now, are you?"

Fear shone bright in his eyes. He wasn't sure what I was capable of, and I could see his mind racing.

Would I shoot him?

Did I have the lady balls to pull the trigger?

In a blink of an eye the fear was gone, replaced by the conceited gleam I was all too familiar with. It was the same dark light I'd looked into when he'd been on top of me, raping me.

I shoved the gun deeper into his chin, my finger itching on the trigger. He didn't get to look at me like that anymore.

"If you think I won't pull the trigger, then you're even more delusional than I thought." My eyes burned into his. "I want you to consider everything I might have thought about doing to you while you were violating me. While you were *raping* me. The pain I was going to inflict on you when I had the chance. The way I was going to kill you when the opportunity arrived. Well surprise, motherfucker, that moment is here."

The gleam vanished.

"You were mine," he spat petulantly. "Mine!"

I leaned in closer.

"I was never yours," I said through gritted teeth.

"They gave you to me!"

He was like a child throwing a tantrum.

"You delusional fuck. They told you to be a protective older brother. Not a raping, violating psychopath."

He laughed then, and I hated him.

"You say you didn't want it, but you did."

"I *never* wanted it," I growled. "You just took it from me, not giving a damn that I didn't want to do any of it."

"Then why did you come when I fucked you?" he leered. His face shimmered with the memory, and I'd never been more tempted to pull the trigger than I was in that moment. "Admit it. You're just as fucked-up as I am. Just as turned on by the struggle."

Hell on Wheels

I shook my head. "Having an orgasm during rape does not equate to consent. And I never, *ever* gave you my consent."

"Your mouth didn't. But your body did."

I cocked the gun. I hated him. And I wanted him to die for everything he'd done to me.

"Cassidy." Chance's voice broke through the pain and rage spinning around in my head.

"He'll never change," I said without removing my eyes from Barrett. My finger itched as it rested the trigger. "He'll never admit what he is. That he's an entitled creep and a raping psychopath. He'll just keep taking what isn't his to take."

"He's going to prison," Chance reasoned.

"No he's not. He's Barrett Silvermane. Daddy will just pay the right people. Just like he always has."

Barrett smiled smugly. It was bloody and ugly, but even the sight of his broken teeth and bloodied lips weren't enough to dampen the rage burning in my head.

Chance crouched down next to me. His voice was calm and sobering. "Killing a man is hard, Cassidy. You need to think this through."

I *had* thought it through. Over and over again while he was pushing into my body and taking a little more of my soul from me. But now, kneeling before him, I paused long enough for my courage to wane.

Slowly, I removed the gun from Barrett's chin.

"I won," I finally said to him. "I'm going to live this amazing life with a man I couldn't love more if I tried. I'm going to fall asleep in his arms every night and then wake up next to his warm body every morning. And then I will make love to him, over and over again because I can't get enough of him. Of the things he does to me. Of the way he kisses me and touches me. And you... you'll be nothing but a faded memory, one that will eventually vanish completely. I won't be able to remember what you looked like. How you sounded. Or what it felt like trapped beneath your touch. It will all be gone. Just. Like. You."

For the first time in my life, I saw the look of defeat cross Barrett's face. He looked like a child who'd lost his favorite toy. He didn't know what to do. What to think. Losing wasn't something he ever accepted, and now that he had no choice, he didn't know how to deal with it. I could see the mental struggle take place inside of him.

It was enough for me. I rose to my feet and looked at Chance.

"Let's go home," I said. "We'll let the police take care of this."

Chance threw his arm around my shoulder, and we began to walk away.

"It's finally over," I breathed with relief.

But before Chance could reply, Barrett's blood-soaked voice reached across the distance between us.

"It will never be over," he mocked. "You'll *always* be mine."

Rage tore through me. But it was nothing compared to the fear that he would somehow get away with this and be free to continue to torture me. Something snapped in my brain. He was right. It wasn't over. It would never be over unless I ended it.

In that maddening moment, all the pain of what he did to me hit me like a junkie's high. The rape. The torment. The years of looking over my shoulder. The terror that kept me running. The fear of him finding me.

One moment I was filled with terror. The next I was calmly walking toward him with the gun raised and pointed right at him.

He grinned at me with his broken teeth.

He was right. It would never be over.

He would never stop.

He would find a way to continue his evil game.

So I shot him.

I shot him dead.

CHAPTER 48

CASSIDY

It was a clear case of self-defense, they said.

And to me it was.

Now that Barrett was gone, I was free to move on with my life without the haunting fear of him finding me and torturing me further.

It wasn't revenge. It was closure.

In the lengthy investigation that followed, further assaults came to light. It seemed Barrett Silvermane wasn't just a monster to me, he had brutalized several other women, stalking and assaulting them then torturing them with threatening messages and sinister gifts in the mail.

No one ever said a damn thing because he scared them into silence.

As a result of the investigation, Kerry Silvermane, the man who was supposed to protect me, lost his political career and found himself facing charges of his own. As more and more details came to light, the media had a field day and tore his life apart for failing to protect Baby Doe from her psychopathic foster brother.

A week after I shot Barrett, Mayor Quinn was arrested for his wife's murder. He eventually confessed when all the evidence against him began to pile up. Chance was right. Vander Quinn was having an affair with Laurent de Havilland and was planning to leave her husband. With the mayoral election coming up, and with several business deals relying on his clean-cut, good guy image, Mayor Quinn couldn't afford to lose his wife of thirty years to a much younger man, *and a known drug dealer*, so in a fit of jealous rage he killed them both.

Laurent de Havilland's body washed up the day of Mayor Quinn's trial. The medical examiner found a bullet in the back of his skull. Quinn had killed his wife as she tried to leave him then waited for her lover to show up so he could plant a bullet in his brain.

Quinn got two consecutive life sentences.

For me the future looked bright. And that future included one fiercely protective biker in a Kings of Mayhem cut.

He married me the following fall, and within months of him putting the crown pendant necklace around my neck, my belly swelled with his baby.

Two months after our daughter arrived, Wyatt and his brothers found my real mother. Her name was Kate and she was living in a trailer in Joshua Tree. We met on a hot night in July, at a bar in the desert. She was fifteen when she gave birth to me. Fifteen and scared. My father was a boy she knew in school, and because her parents were terribly strict, they planned to run away together to raise me. But they were both so young. He changed his mind and instead of running away, she gave birth to me in a deserted roadside restroom then went back to her life. Her parents were none the wiser thanks to her tight ballerina stomach and bulky clothes. She explained that because they were always out at one church event after another, she was easily able to hide her pregnancy and everything that happened afterwards.

She cried when she saw the hope necklace sitting next to my crown pendant. She had given it to me because it was the only thing she could give to me. Her hope for a good life.

After a few months of back and forth, she eventually moved to Destiny to be closer. Now she was becoming more and more a part of our lives.

For Chance and me, life had taken an amazing turn. Now we were living a life filled with love and happiness in the beautiful fisherman's cottage with our daughter down by the river.

It was a life neither of us could ever have imagined. When we met we were both so broken. So scarred. Yet somehow we'd found each other in the darkness and lifted the veil to let the light back in.

The past was gone.

Vanquished by love.

By faith.

And by hope.

EPILOGUE

CHANCE

Something jabbed into my chest.

Again.

Then again.

It was a finger.

A *demanding* little finger.

I held back my grin as it moved from my chest and prodded my cheek, over to my lips, and finally to the side of my nose.

It was my daughter, and she was sitting on my chest, finger-assaulting my face.

I opened my eyelids and found her big blue eyes staring down at me.

"Did I wake you?" she asked in her cute three-year-old voice.

I raised an eyebrow at her. "It was the finger in my nose. Gets me every time."

She grinned at me, and my heart melted like it did whenever Ava smiled at me. I was a sucker for my daughter, and she had me right where she wanted me—wrapped around her finger.

Hell on Wheels

"Mommy's making pancakes. But she says I have to pick the toys up from my bedroom floor before I can have some."

"Best you do that, then," I said.

"But there's so many," she whined.

"If Mommy says you have to pick them up, then you have to pick them up."

She hit me with her adorable dimpled pout. "But it will take for aaaaages."

I couldn't help it. When it came to Ava I would give her the world. But going against my wife would mean a serious case of blue balls. So Ava was going to have to do as she was told.

"I'll tell you what, you get a head start and I'll come and help you."

Her little face lit up. "You will?"

"Of course."

She struggled off the bed and then stood in the doorway, waiting.

"It's not much of a head start if you stand there and wait," I said when she didn't move.

"That's okay, I don't mind," she replied with all the logic of a three-year-old.

I couldn't help but grin because my daughter was so damn cute. But getting out of bed right now wasn't really doable. I had a raging morning wood I needed to calm down first.

"I'll tell you what, you go and start picking up your toys, and I'll pay you two dollars."

"Five dollars."

I laughed at my precocious daughter. "What are they teaching you at preschool? How to hustle?"

She looked at me blankly then repeated, "Five dollars."

I couldn't believe my daughter. I pointed toward the door. "Toys. Off the floor. Now."

She sighed dramatically. "Ohhh-kaaaaay."

She wandered off and I waited a few minutes, strategically thinking about my taxes in order for certain parts of my body to relax. A few minutes later, I was up and dressed and helping my adorable daughter clean up her room. Once finished, I scooped her up in my arms and we headed downstairs to the kitchen for pancakes.

Cassidy was dishing up fat, doughy pancakes sprinkled with both blueberries and chocolate, just how Ava and I loved them. My wife was the pancake queen. It was no accident my jeans fit tighter after marrying her.

The gold band on her ring finger glinted in the morning sunlight. I glanced down at the mirror image of it wrapped around my finger and felt warm with contentment. My life began when she came crashing into it, and now I couldn't imagine a life without her.

After breakfast, I played with Ava until her eyes grew heavy, and she fell asleep at the little plastic table where we were drinking tea with Jeremy the giant teddy bear and Lexie the unicorn. I picked her up and tucked her into bed, where she rolled over and fell into a deep, restful sleep.

When I came down the stairs again, Cassidy stood at the sink doing the breakfast dishes.

She smiled at me, and just like it did with my daughter, my heart melted. Although, this time it melted because of the heat I felt stir in my belly.

My wife was a constant turn-on for me, and it was an effort to keep my hands off her.

I walked up behind her and wrapped my arms around her waist, the palms of my hand rolling over her huge belly. Any day now, our second daughter would be here, and the sound of a newborn would fill our home once again. I nuzzled the back of her neck, my morning wood returning as I inhaled the subtle scent of her.

Hell on Wheels

"Someone is happy to see me," she laughed.

"Wanna see how happy?" I ran my hands up her bare arms. "Ava, is sound asleep, and I have got a serious need to fuck my wife."

"How do you still want to fuck me? I don't understand. I'm as big as a whale."

"But you're my whale," I joked, earning me a direct punch to my right bicep. She grinned, even though she tried not to, because she knew she was the sexiest woman in the world to me.

"I'm serious, Chance. I'm so big I don't even know what my toenails look like. I'm wondering if your second daughter is ever going to come."

Cassidy was just over forty weeks. Her due date was two days ago.

"You know they say sex can bring on labor," I said, running my hands over her peachy ass.

She looked over her shoulder and cocked a sexy eyebrow at me. "You seriously wanna try?"

It was all I needed. I ran my hands down to her hips and pulled them toward me. The move made her bend over, raising her ass and flattening her arms against the counter top. I pushed her dress up to her waist and grinned when I saw she wasn't wearing any underwear.

"I like a woman who is prepared," I said.

She chuckled softly. "Putting underwear on seemed like a wasted effort. It's been two days since you've fucked me; I knew you wouldn't go a third day without it at some point."

"You thought right," I rasped, easing her feet apart.

I slid one hand between her parted thighs, and she gasped when my fingers brushed through her bush and across the lips of her warm, wet pussy. She was creamy and swollen, so I knew it wasn't going to take her long to come. I wasn't the only one who was missing sex.

"I'm sorry I haven't taken care of down there," she said, moaning as I rubbed little circles into her clit. "I was going to wax but—" She let out a loud moan as I slid a finger into her.

"I like it," I said, kissing along her shoulders. "With or without, I'll take your pussy any way I can get it."

My cock ached to be inside her. But I wanted my queen ready for me. I wanted her to come so she was sated when I pushed my cock into her, and going by her little whimpers as my finger rubbed her clit, she was almost there.

"Give me your cock," she moaned. "I'm going to come."

What my queen wanted, my queen got.

She leaned down further so her ass titled higher, and with one smooth thrust, I was inside her. She moaned and licked her lips as her beautiful pussy pulsated hungrily around me with the beginnings of an intense orgasm. I pushed in deeper, pulling her ass against me and grinding hard into her. She cried out and gripped the edge of the counter as she came with violent convulsions.

I would like to say I lasted, but feeling her tight pussy throbbing around me was too much and I came like I had ten seconds to live. I gripped her beautiful ass and thrust into her, one, two, three more times before filling her with a release that burst out from my core.

Pulling out of her juicy body, I helped her straighten and put her dress back into place before turning her around and kissing her. I cupped her beautiful face and savored the feel of her sweet lips on mine.

"I love you," I whispered.

She grinned against my lips. "You might have to love me a few more times tonight to coax this baby of yours out of my body."

It was my turn to grin. "Only too happy to oblige, darlin'."

Hell on Wheels

True to my word, I made love to my queen later that night, and again in the early hours of the following morning. But still our little princess took her time in arriving.

She finally showed up two days later, just before midnight.

When *she* was ready.

And when she came into the world, Anjelica Sasse Calley arrived screaming.

Later the next morning, I stood in the doorway of Cassidy's hospital room and watched my wife with our two beautiful daughters, my heart overflowing with gratitude for everything I had in my life. I didn't regret a thing because everything I'd done and everything I'd been through—all the good and all the bad—led me to this one amazing life where I was a father and a husband, and so fucking happy it almost seemed unreal. The past was gone. Buried behind me where it belonged. Now these beautiful females were my world. My life. My heart. And until I took my last breath, I would give my all, *my everything*, to the most important thing in the world to me.

My family.

THE END

Kings of Mayhem MC Series
Kings of Mayhem Book 1
Brothers in Arms Book 2
Biker Baby Book 3
Hell on Wheels Book 4

CONNECT WITH ME ONLINE

Check these links for more books from Author Penny Dee.

READER GROUP

For more mayhem join my
FB readers group:
Penny's Queens of Mayhem
https://www.facebook.com/groups/604941899983066/

NEWSLETTER

Sign up for my newsletter
http://eepurl.com/giFDxb

GOODREADS

Add my books to your TBR list on my Goodreads profile.
https://www.goodreads.com/author/show/8526535.Penny_Dee

Hell on Wheels

AMAZON

Click to buy my books from my Amazon profile.
https://www.amazon.com/Penny-Dee/e/
B0O2OKT5G/ref=dp_byline_cont_ebooks_1

WEBSITE

http://www.pennydeebooks.com/

INSTAGRAM

@authorpennydee

EMAIL

authorpennydee@hotmail.com

FACEBOOK

http://www.facebook.com/pennydeebooks/

ABOUT THE AUTHOR

Penny Dee writes contemporary romance about rockstars, bikers, hockey players and everyone in-between. She believes true love never runs smoothly, and her characters realize this too, with a boatload of drama and a whole lot of steam.

She found her happily ever after in Australia where she lives with her husband, daughter and a dog named Bindi.